BLOOD ALLIANCE

BLOOD DESTINY, BOOK 12

CONNIE SUTTLE

Published by:
SubtleDemon Publishing, LLC
PO Box 95696
Oklahoma City, OK 73143

Cover art by Renee Barratt @ The Cover Counts

To Walter, Joe, Larry, Lee, Dianne, Sarah and Mark.
Thank you.

~

For the Bearcat
who lived twenty-two-and-a-half years before crossing the rainbow
bridge. *Remember to say hello to your brother and sister for me, and tell
them I'll be along eventually.*

~

And for Erin Lavon Butler
Somewhere in the distance, your light is shining on us all.

ACKNOWLEDGMENTS

As always, this book is the result of collaboration. If it weren't for the support of my editor, my cover artist and my beta readers, it would be less than it is. All mistakes, as usual, are mine and no other's.

About the Author:
Connie Suttle lives in Oklahoma with her husband and a conglomerate of cats. They have finally banded together to make their demands, which has proven disconcerting to all humans involved.

You may find Connie in the following ways:
Facebook: Connie Suttle Author
Twitter: @subtledemon
Website and Blog: subtledemon.com

Blood Destiny Series:

Blood Wager

Blood Passage

Blood Sense

Blood Domination

Blood Royal

Blood Queen

Blood Rebellion

Blood War

Blood Redemption

Blood Reunion

Blood Recall

Blood Alliance

Legend of the Ir'Indicti Series:

Bumble

Shadowed

Target

Vendetta

Destroyer

High Demon Series:

Demon Lost

Demon Revealed
Demon's King
Demon's Quest
Demon's Revenge
Demon's Dream

God Wars Series:
Blood Double
Blood Trouble
Blood Revolution
Blood Love
Blood Finale

Saa Thalarr Series:
Hope and Vengeance
Wyvern and Company
Observe and Protect*

First Ordinance Series:
Finder
Keeper
BlackWing
SpellBreaker
WhiteWing

Queen of Thorns and Roses

Other Titles from SubtleDemon Publishing:

Malefactor

Transgressor

Underhanded*

by Joe Scholes

*Forthcoming

CHAPTER 1

*E*arth, Past
　　　Russian Embassy, Cairo
Ambassador Bespalov

Zaria,

I'm sorry I have not been able to find this information for you sooner. Many of my contacts and sources of information have either been arrested or have disappeared. I did finally speak with someone. He and his daughter worked as janitors at the facility you mentioned, regarding the one you name D'slay.

The father swears that D'slay disappeared and took Irina, his daughter, with him, shortly before the facility was demolished. He is still mourning her absence and says that if Irina were in control of her own senses, she would never have abandoned him.

If you wish to speak with him yourself, his name is Viktor. You said you only needed first names, and I hope this is still true. The government is sending me into retirement in only a few months, and it is my hope that it will not be the same retirement home as that of our mutual friend.

Sincerely—B.

~

Reth Alliance, Current

Queen's Palace, Le-Ath Veronis

Lissa

Lissa? Zaria sounded tentative, as if she thought I might scold her for not contacting me sooner. I knew through Ashe and Charles that she'd been more than busy tracking D'slay and his Sirenali bones, bone dust and a probable stash of the Lyristolyi drug.

Zaria? What do you need? I replied quickly.

Just to talk and run some things past you, she said, sounding weary.

Want something to eat while you're here?

That sounds nice. Can you feed four others besides me? Bleek, Tamp, Ilya and Edden are with me right now.

Of course. Do you want to talk to anyone else while you're here?

If Ashe and Breanne are available, then yes. If you can find Charles, also yes.

She didn't call Charles Father, or Daddy, or anything else. I figured those were names he hadn't earned and might never do so.

Like Griffin hadn't earned them from me, either.

Charles, Bree? I sent. *Your daughter wants to talk to you.*

Be right there, Charles answered first, with Bree's acknowledgement coming shortly after.

Ashe, Zaria wants to talk to us, I sent, knowing he'd come.

Damn, I wish they were this responsive whenever *I* wanted to talk to them.

~

Palace Library, Le-Ath Veronis

Zaria

"D'slay has turned into a problem," I said. "We," I indicated my mates who'd come to the meeting with me, "think D'slay bears a strong resemblance to V'ili."

"Does this mean he's related to the Prophet?" Ashe asked.

"It looks that way. Whether by natural birth or by genetic manipulation, they're likely related."

"Liron and V'ili, the malicious gifts that keep on giving," Bree shook her head.

"I doubt V'ili had enough talent to accomplish much of this on his own," I said. "He would never have created anyone to rival his narcissistic self. It was Liron's idea to create the Prophet—and D'slay, too, in all likelihood."

"You think D'slay has the same sociopathic tendencies as V'ili?" Lissa asked.

"We can't get close enough to him to tell for sure, but he certainly has V'ili's talents for criminal activity and the ability to hide it from everybody. So far, we've only been fortunate enough to follow in his destructive wake. Anyone who's seen him is dead. Quinn and I are sick to death of reading mutilated bodies to learn whatever we can, and that isn't much. He places obsessions before he kills."

"Is he supplying bones and bone dust to criminals?"

"Probably, but once that happens, we can't find them any longer. Plus, he may be handing out the Lyristolyi drug like candy, so criminals can change their appearances whenever they want."

"Do you think he has contact with the Prophet?"

"If he does it isn't much, and Randl agrees. So far, they've had their own agendas, and those plans may complement each other without their paths crossing very often."

"You think D'slay is running interference for the Prophet, don't you?" Charles frowned.

"I do, and he may be supplying the Prophet through back channels with anything he needs or wants to wage his war against us."

"Through other criminals, so we won't have a direct path to either," Lissa concluded.

"Yes. The Prophet hasn't squeaked from inside his rathole for a while, and Randl knows he's plotting something. I've told Randl to stay focused on the Prophet; he doesn't need to add D'slay to the Formidables' to-do list."

"Are you sharing information?" Ashe asked.

"Yes—constantly. Anything that comes up that could be relevant is passed along. Randl is getting his ships back together, and ah, we've built a spaceport for Sirena."

"We?" Charles lifted an eyebrow.

"The Larentii," I said. "They are the only race as a whole who know exactly where Sirena is. It was easier to ask for their help, rather than going elsewhere."

"It's not the first time the Larentii have helped build a spaceport," Lissa frowned at Charles. "They put most of Le-Ath Veronis' together."

"Randl offered them open access to the planet, so the curious ones can visit whenever they want. They found that to be adequate compensation, plus they enjoy the sunlight there. It's a pale shade of green, and they consider it a delicacy."

"What about you? Do you consider it a delicacy?" Bree asked.

"It's fine, and it does have a distinctive flavor," I agreed. "It's like kimchi for the Larentii."

"You're kidding?" Lissa made a face at me.

"Most Larentii have never eaten actual food. I have, and it's the closest comparison I can make," I shrugged. "It's somewhat exotic and a change from the ordinary."

"And nobody has to do the dishes afterward," Lissa smiled. "What can we do to help find D'slay?"

"We've been running from place to place, chasing rumors and investigating criminal activity," Edden told her. He was the diplomat among us, and the best one to speak of our attempts in this search. "It's as if they're baiting us and keeping us unbalanced, by striking here and there, with no clear pattern. What we need is someone to stay and continue an investigation on several likely planets, while others chase these phantoms that appear. Then, they can feed the information back to those on the planets in question."

"Do you have a list?" Bree asked.

"Yes," Ilya said. "These are particularly interesting, in view of the type of criminal activities reported, but once we get there, something else happens on another planet and we're forced to leave before we've done any real work."

"They are baiting you, then," Ashe agreed. "They probably realize that only a few are tracking them at this point, and with an extensive network of criminals in place, they can run you ragged looking for them. I think Bill and a few others from SouthStar might be interested in helping."

"Gavin can put a team together," Lissa said. "I figure Drake and Drew wouldn't say no to some investigative work. There are others, too, who can join either team."

"The Saa Thalarr can volunteer for this," Belen appeared with a beaming smile. "I'd suggest asking for a High Demon to accompany every team sent out."

"I can contact Reah," Lissa offered.

"She says she has someone ready to join my team," I replied. "I've already talked to her and Lexsi. They'll send as many volunteers as we want."

"They'd do anything for you," Breanne said. "You know why."

"They don't owe me anything," I argued.

"Well, it can't be because they love you, surely," she teased.

"I tried to tell them it could be dangerous, and they still want to send help. I said volunteers only, who know what they're getting into."

"Food is ready," Lissa announced. "Who's hungry?"

High Demon Palace, Kifirin
  Denevik Lith

"Grandfather, I know Grandmother Breszca's death still troubles you," Reah told me. She and I sat in the kitchen, having a snack that she'd cooked for us. Not many were served by the Queen of Kifirin nowadays —she was too busy running the planet and barely had time for sleep.

She was right; Breszca had been gone for years, and still I felt an absence in my life. She was missing, and there was a hole—a gap in me where love belonged. Recently, I'd begun thinking about Baetrah, and giving myself to its flames to relieve the emptiness of my life.

I'm sure Reah and Lexsi had noticed; few things got past them. Therefore, Reah had invited me to share a treat with her in the kitchen, which was oddly empty of all servants at what should be a busy time of day.

"Lobster crisps are my favorite," I forced a smile as I bit into the tasty treat.

"I know. I have a favor to ask of you, Grandfather," Reah said. Lifting my eyes, I blinked at her sudden seriousness.

"What's that? Please tell me it's not another offer to sit on your Council. I've done that already, and it wearied me, listening to all the argument."

"I know that, too," she agreed. "I think this favor may be more to your liking, although I will warn you up front that it could be quite dangerous."

"Dangerous?" I almost agreed right then, without even knowing what it was. Dangerous sounded as if I could serve a purpose and forfeit my life in a better way than jumping into a volcano in humanoid form.

"Yes. Very, according to the one who is coordinating this search."

"What search is that? And who are we talking about?" I crunched into a second lobster crisp, its delicate pastry cooked to perfection, the lobster and cream sauce inside both savory and perfect on my tongue.

"The search is for one of V'ili's get—a Sirinali named D'slay."

I stopped chewing for a moment as I considered this information. V'ili had been next to impossible to track and kill. He and Cayetes, the master criminal he'd served, had left a trail of crime, bodies and dead or destroyed planets in their wake.

"That's—certainly dangerous," I dipped my head in a half-nod. "You want someone who isn't susceptible to Sirenali obsession, I take it?"

"That is certainly my goal. We need several volunteers, but none more important than the one serving on this particular team."

"Which team is that?"

"The one who started the hunt for D'slay. Zaria."

"I'd say that Zaria deserves the best High Demon you can send, then," I said.

"That's why I want you to go with her. I've got others from the army who've volunteered to go out with other hunting parties. I need someone I can trust with my life to go with Zaria, because she is more than important to Kifirin—and the Crown."

"I haven't trained with the army in a long while," I pointed out.

"It will come back to you. When is the last time your full Thifilathi was set free?"

"Mostly, my smaller Thifilathi goes out on full moons," I confessed. "It became a habit because Breszca was terrified of the taller one."

"I doubt Zaria or anyone on her crew will worry about your full Thifilathi."

"Larentii are seldom worried about that sort of thing," I conceded. "When should I go?"

"Lissa is hosting Zaria and four of her mates at a meal right now. You can go and introduce yourself, if you want. You can take the rest of these crisps, too; you're not the only one who loves them."

"How long do you suppose the search will continue?" I asked as I rose from the small kitchen table.

"I don't know, but should it last for more than two years, then I beg you to stay until two years are up."

"Then it will be so, Granddaughter." I leaned down and kissed her cheek, making her smile.

"Crisps," she held the tray out to me. "Give them to Lissa, first. She adores these."

∼

Queen's Palace, Le-Ath Veronis
    Lissa
    Grandfather is on the way, Reah sent. *I've asked him to join Zaria's crew.*

Denevik Lith is on the way, I informed Zaria. *He's Reah's pick as your High Demon crew member.*

Ah. I feel there's another reason for sending her Grandfather, and it's not only because she trusts him.

Breszca died years ago, and he's still in mourning, I said. *Perhaps activity will break him out of that mood. I'm sure Reah is concerned that he's considering Baetrah to end his life.*

That's a downer, Zaria sent a mental sigh.

"Queen Lissa, Reah sends her regards and ah, a half-tray of lobster crisps," Denevik appeared near my seat at the table and offered the tray of food.

"Oh, my favorite," I said, reaching for one of the treats. "Sit down, Denevik. I'll have someone else bring a plate for you and carry your tray around the table."

"I hear you're going to join our search team," Zaria pulled out a chair with power so Denevik could sit three seats down from her. He might negate someone else's power, but not a Larentii's—or one of the Hierarchy. Zaria—we still didn't know whether she could be a member of the Hierarchy, but there were strong suspicions by most of us in that group.

As for her status in the Hierarchy (if she were a member), none of us could guess at the level. With some genetic manipulation from Charles, she was my daughter, Bree's daughter, and the daughter of a Vampire Queen long dead. I still didn't know who the reincarnated version of Sarita was, although I felt Bree and Charles did.

Travis and Trent were more than happy to be related to Zaria, as were my other children, but my High Demon child, who went by the name of Vik Roth, loved her the most, I think.

She'd seen something in him, and she and Quin had gone back in time to negate his death and heal him of wounds that affected him most of his life. All that was before they were aware they were half-brother and sister.

Vik would follow her to the depths of hell, if she asked. She'd put her life on the line before she'd ever ask that of someone else. I realized that she'd inherited that quality, at least in some small measure, from Breanne and from me.

While my children accepted her as family without question, she and I were still coming to terms with our relationship. The same held true for Breanne, and to some degree, Ashe.

How Charles viewed all this, I had no idea.

I have three daughters, Charles sent, as if he knew what I was thinking. *I was only able to see them once in a while, and for a few stolen moments. Don't let the opportunity pass to form a bond. I've failed in that way, and it eats at me.*

Could have fooled me popped right out before I could stop myself.

I deserve that, he agreed. *At least Kiarra, Conner and I have some sort of relationship, now. My youngest daughter—I should have known that she'd be the skeptical one.*

Zaria isn't one to be fooled, I sniped.

She has that from her mothers, Charles acknowledged.

More Breanne than me, I said. *Zaria and Bree can see through just about anyone.*

Sarita was good at reading people, Charles told me. *She knew Wlodek loved her and that Merrill didn't. She tried her best with Wlodek, but it wasn't enough. Merrill had her heart and he rejected it.*

I know that feeling. Merrill had done the same to me, until Bree came along and *Changed What Was.*

I didn't mean to bring up old wrongs. I certainly don't want to be the reason you and Merrill have an argument later about it.

Charles, go soak your head, I huffed. *You didn't have anything to do with that, anyway. My own father did.*

As he did with Sarita.

I went still. *Griffin did that to her, too?*

Merrill requested it; Griffin complied, just as he did in your case.

My father was responsible for her suicide?

She may have done it eventually, even if Merrill had accepted her. She wanted children, and that could have eventually convinced her to walk into the sun. With Merrill and Griffin's interference, her life ended sooner than it should have.

No doubt that affected the timeline.

It did. It made me realize that I needed a third daughter. It was only fitting that Sarita get the child she always wanted, to right the eventual wrongs that came because of past interferences.

I'm still not sure how I feel about becoming a mother again when I had no idea it was done.

You should have heard Breanne, when she told me in ah, plain, if profane, words, that I kept this from her far too long.

I think Zaria takes after Bree more than anyone, I said.

Don't sell yourself short, Lissa. Have you told Zaria that she has her own suite here at the palace?

I haven't finished decorating it—I wanted to find out what she likes, first.

Then tell her and let her make those final decisions. You can help, once you know what she wants.

She'll be off again before, I began.

Tell her now. Ask her to stay for a day or two and rest. She's tired and needs it.

"Zaria," I said aloud. She and Edden had been talking quietly with Winkler, who'd sat across from both.

"Lissa?"

"I—you have your own suite here at the palace, but I haven't finished decorating it, yet. I wasn't sure what you'd like, but we can have it ready for you in no time. Will you stay for a day or two, at least? I think you need some rest, and your other mates can catch up with you if you want. Besides, I think Nissa would like to see you."

"Really? I'd love to sit and talk with her," Zaria sighed. "We only met one time and didn't get to spend more than half an hour together."

"I'll make sure Grey House lets her and her husbands come for a visit tomorrow, then." I smiled, because seeing Nissa, Toff and Trik would be wonderful, and seeing them with Zaria would be even better.

In fact, if I worked things out right, I could get all my children here, and we could have some family time. Yes—that would be excellent.

"Really? They can all come?" Zaria read me like a book.

"I think I can get them here," I smiled at her sudden excitement. She'd grown up as an only child, and I was coming to realize how lonely that had been.

Well done, Charles sent. *You've made our daughter happy for the first time in months.*

~

King's Palace, Karathia

Rylend Morphis

"I worry that something will happen," Vik paced before my desk.

"By something, I assume you mean somebody will figure out who you really are? Can that be a bad thing?"

All seven feet of him stopped dead center of my study and blinked at me. "I can only imagine that Reah will be more than pissed, and I've come to terms with the fact that she's with someone else, now."

"It's not fair to you, dude. Besides, Zaria wants to see us. That means you, too."

"If I go for anyone, it would be her."

"Then come. I can provide a disguise, if Zaria won't do it for you."

"Zaria will if I ask her."

"Then come. Randl can do without you for two days, at least. Besides, Travis and Trent are coming, and they'll have Sabrina with them."

"Fine. I'll go. It'll be nice to visit old stomping grounds."

"Come on, then, bro. Go pack or something. I've already arranged to leave Dad in charge. I'll be leaving in about an hour. Want to come with me?"

"Sure. Let me grab my stuff and I'll be back."

~

Grey Planet

Nissa

"Pack your swimsuit," I told Trik. "Stop worrying about pale legs. I can give you a fake tan if you're that self-conscious."

"I've got mine," Toff wandered in, with three shirts and swim trunks hanging off the points of his wings, while he carried a stack of jeans and shorts to pack.

"If you ever decide to change professions, I think I can get you work as a valet," Trik teased him.

"The humanoid kind, or the one that stands in a corner and serves as a catch-all?" Toff lifted an eyebrow at Trik.

"Your choice," Trik laughed. Toff hurled one of his shirts at Trik, who deftly employed his wizard's power to fold it in midair and allowed it to plop gently onto the bed with a rustle of cotton.

"This is going to be fun, isn't it?" I smiled at Toff and put my arms around his neck. He smiled and leaned down to kiss me.

Yes, it *was* going to be fun.

～

Sirena

Travis

"Zan, you're invited. Don't be a martyr and say it's only for family," I barked. "Get your stuff together, and make sure Perri is ready, too. You'll be Quin's guests at Avii Castle. Perri can visit with her brother while we're there."

Zanfield looked surprised by my words. "Look," I softened my tone, "I got mindspeech from Zaria. She specifically invited you. I don't want to be the one to tell her you refused."

"She asked for us to come?"

"Yes. Now, go pack. Bring your swimsuit. We can go swimming either in the palace or at the beach outside the light palace."

"On my way," Zan grinned and loped out of my quarters.

"Do we need anything formal?" Sabrina leaned into the doorway to ask.

"Bring at least one outfit; I'm hoping for a trip to Desh's," I grinned at her.

"Oooh, that sounds nice. I'll go grab something."

~

Lissa

"Wayne, please mind your manners," I said. "You still have to go to school; Master Morwin won't let you skip your lessons, you know."

"Mom, where will everybody sleep?" Wynter asked.

"Some will stay with Aunt Quin," I told her.

"Is Nissa staying here with us?"

"She is."

"Good."

"You just want to play with Trik," Wayne accused his sister.

"He's fun. You're not," Wynter sniffed.

"Don't start," I shook a finger at my youngest. "If you want to spend time with our guests, you have to behave yourselves." Had I been this frazzled with Travis and Trent? As I recalled; they'd been into most everything, but they'd been united in their misdeeds, at least. Wayne and Wynter were always sniping at one another.

Winkler, your seven-year-olds are acting up again.

It's normal, came back in his usual drawl.

How long does this normal *last, then?*

Until they go out with the pack the first time.

Great.

Sometimes after that, too.

Oh, lordy.

I want to be on one of Zaria's search teams, Winkler informed me.

Are you sure?

Yep. I can do legwork and sniff around. I think I can get Weldon and a few others to help, too.

Take a couple of vamps with you. Couldn't hurt, huh?

I'll talk with Rigo.

You do that. Rigo would be a good choice, either for advice or to join in.

That old vamp knows a few moves.

Yes, he does.

When is everybody showing up?

Could be any minute. Ry was so ready to come, he grabbed Bel Erland and started packing. Erland will hold down the fort while they visit. Travis and Trent may be right behind those two.

I don't think I've ever seen a family reunion come together so fast, Winkler teased.

Maybe we should do this more often, then.

Maybe we should.

~

Avii Castle

Zaria

"Quinnie Bee," I held her for a long, satisfying hug, while Justis stood a few feet away, smiling.

"When will Perri and Zanfield get here?" Quin pulled away to ask.

"Could be any time," I said. "It's so good to see you."

"We have more suites available, if Lissa needs space," Justis offered.

"I'll make the offer; some may want to come here, just for the view."

"He won't say it, but he enjoys the company," Quin laughed.

"I think we may be invited to Desh's for dinner tonight," I turned toward Justis. "And you may get the ox-roast you're so fond of."

"That sounds intriguing," Justis said. "Come, have tea or coffee with us and we'll watch the boats from the balcony."

"You know I want coffee," I said.

"I do know that," he chuckled. "Come, the weather is quite fine, and I'll have the drinks delivered from the kitchen."

I watched as a guard dipped his head to the Avii King and walked out to place our order. Quin hooked her arm with mine and together we walked toward the King's private balcony, where the weather really was as fine as Justis said.

"Zanfield and Perri just arrived," Dena strode in behind us, dipping her head to Justis.

"Send them to join us," Justis told her. "Is Zanfield wearing his uniform?"

"No, my King. He ah, was told he had to remain as incognito as possible."

"Good. I didn't want to explain things to the entire castle."

Dena stifled a laugh and went to do as Justis asked.

"I like him—Zanfield," Quin said as she and I took seats in the shade of the castle behind us.

"He's an honorable man. Not easy to find, nowadays," I replied. "I like him, too."

"A quirky, honorable man. Certainly not easy to find anywhere," Quin agreed. "What color will his hair and eyebrows be this time, you think?"

"No idea. I think Perri indulges him nowadays—a witch's power won't damage his hair like dyes will."

"The guards said we'd find you here." Tamp, Ilya, Bleek and Edden, with Denevik trailing them, walked out to join us. "They ordered extra tea and coffee."

"Save room for Desh's tonight; I just got confirmation from Reah and Lexsi that they've reserved their banquet room for us."

"We'll need more chairs," Quin half-rose from her seat.

"I'll take care of it." I waved a hand and ten more chairs, matching what Quin already had on the balcony, appeared around us, in addition to a large round table, where tea and coffee could be served.

"You always think of us," Tamp leaned down for a quick kiss.

"Denevik, are you overwhelmed, yet?" I asked my High Demon conscript.

"I'm trying not to be. Only time will tell whether I'll be successful."

"You take after your father, don't you?" I asked gently. He had the dark hair and eyes of Lendevik, once the King of Kifirin.

"Glindarok says that I sometimes shock her with how much I look like our father." Denevik didn't try to hide his sorrow at that fact.

"You couldn't have saved him; you'd have died beside him," I said. "I know this is little comfort, but that plot was designed by rogue Ra'Ak, and they'd have killed you if you'd learned of it before it happened."

"Cursed all the way around, then," Denvik sighed and took a chair beside Tamp's.

"Don't let the past destroy your future," Quin told him. "May I touch you?" She was off her chair and walking around the table to reach him.

"It will do you good," I told him as Denevik hesitated. After a few moments, he nodded and closed his eyes as Quin reached out to hold his head in her hands.

He needs this, doesn't he? Ilya sent.

Yes. Quin glowed, even in the bright light of day, as she offered what healing she could to a mind long eaten by guilt and self-recrimination. Denevik's dark hair lifted in the breeze from the sea far below, as lines of worry disappeared from his face.

By the time Quin had removed her hands, he looked far younger than he did when he first sat down.

"Thank you—I didn't realize," Denevik blinked at Quin.

"You're welcome," Quin patted his shoulder and walked back toward her chair.

Three winged servants flew up to the balcony, each carrying a covered tray. Their feet touched the balcony gracefully; Quin motioned them forward to set out tea, coffee and snacks for us.

"There's food? I'm in," Zanfield arrived, sporting orange hair, purple sideburns and eyebrows, and a hoop of gold in one ear.

"Zanfield, did someone tell you about Earth pirates?" I asked, eyeing the earring.

"I saw images—Travis and Trent sent them," Zanfield grinned. "I thought about putting two Tiralian crystals in the hoop, but they said that was overkill."

I had no part in any of that, Vik appeared on the balcony with Rylend Morphis. *It was all Travis and Trent.*

Did you not warn them that Zanfield would have an earring by the end of the day? I asked. He grinned in response.

They had a bet going how long it would take.

I really, really want to slap my forehead right now, and I can't. "Zanfield," I said aloud, "the earring looks good, but if you decide that you want to change your look someday, I can heal the hole in your ear. Or Quin can. Just ask."

"She can put the hole back, too, if you change your mind again," Vik volunteered. "Just don't ask more than twice."

"There's a slight problem," Teeg San Gerxon announced as he appeared next to Rylend.

"What's that?" Vik asked. I already knew from reading it in Teeg's face. Irina's body had been found; I recognized her image in Teeg. He still didn't know her identity, but testing on her body revealed that she died of radiation poisoning, and that she was originally from Old Earth.

CHAPTER 2

*Q*ueen's Palace, Le-Ath Veronis

Lissa

"Where was the body found?" I asked.

Zaria, Gavril, Ry, Vik and several others had brought the news to me shortly after Gavril's arrival. In my house, surrounded by family, he was Gavril and not Teeg.

"Sawnee," Gavril replied. "Ten minutes before I left to come here, I got word from the CSD's Forensics Department that she was from Earth—Old Earth, actually. The toxins, heavy metals and such in her body verified it. We're worried that she came in contact with radiation on one of those abandoned worlds that Randl may have investigated."

"Or one that the Prophet currently lives on," Vik growled. "He appears to thrive on that filth."

"Do you suppose that D'slay asked his ah, relative to house his paramour?" I asked Zaria.

"I don't know. Quin and I ought to see the body, though. Maybe we can tell something from it."

"I think I'd like to see this for myself," I said. "Can we go now, so I'll have time to get my appetite back before dinner?"

"I'll take us," Ry offered.

"Then let's go."

With power, Zaria lifted one of Irina's hands, followed by the other. She examined the body while Quin studied the woman's face. I wondered if D'slay really cared for her—most women who found themselves companions of Sirenali usually had bite marks or scars from old bite marks all over them.

Irina had none of that.

When Zaria's hand passed over Irina's abdomen, however, her head jerked up and her eyes stared straight into mine. *Irina gave birth,* she told me. *Several times.*

D'slay's?

Not completely—no.

Who else, then? I asked, although afraid of the answer.

There's the touch of Sirenali about them, and ah, something else.

What something else?

Krelk.

Those things? I hesitate to call them people, because they're so primitive they're barely beyond living in caves.

This worries me.

If it worries you, then I'm worried, too.

We have to find D'slay before he spreads more of himself around, if you get my drift.

"Thank goodness you are both here," Valegar arrived.

Zaria's eyes widened at his appearance, while I gasped at his scent. This Valegar was roughly fifty or sixty years older than the one I'd seen in the past three months. He always allowed me to scent him. That's how I knew he came from the future, just as Zaria would know by looking at him.

"I must take Zaria with me briefly," Valegar told me. "She will be back in five minutes or less."

Both disappeared, while Quin came to stand beside me. "Nothing good will come of Irina's alliance with D'slay," she sighed.

~

"Is it anything you can talk about?" I asked Zaria when she returned—in less than five minutes, as Valegar promised. There was no way to tell how long she'd actually been gone; like anyone who held the power she did, she could bend time.

"No."

I didn't point out that she appeared pale and troubled. "You need a drink," I told her, pulling her toward the door of the forensics lab. "Come on, let's get out of here."

"Quin?" Zaria turned to her adopted daughter. Quin came and hugged Zaria.

The moment we were out the door, I folded us back to Le-Ath Veronis.

~

Desh's Restaurant, Tulgalan
Vik

Reah and Lexsi were both at the restaurant—sitting near Mom and having a conversation with her, Zaria, Nissa and several others. Reah, well, that door was closed, but I watched my daughter carefully. Was there any love left in her for me?

Better not to think about that.

Zaria was subdued after what she'd seen earlier—both in Teeg's forensics lab and in whatever future she'd visited with Valegar. I'd never heard of a Larentii coming back to warn anyone in the past of anything; they always let things play out. I doubted Valegar would make such a move without discussing it with his father, Chief Archivist Nefrigar. Nefrigar was one of Reah's mates, and probably knew all about my continued existence, because he considered Zaria his daughter.

Does Nefrigar know? I sent to Zaria.

Know what?

That I'm me.

He does. He hasn't told Reah, if that's what you're asking.

Maybe he should. That way I might stop worrying about it. He could tell her I understand that the door's closed. I would like to see Lexsi now and then, though.

Zaria was quiet for a several moments. The next voice I heard shocked me. *Tory, I've known for a while,* Reah informed me. *Lissa told me.*

I'm sorry. I don't want to intrude on your life, I said.

Stop worrying about that. Do you want me to tell Lexsi? I think she'd like to hear that her father isn't dead.

I'd like that a lot.

Come to dinner, at the palace tomorrow night; you can tell her then. That is if she hasn't already figured it out for herself.

She's really smart. She gets that from her mother.

Lissa said things had really changed with you.

You can thank Zaria and Quin for that. They emptied themselves healing me—of all sorts of things.

Nefrigar explained that when I asked him. He said only Zaria could change some of the things that happened in your past. No ordinary Larentii would even try.

So much of my life has been a waste, I admitted. *Zaria, Quin and Randl found something to salvage. I'm grateful. I enjoy what I do, now, and the ah, connections I now have.*

I know that's secret—even Nefrigar won't talk to me about it, so I don't need to know. He says it will help keep us safe, and that's all that matters.

Thank you for understanding—and for talking to me. I was worried things wouldn't go well if you found out. It's good to have a Lith descendant on the throne again. You're a good fit—not just for the Crown, but for the entire planet. And it's appropriate that you're the caretaker, when you're the one who saved it.

Zaria saved it last time, Tory. You know that.

Then I suppose it's a good thing she and I are related. That means Lexsi is related to Zaria, too.

Did I miss something?

She didn't know.

I ah, I hesitated. Her father took DNA from three women to create Zaria. Lissa is one of those three. I'm related to Zaria through Mom.

Are you kidding me? Really? Lexsi will be over the moon. Wait. Who is Zaria's father?

I suggest you talk to Zaria about that. It's not my secret to tell. How are the older girls?

They're fine. They barely blame us for Jaydevik's death any longer, although they're at Glinda's manor more often than the palace.

Reah, they shouldn't mistreat their mother this way. They had all the best things, because you were putting money into the royal coffers with gishi fruit sales.

What can I do about it, Tory? Force them to love us? They were never intended for us—not at the time. All of it was done without our knowledge or permission. There's no way to take that back, no matter how sorry Kifirin is now. He's a different person—like Edan Desh is a different person.

Like I'm a different person, I admitted. *I didn't know back then how many things were wrong with me—how much they'd managed to fuck me up. I'm sorry for all of that, if it means anything to you at this point. Zaria says it had to do with the many times they had to replace the controller, because I kept trying to break free of it—or my Thifilathi did. It—damaged much of my brain.*

They did that?

Zaria says she saw nineteen changes of the controller. After she and Quin healed me, she asked if I wanted the scar on the back of my neck removed. I told her to leave it—as a reminder.

A reminder of what?

Of how lucky I am right now, no matter the circumstances. That Zaria was willing to bend time to pull me back, and then ask Quin to help heal me.

Come to dinner at the palace tomorrow. Bring Zaria if you can. I'd like to see both of you.

I don't want to disrupt your life.

You won't.

I'll ask Zaria. Anyone else you'd like to see?

Denevik, if he's willing.

Then I'll ask both.

Zaria

"Ilya and Tamp will want whiskey. Edden prefers wine and Bleek will have whatever's available," I said when Travis and Trent invited me to the palace library for an after-dinner drink. "Vik is coming too, isn't he?"

Trent grinned, letting me know that all of my siblings would be there, with spouses or significant others in tow.

"Reah's coming," Travis arrived after going to ask. "Lexsi and Kory will come with her."

"She had a short conversation with Tory during dinner," I said. "So she knows, now."

"Cool," Travis high-fived Trent.

"You had a bet going, didn't you?"

"Yep," Travis chuckled. "Only we bet with our dads. They just lost."

"How late will this shindig last?" I asked, meaning the drinking in the library.

"Maybe an hour or two. Why? You have someplace to be?" Trent grinned.

"I do. I made a promise—to bring Irina home if she were found. That means a trip to the past."

"Want company?" Vik asked. He and Ry had walked up to us as I answered Trent's question.

"If you want to come."

"I think we want to come, too," Trent said.

"How about going now and having a drink here afterward. You can bend time," Ry pointed out.

"I have to tell Teeg that I'm taking the body, first," I said.

"You have to tell me what?"

"Hey, bro. We're taking Irina's body back to her father. Want to come?" Travis punched Teeg on the shoulder.

"Have you considered *Changing What Was?*" Teeg frowned at me.

"Honey, I don't think that's wise. I think she'd be so messed up it would take a lot of power, and I get the feeling that D'slay would just come looking for her again."

"He can bend time?" Vik asked.

"I doubt it, but I think he's found someone to get around that for him."

"Who? And that sounds scary," Vik said.

"It is scary, and I'm hesitant to tell any of my theories just yet. Some are more frightening when they're spoken aloud."

Can you expand on that? Ry sent mindspeech.

Larentii and Saa Thalarr aren't the only ones who can bend time and create a nexus echo, I responded. *I'm feeling that sort of residue in places where D'slay has been.*

More rogue gods?

I don't know, yet. If it is, it's not somebody we're aware of.

"You're right not to say that out loud," Ry agreed. "Are you comfortable taking a crowd with you, to deliver the body?"

"If you can't conceal yourselves, I can do it for you," I told him.

"I've already notified Tybus to release the body, and told him we'll be there shortly," Teeg said.

"Good. Damn, this day has been several decades long," I complained. Nobody laughed.

～

"I'm expecting ah, visitors," Ambassador Bespalov informed me when I appeared inside his study. The coffin containing Irina's body settled in a bare space on the rug nearby.

One look at his face, lined from years of worry and fear, told me these wouldn't be welcome visitors.

"Have you ever considered relocation?" I asked him.

"Where can I go where they will not find me?" he swept out a hand.

"I can go quietly now, or wait for the sly poison, the hidden knife or the sniper's bullet from far away."

"We can convince them that you're—not worth seeking," I sighed.

"How do we do that?"

"We can leave a body behind that will convince them," Ry let his concealment spell drop. Bespalov blinked; he had no idea he had hidden guests.

"What body?"

"I think Irina will commit a final, heroic act," I said. "I promised you I'd bring the body back. I never promised her father."

"It will save your life and make some amends to what she may have become involved in," Vik said.

"They're here," Travis warned, as headlights flashed the window in Bespalov's study.

"Where would you like to go?" I asked him.

"I speak Japanese fluently," he said.

"Good enough."

Ry was ahead of me with the body. He'd already positioned Irina's body on Bespalov's desk chair, then shrunk the coffin down to a tiny size that would fit in his hand.

"Need a gun and a bullet hole," Vik said, as Ry worked his spells.

"What, exactly, is he?" Bespalov whispered to me.

"He's the King of Karathia, and my half-brother," I shrugged. "I'll change the likeness, the blood type, fingerprints and everything else, once he's done."

"I can see that you'd work quite well together. Who are all these others?"

"Also my half-brothers. Your guests are about to knock on the door. We have to hurry."

"Ready for you," Ry turned with a grin.

"On it," I told him, and employed power to change everything about Irina, until she looked exactly like Bespalov, down to the tiniest, well-trimmed hairs in his nostrils. Blood dripped down the replica's face, while the gun, with exactly one bullet fired, lay on the floor as if dropped by a lifeless hand. Even the powder burns on the hand were exact.

By that time, our visitors had gotten tired of knocking, and were blasting the door with automatic weapons to gain entrance.

"Anybody want sushi?" Trent joked as we folded space to Japan.

"Why didn't you take me?" Ilya demanded when we returned to Lissa's library.

"I thought it might be difficult for you to see Bespalov. He has to live out his life and be reborn, honey," I bumped my forehead against Ilya's chest.

"And you used up a lot of clout to rescue my son." His arms came around me, then.

"At least he won't die in some hellhole prison," I mumbled against Ilya's shirt. "I arranged to send Irina's father a letter with some proof of her death—as a last act of Bespalov's, to keep his promise."

"I should have known you would leave nothing to chance, and give as much closure as possible," he murmured against my ear.

"I'd have done the same," Lissa now stood beside us. "Teeg says there's a full report now in his forensics files. I assume that was the last loose end tied?"

"Yes. It's everything Quin and I learned from Irina, that could go in the official records."

"Leaving out D'slay and unscheduled pregnancies, I assume?"

"Yes."

"Come on, both of you. Come have a drink with me, then go to bed. I can see you're exhausted."

We followed Lissa into the library, where Vik, Ry and the others who'd gone with me described what had happened, and what we'd done about it.

"Wine or something else?" Lissa asked.

Ilya and I looked at one another, then turned back to Lissa and said in unison, "Macallan twenty-five, if you have it."

~

Lissa

"I don't think we'll get much of anything out of her, unless she wants to tell us or we need to know," I answered Winkler's question as we got ready for bed.

My werewolf was just as curious as I was about what Zaria had seen or done when she visited the future with Valegar.

"Did you know that every last one of your mates has offered to act as her step-father-in-residence? It appears that she doesn't have much to do with her actual father, and, well, sometimes a father figure may be needed."

"Merrill volunteered first," I sighed and unpinned my hair. "You'd have to fight Wellend, you know. He would have been her second father, had things been allowed to happen naturally and without the Lyristolyi drug's interference."

"We know that. Here's what we've discussed—with Connegar and Reemagar weighing in, of course."

"What have you discussed?"

"Who her Larentii parent would have been. So far, nobody has come forward, and we're wondering about that."

"Have they consulted the Wise Ones?" Now I was curious about this, when I hadn't considered it before. Charles might know, but he'd never tell.

"Since Connegar is related to two of the Wise Ones, of course they've been consulted."

"And?"

"The information has been hidden, according to them."

"Then Charles is right in the middle of that, I have no doubt."

"That's my guess," Winkler agreed. "I think it's to prevent a Larentii from stepping forward to assert his claim of parenthood."

"Because nobody needs to get into a rumble with the Mighty Mind," I shook my head. "What a mess. And for the record, I think it's unfair to keep that information from a parent, or even who should have been a parent."

"I agree. I'd be pissed if I found out that somebody withheld information like that from me."

"Zaria treats Wellend like her father. I think she'd treat a Larentii parent just the same."

"Right again," Winkler grinned. "Aren't you ready for bed, yet?"

"Look, if I could just drop my clothes and be ready, I would. I have to get this junk out of my hair and a bunch of other stuff."

"Stop doing it manually, then. Time's wasting." He tapped his wrist, as if he wore a watch.

"Says the horny werewolf. And you haven't worn a watch in centuries."

"Sometimes I miss it," he grinned and walked around the bed to pretend-stalk me. "Now, take off those clothes or I'll do it for you."

"I thought you'd never offer," I laughed and jumped into his arms.

~

Zaria

"We need more time together," Nissa told me as she, Lissa and I sat in Lissa's arboretum to have breakfast the following morning. "It's nice to do this now and then, without the guys hanging around."

"You have that right," Lissa grinned and sipped hot tea with honey.

"The kitchen did wonders with vegetarian biscuits and gravy," I said.

"Reah taught them how to make the gravy. I showed them how to make biscuits," Lissa said. "Reah is really good at converting recipes."

"Kiarra and Conner love it when Reah cooks," I agreed.

"Do you find it strange that all three of Wisdom's daughters turned out to be vegetarians?" Nissa asked.

"Luck of the draw, I guess," I shrugged. "He isn't vegetarian, last I checked."

"He's not," Lissa confirmed. "I think it has something to do with what all of you became."

"I suppose so."

"Sorry I'm late," Breanne arrived to take the fourth chair at the table.

"I kept the food warm for you," Lissa told her. "The biscuits and gravy are vegetarian and come highly recommended."

"I love them, and especially when they're paired with scrambled eggs," Bree breathed as she set the napkin on her lap and uncovered her plate.

Ry tells us that you think someone has been implementing nexus echo around D'slay's comings and goings, and maybe bending time, Bree said as she cut into half a biscuit with the edge of her fork.

It has that feel about it, I agreed. *I just can't tell who did it. Larentii often leave a marker when they place theirs, so another Larentii will recognize it. With them, it's not hard to determine. This—it isn't Saa Thalarr and it isn't Larentii, not that I can tell, anyway.*

That leaves the Hierarchy, or someone powerful enough to place nexus echo, then, Lissa said. *What about D'slay, or the Prophet?*

Since they're Sirenali, I can't pinpoint that about either of them, I replied. *They're at the top of my suspect list, but how will we figure out if it's them or someone else, unless we stumble over them in our blind searches?*

"That's a good way to describe it—blind searches," Bree shook her head and took another bite of her food.

"If there's any way I can help you, let me know," Nissa offered.

"It may take all of us," I told her. "Like sending out all the ranch hands to round up strays."

"Possibly the most evil and important strays," Lissa confirmed. "This isn't something we can let go, that's for sure. The ASD is dealing with six planetary uprisings as it is, and the Prophet and D'slay are likely behind all of that."

"This doesn't include anything happening on non-Alliance worlds," I said. "Those have been ignored lately, so the ASD and CSD can tend to problems within their own Alliances."

"We only have so much manpower available," Lissa said.

"I'm worried we may have to begin conscripting more for longer periods than is already happening," I agreed. "For now, it's five years. If things get worse, I'd suggest moving it to seven or ten years, and opening it up for vampires and shapeshifters to join."

"We don't have that now?" Nissa asked.

"No. They worry about the vamps only being available during the night and shifters being, well, not humanoid at the full moon. Add to that the fact that vamps and shifters having a decided strength advantage over normal humanoids, and you have a problem," Lissa said. "This isn't Old Earth, where many shifters served in the military and managed to hide what they were."

"The Alliances could train them separately," Nissa suggested.

"Something to mention to Ildevar and Teeg," I agreed.

"It'll take a majority vote at the next conclave, and that won't happen for eight years," Lissa huffed. "Unless we can put an emergency meeting in place, and that will require another majority vote—electronically, of course."

"Then I hope the minds of the majority are still their own and not obsessed," I grumbled. "If that's not the case, we could be in real trouble."

Breanne exchanged a glance with Lissa—they were concerned about this, just as I was. "Another thing that worries me," I said, "is this; what if some of them made a deal with the devil—to get re-elected or stay in power or to take over?"

"That bears looking into," Lissa agreed.

"Send recent images of all planetary leaders to Quin. We need to get started on this now."

"What can we do about obsessions? We can't form an assassination squad to take out the ones affected," Nissa observed.

"We have only two who may be able to change anything of that sort," Bree pointed out. "And employing either one will certainly draw unwanted attention."

One of those she mentioned was me. The other was Ashe's mate, Kay. While Bree could technically count as the third one who could intervene, she was one of the Mighty and held back from interfering more often than not.

"I suppose there are subtle accidents that can be arranged," Lissa snorted. "Rigo is the one to talk to about that."

"Let me think on that," I said. "Maybe there are other ways around it."

"Such as?" Bree turned to look at me.

"Well, I can make a temporary replacement resemble the real thing, right down to their toenail fungus," I replied. "If we remove a leader—temporarily, of course, and place our spy in their seat of power, maybe we can find out where the obsession came from and what the ultimate goal is."

"Somebody not susceptible to obsession," Lissa breathed and a light appeared in her eyes. "That's genius. We can keep the real leaders sequestered somewhere comfortable while we practice subterfuge."

"I think I can replicate the feel of an obsession around a replacement, so the one who placed it can be fooled," I added.

"There is a definite feel about them," Breanne agreed. "Slimy feeling, too."

"Exactly."

"Who is immune to an obsession—that is available to do this?" Nissa asked.

"I'll have to consider that," Bree said, "because it could be considered interference by some of them."

"Will some of the Larentii interfere on our behalf?" Lissa appeared thoughtful.

"I doubt Kalenegar will allow it, unless one of the Three give permission."

"Some of the very old vampires are immune," Lissa said. "But someone will have to make that determination before we consider sending them out."

"I imagine the number of those immune to obsession may be relatively small, compared to the numbers we may actually need."

"And there's the problem of making sure they have the skill set to actually sit in a seat of power," Nissa pointed out.

"Right on," I held up a hand for a high five.

"Is this a high five?" Nissa laughed and slapped her palm against mine.

"Yep."

"I know several vampires who have that skill set," Lissa sipped from her teacup. "All of them former Kings of Hraede, and all of them ancient."

"Successful kings, too, I might add. I've worked with Halimel. He's probably the most patient man I've ever met, and quietly steers people in the proper direction, making them think it's all their idea rather than his," I agreed.

"A sign of true leadership," Bree nodded. "They're all good at what they do. That's why they were turned."

"Kell would be a good candidate, too. He turned Rigo and taught him everything he knows."

"Will the ASD be willing to let Kell do something like that?" I asked. "They tend to frown on suggestions of taking over governments, no matter how temporary or necessary."

"I think we could have a talk with Ildevar," Lissa said. "He may see the sense in it, especially if the obsession of a head of state could destabilize an entire region of planets, instead of one or two."

"You mean the regional hubs?"

"Yes. Distribution of goods is routed through those, and they're major space stations for passenger travel, too. If the massive amounts of tax money paid by any of those hubs is interrupted, that means the Alliance won't be able to operate as it normally does."

"And it will affect every planet that deals with that hub for anything coming in or going out," I acknowledged. "Some of those could face real hardships if they don't get food, drugs or other vital necessities shipped in, or if new tariffs are levied that make it too expensive for them to afford."

"Bingo," Lissa tapped her nose. "For now, the laws are relatively lax on tariffs charged by hub planets, and they've always been on the honor system. An obsession could take advantage of those loopholes and we could have real shortages and less movement of goods and people. That, in turn, will affect shipping companies, tons of employees could lose their jobs, businesses who manufacture the goods will be forced to cut production—the list goes on."

"You know Hraede is one of those hubs, don't you?" Breanne stated quietly.

"We'll check the current monarch when we check the other hubs," I leaned back with a sigh. My to-do list was piling up again, and I was still weary from putting out too many recent fires.

I didn't tell anyone that I already had a special request to check on Hraede—from the spirit of Hraede itself, which was embedded in a gold coin at the top of three that had taken up residence on my left shoulder blade. Therefore, I would go to Hraede first.

Those three planetary spirits had asked to stay with me; the others had chosen among Randl's *Formidables*, although he carried the majority of them himself. In gold and silver, those coins covered the sun and moon tattoos on his back and brought them to life—for those who could see them.

Not everyone could, unless they chose to be seen.

Vik carried one, as did Travis and Trent. I wondered if they'd told Lissa. It didn't matter if she knew—she wouldn't reveal those secrets.

The other two I carried?

Karathia and Kifirin, because I'd already championed both those worlds, and they were pleased by my efforts on their behalf. "How quickly can I put Halimel in place on Hraede?" I asked.

"You think it'll be necessary?" Lissa made a face as if contemplating my question.

"I think it will be," Breanne answered before I could. "Rigo may be needed elsewhere. Halimel will be a good fit on his homeworld. They didn't call him Halimel the Wise for nothing, you know."

"Only because they couldn't call him Halimel the Great," Rigo walked into the arboretum; Lissa had sent mindspeech and asked him to join us.

"Yes, only Rigo is the Great, followed by the Wise, the Just, the Fierce—you get the idea," Lissa teased him.

"All the members of the Order of the Night Flower are

distinguished in their reign of Hraede," Rigo teased her back. "That's why we were turned, you know."

"I thought you were turned so you could kiss my fingers," Lissa grinned at him.

"A worthy reason, indeed. Now, you think Halimel will be needed to stand in for Hraede's current King?" Rigo turned to me.

"I think that may be the case. I have it on good authority that things aren't quite right there, with the seat of power."

"May I come with you to assess the situation first?"

"I was hoping you'd come if I asked," I said.

"You do not need to ask. I will be honored to accompany you, as will Halimel."

"How soon can you both be ready?" I asked.

"We can go within the hour, if you'd like."

"I'll come, too," Lissa said.

"See, easy as that," Rigo spread his hands and smiled.

CHAPTER 3

H raede

Lissa

"I dislike this dalliance, to be sure," Rigo murmured. He and I sat in a tea shop roughly a mile from the palace; we'd arrived to find King Larvalis engaged in various compromising acts with a lover.

A lover who wasn't Larvalis' Queen, and who was also pregnant with Larvalis' heir. So far, the Queen was barren, or hadn't bothered to try because Larvalis wasn't up to par with other Kings of Hraede.

Halimel had taken Zaria to a nearby shop that sold scarves and jewelry, so Rigo and I could discuss the implications. Up to now, Hraede was the most stable hub in the Reth Alliance. Poor leadership, combined with a potential obsession, could change all that in a hurry.

"We should take a look at his lover, too," Rigo whispered.

"She could be involved," I conceded. "No matter what, Renellia's pregnancy is a scandal waiting to happen."

"If we remove her, too, we'll need a replacement."

"How often do you suppose he visits her?"

"We can find that out easily," Rigo said.

Yes, we could, unless he is too obsessed to reveal that information. Either way, Rigo was right. We have to find a replacement for her,

35

since others know of her and would become suspicious if she suddenly disappeared.

Whether the Queen would be a problem, we had yet to discover.

"You're considering Mephista, now, aren't you?" Rigo smiled and covered one of my hands with his.

"Yes. How does it feel to come back here, when you once ruled the planet?" I asked him.

"I like seeing things from this side of the palace walls," he sighed. "Back then, I was surrounded by bodyguards, and every conversation I had with anyone in a shop such as this was always an exercise in obsequiousness or fear."

"I dislike the bowing and scurrying myself," I agreed. "It's why I like to go out disguised."

"Had I known back then how to successfully disguise myself, I'd have done it many times. Perhaps it's a good thing Kell never taught me those things until after I was turned."

"You were slightly more vulnerable back then," I pointed out. "I'd really hate it if you hadn't survived long enough to be turned."

"Kell saw to it that I wasn't embalmed, and my body lay in state for three days at the palace until it was placed in the royal crypt. I woke seven days later."

"Fancy," I waggled the fingers of my free hand at him. He responded by lifting the hand he'd covered and kissing my wrist.

"I know the circumstances of your turning," he held my fingers against his cheek. "Gavin and Merrill explained all of it to me."

"I hear my early diaries are in the Larentii Archives," I shook my head and pulled my hand away. "Ashe 'fessed up. Nowadays, I don't have to record anything—Connegar and Reemagar do it for me, and that information goes straight to Nefrigar, who catalogs it for the Archives."

"The Larentii Archives are wondrous," Rigo smiled. "I've barely seen a fraction of what is there; Connegar takes me whenever I wish to go."

"Let me guess—you've studied the section on poisons extensively," I teased.

"Why not? I've learned a few things and refined much of what I already knew. Something you may not suspect is that I also studied extensively in the antidote section."

"I knew I loved you for a reason."

"Tiessa, you make my heart young again. Come, I see Hal and Zaria returning. Perhaps Renellia and Larvalis have exhausted themselves with their cavorting."

"Cavorting. Now there's a word you don't hear every day," I said, rising from my seat.

"It's politer than saying fucking like plains-faphets," Rigo informed me.

"It astounds me that you can say the word *fucking* as if it were a proper royal decree," I snickered.

"Larvalis is on his way back to the palace," Zaria said when she and Halimel reached our table. "We can arrange to be hidden inside his chamber when he arrives."

"Then take us," Rigo intoned. "I'd much prefer being skinned alive than to scent his stench before he showers."

Those words told me exactly what Rigo's true thoughts on Larvalis and his reign were—as politely as he could put it. Until recently, I'd called Larvalis classless and ineffective. He'd become dangerous in a short amount of time, and that either meant he was being manipulated by someone in his court, or he'd been obsessed. While I considered which of those two things it could be, Zaria transported us to Larvalis' suite in the palace.

Rigo wasn't wrong about the stench; until I forced a shield up, Larvalis stank of sweat and sex. He began removing clothing and dropping it on the floor as he made his way toward the massive bath inside his suite. An attendant followed behind him, picking everything up to have it cleaned.

Towels and bathing items were carefully laid out in the bath; Larvalis, now naked and not much to look at in that condition, slipped into the water of the bath and ordered a glass of wine.

The attendant bowed and left the room to fetch the King's favorite beverage.

He isn't obsessed, Zaria informed us. *There is a new courtier who whispers in his ear, however.*

Can you tell us anything about the courtier? Rigo asked.

Larvalis doesn't know much, other than Sworden kisses his ass and provides advice free of charge, Zaria replied. *Something about this feels— really off. I've* Looked *already, and there isn't anyone by that name who comes up.*

Then we must visit Sworden, too, Rigo growled in mindspeech. *Along with the Queen and the lover.*

Do you know where Sworden is? I directed my question to Zaria.

He has a suite in the royal wing. Want to go now?

Let's go.

Zaria

Something prickles my mind about Larvalis, Halimel sent the message only to me just before I moved our party to Sworden's suite.

I've placed a perimeter spell, so I'll know who comes and goes, I told him. *And I've placed a shield around Larvalis, so he doesn't get croaked while we're visiting his friend.*

Get croaked?

Did in? Bite the dust? Take a dirt nap?

I watched Hal's mind work as he sorted out the idioms I'd flung at him. *Ah,* he said after only a second or two. *I like* get croaked *best. It was the most difficult to decipher.*

So you like a challenge, huh? I asked while we were in transit to Sworden's rooms.

I do like a challenge, he agreed as we studied the sleeping form of Sworden, whose windows were completely darkened to keep all light from entering his bedroom.

Well, I'll be damned, Lissa hissed in our heads. We were looking at a vampire, asleep during the day. No doubt he'd laid compulsion to not be disturbed during the day, and kept his doors locked during that time.

Want to take him with us and question him at nightfall? Rigo asked while lifting an eyebrow at Lissa.

I'll send him to my dungeon now, Lissa said. *That way, we can question him whenever we want.* We watched as Sworden disappeared. *That was enlightening,* Lissa breathed. *Shall we go to the Queen, next?*

The Queen was having tea with three friends in the palace library. Mephista sipped from a delicate, hand-painted, gold-rimmed cup that was part of a set hundreds of years old.

While her movements were graceful, her words charmingly polite and her afternoon dress elegant and refined—inside, she was a brittle tangle of regret.

Her beauty and pedigree had convinced Larvalis to offer her marriage and the position as his Queen, because he liked how they appeared in public. She'd been pushed to accept the offer by her own father, who had designs on having a grandchild on the throne.

Mephista was determined not to have a child, as revenge against both her husband and her father.

What a train wreck, I told my companions. *She knows about Renellia and doesn't care. She wants nothing to do with Larvalis.*

Halimel, who stood beside me, appeared thoughtful.

I have a suggestion, he told me.

What's that?

I think Alrenardo would be a better replacement for Larvalis. He hadn't taken his eyes off Mephista once while he spoke. I understood why, too. Al loved auburn-haired women, and Mephista's natural, auburn waves were piled stylishly atop her head, with a jeweled pin placed strategically for the best effect possible.

Alrenardo will be a better fit to replace Larvalis, Rigo echoed Hal's opinion seconds later.

Which brings up the replacement for Renallia, Lissa said. *Who?*

Someone who won't mind not having sex, I said.

Al can visibly send Renallia away, so her replacement can be situated at the summer palace, Rigo suggested. *Anyone can be made to look like her.*

I'd worry about them—they can be used to blackmail Larvalis—or

Larvalis' replacement. The one we send has to be able to take care of themselves, Lissa sighed.

We can also send guards, who will be able to do the same, Halimel said. *It's not uncommon to do so.*

Where should we keep Larvalis and Renallia in the meantime? Most of the places I knew had problems in one way or another, and I certainly didn't want their stain on Sirena's soil.

I'll think of something, Lissa said. *Come on, we have Alrenardo to inform, Sworden to question and Larvalis and Renallia to deal with before we can replace them.*

Vik

Denevik agreed to come to dinner at the palace on Kifirin. He and I met in Mom's library, while we waited for Zaria to join us. She surprised us by bringing Halimel with her.

"Long day?" Denevik asked after studying their faces.

"I used to think that bending time would be a blessing," Halimel breathed. "I no longer consider it such."

We went to Hraede to handle a delicate situation, which turned into a snarled mess, Zaria informed me in mindspeech.

Did it involve the idiot currently on the throne?

It did and still does. I'll try to explain it later. We'll be checking on all the hub worlds before this is over.

Because interruptions on those worlds could cause a cascade of events, huh?

Something like that.

Nothing like starting wars over shortages and discontent, eh?

And those wars, as devastating as they could turn out to be, could be a distraction from other things.

Don't scare away my appetite, I warned. *I haven't had anything cooked by Reah in a long time.*

Sorry. Hal and I are a bit testy after questioning the vampire who's been whispering in Larvalis' ear for the past few months.

You're kidding?

Not.

Come here. You need a brotherly hug, I told her.

I'll take it, she said and allowed me to squeeze her against me.

"Don't squash your half-sister," Denevik mumbled.

"I won't," I said and let her go. "Now, who's taking us?"

"You can do the honors," Zaria said.

And so I did.

Zaria

Reah served a fish course, a beef course and, for the lone vegetarian (me), she served a noodle dish in a delicious sauce, then a type of mushroom that grew larger than Vik's palm, which had been sautéed in red-wine and seasonings, and served with tiny, herb-crusted potatoes.

"Is that good?" Hal, who sat on my left, asked.

"Want a taste? It's awesome," I told him.

"I'll try it."

I cut a piece of the mushroom, made sure it was coated in the red-wine sauce and offered it to him.

His eyes lit up as he chewed.

"That is delicious," he said. "I would definitely eat that again."

"I can serve it as a vegetable course in the future," Reah beamed at us. "The mushroom has a denser consistency than most, so it's perfect to serve in this way."

"The sauce is good with the potatoes, too," I said. "Ilya and I will beg for this recipe."

So far, the topic hadn't turned to Vik being Torevik Rath, Lexsi's father, and still among the living. I'd watched Lexsi when she wasn't aware of my gaze; she knew something was up but hadn't speculated.

Yet.

Who is Vik? Really?

Lexsi's mindspeech didn't surprise me.

Do you want to hear it from me or from him?

Please tell me it's Daddy, she begged. *He's tall, like Daddy, but he doesn't look the ah, same. I know you could have saved him if you wanted to. Tell me you did that.*

I opened a channel to Vik, allowing him to hear her words.

It's me, baby, he told her. *Zaria made me look different, well, because.*

I barely recalled that Lexsi could turn to mist, just as her grandmother, Lissa, could. She was beside Vik's chair in two blinks, with her arms wrapped around him and sobbing her happiness onto his shoulder.

He pulled her onto his lap and soothed her with words so soft I barely heard. Words of love. Explanations of how proud he was of her. So many things that he hadn't been able to say to her before.

Kory, who'd kept his seat across the table, now listened intently while Reah whispered in his ear. I saw his eyebrows shoot upward as he learned what Lexsi had only realized moments earlier.

A sly smile tugged at Denevik's mouth; Vik had already told him. Halimel knew because I'd explained things to him before meeting with Denevik and Vik.

And, because the food was too good to waste, Hal and I kept eating. After all, we'd skipped at least two meals before coming for dinner.

~

Lissa

"So we have another group of vampires on Hraede, posing as the Rith Naeri?" Merrill, Gavin and Tony joined Rigo and me in the library. Merrill was the one who spoke, however, after I explained what we'd learned from Sworden.

"Except these vampires have a very different view of what the Rith Naeri should be doing," Rigo fumed. I'd never seen him this worked up about anything. "We kept our deeds secret. How did they learn of this?"

"I'll ask Zaria if she saw that in him when she gets back from

Kifirin," I said. "Then, Rigo and I need to sleep, and then we need to start hunting the others in Sworden's fake group of vampires."

"Zaria says that Sworden is only a lackey in the group and knew little," Rigo reminded me.

"I know. Honey, I'm so tired I can't even think straight anymore."

"What if every hub world now has a secret group infiltrating the ruling offices?" Gavin asked.

"I'm worried that this is exactly what's happening," I said. "While Larvalis is gullible enough to take Sworden's advice without compulsion, others may not be as malleable."

"I doubt anyone is as malleable as that incompetent fool," Rigo hissed.

"Why don't you two rest while we investigate for a while?" Merrill offered. "I can take Kiarra, Adam and Gavin with me. We know where all the hubs are, and Kiarra will know if something is wrong, even if she can't read those in power as easily as Zaria can."

"Thank you. Rigo and I will appreciate updates when we wake."

"I'll see that you get them, Cara," Gavin promised.

When they folded space, leaving Tony, Rigo and me in the library, I yawned.

"I can get you both to bed," Tony told us. "You look like you could sleep standing up."

Zaria

Vik stayed to talk with Reah, Denevik and Lexsi. Hal and I begged off and returned to Le-Ath Veronis.

Lissa is asleep, Tony informed us when we landed in Lissa's library and sent mindspeech. *You should get some rest, too. Gavin, Merrill and a few others are out checking the other hubs right now. You may have new information when you wake.*

Good. We're going to bed. Wake me if the apocalypse happens.

And only if the apocalypse happens, Hal added. "Come," he said aloud. "I can mist you to your suite. Mine is down the same hallway."

"Then what's the holdup, dude?" I leaned against Halimel.

"There is none, my lady," he whispered and turned us both to mist.

~

"Love or breakfast. Which would you prefer?"

Edden's breath warmed my ear and woke me at the same time. "Who turned the air frigid?" I mumbled, refusing to open my eyes.

"An unexpected cold snap occurred while you slept," he chuckled. "It is late fall on Le-Ath Veronis. So far, the residents are enjoying the chill in the air."

"Because they're vampires and don't feel it," I complained.

"It is their nature," Edden agreed. "Shall I fetch another blanket for you?"

"How is it," I began, while attempting to open my eyes and sit up at the same time, "that all three of my mothers were vampires, and not one of them graced me with the ability to not feel the cold? Never mind, I'll warm the air myself."

"How do you know your third mother was a vampire, and in the past tense, my love?"

"I can read Lissa when I want to," I mumbled like an obstinate child. Employing power, I warmed the air in my suite considerably. "I also saw that she's been reborn, but Lissa doesn't know who she is, now."

"Do you have any idea who it could be?"

"None yet. I'm working on it. I'm also starving."

"Then we'll find breakfast for you."

"No, I think I'd like a kiss, first."

"I was hoping for that."

Edden is a diplomat of the highest order. Not only did I get love, but breakfast in bed shortly after. Giving him mindspeech was one of my better decisions.

~

"Hey, crew," I said, walking into the library with Edden. Ilya, Bleek, Tamp, Vik, Denevik and Halimel waited there for me. I wasn't surprised that Halimel chose to come to the meeting; we waited for Lissa, Rigo, Merrill and several others to join us. We'd discuss their findings on other hub worlds.

Tea, coffee and snacks had been laid out for us; I poured coffee for myself while Vik stacked a small plate with cookies.

"Things went well last night, I take it?" I asked him. He grinned in reply. *Thanks for smoothing the way*, he sent, before giving me a wink and moving away to find a chair.

Anything for you, bro, I teased.

Travis and Trent walked in with Lissa, followed by their fathers, Drake and Drew. Gavin, Merrill, Rigo and Kiarra came in after those five.

"We've found four other hub worlds that are acting suspiciously, as if obsession has been laid," Lissa announced. "Others could be targeted, too. I've already sent images taken yesterday of all the leaders of hub worlds to Quin; she should get back to us at any moment."

"We're here," Quin, announced. Her smile was aimed at me, however, as she and Justis walked into the library, royal-red wings folded tightly against each back.

I patted the sofa cushion next to mine; Quin and Justis joined me on the couch I'd chosen. My crew had elected to stand during the meeting, so they filled the space behind the sofa.

"What can you tell us?" Lissa asked Quin.

"The four you suspected are obsessed," she pulled her comp-vid from a pocket and handed it to me, so I could look at their images, too. "So far, the others aren't affected by obsession, but three are under some kind of duress."

I thumbed through images of two Queens, one President and a Prime Minister. Each of them bore an obsession, although the type of obsession was never evident. Part of the Sirenali curse, that even the most powerful couldn't get past the obsession to see the content of the original commands.

"I need to go to each of these worlds to see if there is anyone around these leaders who recalls seeing D'slay, or whether we have other Sirenali to contend with."

"I think we should infiltrate all of the hub worlds, to see if and when they fall under an obsession, or to stop it if we can." Lissa sounded angry; I didn't blame her. Something was afoot, and I figured it would be Alliance-wide war before it was over.

"I think the Prophet and D'slay are working in tandem, even if we can't put the two together," Vik snorted. I turned my head to look at him, only to see a curl of smoke escape his nostrils. His Thifilathi was upset, and that was a good indication that Vik was right on the money.

When Quin and I had healed him, we'd reset everything about him, including his ability as a guli, or High Demon truthsayer. Another thing he had that many High Demons no longer listened to was what they'd been intended for in the beginning. They knew, through instinct, when the dark races posed a threat to any others.

His Thifilathi knew that Sirenali, combined with other forces, were threatening everything. In the past, that was supposed to be a sign for the High Demons to mobilize and quash the offenders.

Most High Demons no longer paid attention to that small voice within them. Vik was listening carefully to everything it said, likely amplified by the spirit coin he carried on his chest.

"I agree with Vik," I turned back to Lissa. "They're working in tandem, whether they realize it or not."

"You think a master hand crafted this, don't you?" Kiarra studied me carefully. "I think the same," she added.

"We probably agree on who that hand was attached to in the beginning," I told her. "I can't begin to tell you how much that infuriates me."

"It's like land mines left behind after the war is over," Lissa sighed. "Planted by design, because they never want to give up the fight, no matter what."

"A hollow victory, indeed, if you can even call it that," Charles appeared beside Kiarra and pulled her close to kiss her cheek. He'd been present as a father in her life far longer than he'd been in mine. I wasn't jealous; I merely wondered why.

I had to be sure of some things, he sent to me, as if he'd read my thoughts. *You'd never have conquered the Metal Library if you hadn't been worthy.*

You realize you keep digging the hole deeper, I snapped at him. *Perhaps you should go hide in it.*

That is the Mighty Heart speaking—with the passion she possesses, he informed me.

Right. And that is Wisdom, telling me this with the cold, calculated, unfeeling sentiment that he's so famous for.

I don't mean to do this to you—to both of us. I'm sorry for the hole I've left in your life, and for the confusion I handed you with the mystery of your parentage. I should know better.

Well, I guess Wisdom doesn't know everything, now does he?

Far from it, he agreed. *Sometimes, Wisdom means the willingness to accept your mistakes and learn from them. Wisdom means learning—constantly. I suppose it's far too late to take you fishing, so father and daughter can bond.*

I'd be healing the fish you caught and arguing about catching them in the first place.

Now, that's the daughter I love so much, he replied, a slight smile forming on his lips.

Do you?

Do I what?

Love me?

Daughter, I love you so much it hurts. That's why I didn't rush in every time you skinned a knee or got into a jam. You had to learn to fly on your own. I only interfered with the giving of the drug. I needed you at this point quickly, and that's the only way it could happen. I'm sorry for any pain that brought you.

You know, I wish I could believe that.

I understand why you don't. It was a great risk to my heart, and now I pay the price of it.

Will you answer a question, then?

Anything.

Who is the reincarnated Sarita?

Ah. I should have expected that dagger in your hand, he said. *You know her well, daughter. She sits beside you now.*

With that, Charles disappeared—as if he couldn't bear to see the shock on my face. "Is something wrong?" Quin touched my hand, sending a jolt of recognition through me. Charles had blocked that information from both of us—until now.

CHAPTER 4

Z aria

"It's fitting," Merrill raked fingers through fine, black hair. "As she was one of your mothers, now you are hers."

I'd asked to see him alone after our meeting. He'd turned Sarita centuries ago on Old Earth. He'd had no idea who she'd become, once reborn. I figured there was more to this story, too, because it was a given that Liron never provided Quin with a soul. Someone else had done that, and I suspected my father.

"I don't think this information should be given to Wlodek," I shook my head at Merrill, whose bright, blue eyes confirmed my decision.

"He is past that, I think, but there's no reason to tempt fate. It will only upset both of them to know this."

"Agreed."

"Thank you for telling me, though. I've worried about her over the years. Now I know she is loved and in the best of circumstances."

"I was hoping you'd feel that way."

"What are your plans for the rest of the day? Don't tell me you're going to rush off to four worlds to deal with obsessions," he chided. "Child, you are exhausted. Come to NorthStar and stay for a few days.

You can always bend time, if necessary, to deal with the problems we face."

"I know." I hung my head. I'd driven my crew just as hard as I'd driven myself, too. "Can I bring my crew? They're just as weary."

"Of course. Bring anyone you want. We'll expect you for dinner." He smiled, patted my shoulder and folded space.

~

"We're going to NorthStar for a few days."

"My love, I am grateful you accepted the invitation," Tamp breathed a sigh.

"Merrill pointed out that all of us are exhausted. I can bend time if it's necessary. We'll take five days off and see how we feel."

"Ah, rest for all six lobes," Bleek's four arms settled around me for a tight hug.

"Honey, I just want to float in the pool," I told him. "That sounds like heaven right now."

"I can do some reading," Edden breathed. "I'm so far behind on my book lists."

"Will there be anyone available for sparring?" Ilya asked.

"I think we can find someone who'll wave a sword at you," I shook a finger at him.

"I'll do it," Vik walked in, wearing a grin. Denevik strode behind him; I could see those two were becoming fast friends.

"Good enough," Ilya fist-bumped Vik.

"Guess who's going to replace Renellia on Hraede?" Vik grinned at me.

"No idea," I said.

"Nissa is doing it, while Trik and Toff act as her bodyguards."

"Nothing like getting the hairs singed off your nose if you act up around those three," Bleek laughed.

"Well, Lissa said it should be someone who could take care of themselves," I said. "Did they volunteer? I'm surprised they allowed them away from Grey House for such an assignment."

"Ah, Mom offered to bend time," Vik cleared his throat.

"That's a solution, then. Is everybody packed up?" I asked. "They're expecting us for dinner. It's casual," I held up a hand before Vik could offer to change out of jeans and a pullover. "Dinner is served poolside —Kiarra sent mindspeech half an hour ago."

"Who else will be there?" Vik asked.

"No idea. Don't get cold feet, bro."

"No cold feet here," he declared.

"Then let's go." I folded everybody to NorthStar, landing us beside the pool, as directed.

Vik

I had no idea that Valegar, Nefrigar and Pheligar would be at NorthStar, or that Nefrigar would bring Reah with him. I thought we'd left things on a good note on Kifirin, and that I'd likely see Reah only now and then, when I visited Lexsi.

Did you know about this? I accused Zaria in mindspeech.

Val may have told me—at the last minute. I hope this doesn't make you feel uncomfortable.

I'll get over it.

If you need help, let me know.

I wanted to snap at her for leading me into this, but it hadn't been her plan. Nefrigar and Pheligar probably conspired to bring this about.

You lack patience, young demon, Master Morwin used to tell me. There was nothing for me to do here except suck it up and behave.

"There is a proposition in this, you understand," Edden held out a glass of bourbon.

"What are you talking about?" I took the offered glass and downed half its contents.

"One of the affected hub worlds is Galk."

Galk. Where the Queen ruled and the King either hid in the library or went fishing in the ocean from his private yacht. "Which one is affected?" I asked before emptying my glass.

"Both."

That statement brought a stream of smoke from my nostrils. Reah was a close fit for the Queen of Galk. Her husband towered over her, much as I did over Reah.

Fuck.

Neither of us were susceptible to a Sirenali's obsessions—because we were High Demon. Perfect to substitute for the royal couple. At least they didn't appear to have much to do with one another, unless they were at a function which required it.

"Does this mean Lexsi will be in charge of Kifirin while Reah is gone? Does Reah know they want to put her on Galk?"

"I imagine she'll know soon, if she doesn't already. Her Larentii mate keeps her well-informed."

"Are you sure you don't want to come, too? As an advisor?"

"Only if there is no other option. I fear that duty may call me elsewhere in this."

"Who am I supposed to talk to, then?" Mom would say I was whining. I suppose she'd be right. Dave was still on Sirena; maybe I could ask for his company.

"Perhaps the Blevakian will agree to act as bodyguard?" Edden wanted to snicker, I could tell.

"Hell, he can be King in my place, and I'll act as bodyguard."

"There's something else you should know, too," Edden forced himself to be serious once more.

"What's that?"

"I believe your mother may take Prime Minister Fallah's place on Corez."

"Corez has been hit? That's awful. I've been several times to relax and unwind from the job."

"Even worse is that Fallah has been afflicted by an obsession. She is a strong leader, and Corez is just as stable as Hraede, nowadays. That would be a terrible blow to the Alliance."

"I get that. Why can't I go as Mom's bodyguard, then?"

"Because she has many mates, and at least two or three will insist on going with her. I believe Winkler, Rigo and Gavin have already submitted their reasons why they should go, although her Falchani mates are also attempting to fight their way in."

"Who'll watch Le-Ath Veronis?"

"Ah. The looming question," Edden smiled mysteriously. "I may have a guess, but nothing solid to base it on."

"And you won't tell me, will you?"

"It's only speculation at this point, so I'll keep it to myself."

"Fine."

"Tory, can we talk for a few minutes?" Reah's hand was suddenly on my arm, sending a jolt of electricity through me. We hadn't touched since—well, since we'd made Lexsi. Nobody had called me Tory, either, except Mom and only when we were alone.

My Thifilathi, too, was in immediate need at Reah's closeness. I forced it back.

"Sure." I handed my empty glass to Edden, who accepted it with a raised eyebrow and mute speculation.

Reah led me toward the front lawn, which was covered in decorative trees, each providing a canopy of privacy for NorthStar's residents. She stopped beneath a star-leaf tree, its supple limbs hanging down around us, similar to that of a weeping willow's.

We didn't need a divorce or separation; according to Alliance records, Torevik Rath was still as dead as a doornail. Mom's old phrase still made little sense, but it's the one that came readily to mind.

"Nefrigar is telling me that Edden may have spoken to you about Galk," Reah began. My shoulders lost some of their tenseness at her opening.

"He did."

"We should go."

"I," nothing more came out of my mouth. It was as if my brain were no longer connected to anything else in my body, and had forgotten how to form words or think, even.

"Tory, I know there's plenty of awful history between us. That doesn't mean we can't get along now, does it? Deep down, we know one another, don't we? We share the same heritage; we know what the other is and what they're capable of doing. You're different now. I think I am, too. Being able to keep Lexsi close to me has meant so much, and one day, she'll rule Kifirin. I couldn't have done that without you."

"It makes a hell of a difference when gods aren't fiddling with your reproductive system, doesn't it?" I winced when I considered how insensitive my words were.

"You're right," Reah agreed, brushing aside my callousness. "Nefrigar thinks this assignment won't last more than two months; he and the Wise Ones feel some sort of break is coming, but they can't say whether it'll be good or bad."

"So this is important," I dipped my chin in a thoughtful nod.

"Yes. I think it is."

"Then I'll do it."

"Good. We can make plans the last day you're here; Nefrigar says he'll bring me, and we can go to Galk afterward. Someone else will take away the obsessed King and Queen and we'll slide into their places. Grampa Denevik may come as a bodyguard."

"This could be dangerous, you know," I warned her.

"I know. We've done this before, remember?"

"Reah, when was the last time you went on an assignment?"

"A while, I suppose."

"Just—watch out for yourself. I'll watch your back as often as I can. Are there any others we can bring along? I get itchy every time I think about Galk."

"Something of your mother showing through?" Reah's eyes narrowed in conjecture.

"It happens now and then," I shrugged. "I'll talk to Zaria—maybe she'll find others who can come as extra bodyguards or something."

"I wouldn't mind a little help. More eyes and ears will only assist us in finding villains."

"I wish Ry could come with us," I sighed. "He's excellent at disguises and intrigue."

"How about Bel Erland instead?"

"He'd be a good one," I agreed. "What about Wyatt?"

"You don't mind your nephews coming along?"

"Are you kidding? They've both worked with the BlackWing Pirates. I'm proud to claim some kinship with them, whether they know who I am or not. They're your sons, Reah. Are you sure you don't mind?"

"They've offered their services to Lissa and Zaria. They're grown. They can make up their own minds."

"Plus they can be trusted. Are they immune to obsession?"

"Zaria confirms it, because their mother is part High Demon."

"You are an amazing mother, you know that?" I grinned at her.

"Thank you. I'm not sure you've ever said that to me before."

"If I haven't, then it's because I'm a difik. Come on, let's go eat. I'm starving."

Reah allowed me to take her elbow and steer her toward the back of the house, where we could hear laughter and conversation.

Zaria

"Are you prepared to allow Wyatt and Bel Erland to go with them?" Edden spoke softly next to me when Reah and Vik returned. We watched as they talked and filled their plates with food before joining Nefrigar, who was sitting on the pool deck absorbing sunlight.

"I am. Denevik will go with them, too, And I may have two others to send, but I'll fit them in as unknown spies and allies for those five."

"Have you decided what we'll be doing?"

"I have."

"And?"

"We're going to Kwark."

"Yes. I can see the sense in that."

Edden knew quite well that Kwark was the centrally-located hub to all the others, and closest to Galk. I suspected there was some foul purpose for the enemy to choose those two. Also, Kwark's Queen had five mates, who also served in some capacity in her government. She was the only one obsessed, but all five mates would be taken with her and kept safe.

"Who will be covering for Lissa?" Edden asked. He already suspected; his guess merely hadn't been verified.

"Bree. She's done it before. Nobody will know it isn't Lissa there on the throne of Le-Ath Veronis. You should have placed a bet on your guess—it was a good one."

"It would have been my choice, had I been Lissa. Also, the fewer people who know, the safer both will be," he added.

"You were the best High President Kondar ever had," I told him.

"You're too kind."

"And truthful."

"How will we hide Bleek's extra arms?"

"Oh, I have a plan," I smiled.

"I like your plans, especially if they make you smile."

"How *will* you hide my extra arms?" Bleek joined the conversation.

"Honey, the tech is readily available, and the consort you'll replace is having a birthday party next week."

"You mean a biotech conformer?"

"Yep. Except it will be fake and look like the real thing."

"I love you."

"I love you, too. Even if you have six lobes."

"Can I have the real thing afterward, to have six arms?"

"Only you would want that, but sure."

"I assume that Randl's crew will now be looking for evidence of D'slay, in addition to the Prophet?"

"That's the plan," I sighed. "They'll coordinate through me and I'll give him any information that Lissa, Reah, Nissa and the others gather on their hub worlds."

"I hope that this many of us, placed on strategic worlds, will find something of value," Tamp arrived with a fresh glass of wine for me. Ilya was right behind him, offering me a small plate of sliced gishi fruit.

"Zaria?" Kay joined my small group, with Ashe right behind her.

She was staggeringly beautiful, and her soul shone behind bright-blue eyes that only the Elemaiya could produce.

"Kay," I left my wine and gishi fruit hanging in midair, so I could hug her.

"I think I can help somewhat," Kay told me when I let her go. "You'll need to know what the obsessions are that were placed on hub leaders. I may be able to get to those if I change aura lines."

"Now there's an idea," I nodded. "That could make our presence much more convincing, if we knew what they'd been ordered to do."

"I think so, too," Ashe agreed. "Kay had already offered to help those affected on hub worlds, and they'll be kept safe within the boundaries of SouthStar while we're doing our spying on their attackers."

"Good. Thank you for offering to house them," I said. "I was worried about that."

"I know you were—Lissa told me. I'll coordinate with you and the others when it comes time to remove the leaders you're replacing," Ashe went on. "It'll be a smooth transition, and the leaders will be placed in stasis until Kay can change aura lines for each of them."

"We'll explain that their exile is only temporary, or they could end up obsessed again, and I doubt anyone will want that," Kay said.

"Not when we can supply them with evidence of their behavior after the obsession," Ashe snorted. "They won't even recognize themselves or their actions."

"I assume you'll have the assistance of Nefrigar and the Larentii in handling that?"

"Yes. A Larentii's playback of any event is unquestioned in its veracity. Anyone who thinks otherwise is only deluding themselves."

"Then let's hope they behave rationally when you explain things to them."

"We'll find a way," Ashe offered a crooked grin. "Don't worry about that part—we'll handle it."

"Good."

"Let's eat," Kay leaned into Ashe.

"I was hoping you'd say that." They walked toward the buffet table, where plenty of food waited.

"Don't forget you're here to relax, dearest," Valegar took Ashe's place. "If you need help, I will do what I can."

"Let's sit down," I said. "I'm tired of standing."

"I will move us," Val offered and did so without ruffling so much as a hair on any of us.

Lissa

"Reah and Tory are going to Galk," Bree informed me as I tossed another silk tunic on the bed. I'd have to change the style of it with power, but I sure didn't want to wear somebody else's clothes while I was undercover.

"Have they worked that out, then?"

"They had a talk, according to Nefrigar."

"Zaria and her bunch are going to Kwark."

"That's suitable—a Queen with five consorts."

"Ashe will be housing all the leaders being replaced."

"Good idea."

"Who's going to Corez with you?"

"Winkler. Gavin, Rigo, Drake and Drew."

"Who'll act as First Advisor, then?"

"Rigo. He has the most experience, although Winkler's tail is in a knot over it."

"So, which two are the Secondary Advisors, and which ones are guards?"

"Gavin and Winkler are acting Secondary Advisors. Drake and Drew will carry traditional weapons, as the guards do near the royal couple."

"I hear those swords are merely decorative, and their edges are as dull as watermelons."

"Then somebody's in for a surprise if they try to attack us."

"Like dragons won't be enough if somebody tries that?"

"They'll have blades out, first. Dragons are the weapon of last resort."

"Sirenali can be incinerated by a dragon's fire, just like anybody else."

"You're really into this, aren't you?"

"I just don't want to take any chances," Bree sniffed.

"Will you be all right here, taking my place?" I asked her. "The first time wasn't a good memory for you."

"Everybody who needs to know will know, so that will eliminate any problems. Plus, I have a few mates who don't mind being disguised as the ones you're taking with you—in public, anyway."

"Now there's an idea," I grinned at her. "Nobody will know we're gone except the rest of my bunch."

"Whose lips will be sealed—I can make sure of it. Who will take President Yilisis' place on Murazal?"

"Well, you know how flamboyantly wealthy he is," I said.

"He's that, all right. Doesn't mean he can't govern when he sets his mind to it, though. That's why he was elected—because he's fair and firm."

"Zaria has asked Travis and Trent to act as bodyguards for Zanfield Staggs. A few others may be sent from Randl's staff. There's a new pod'l-morph recruit that may be put into play on this assignment."

"Zanfield agreed to this?"

"Are you kidding? He can't wait."

"But what about the ah, potential for obsession?"

"I think Zaria may have taken care of that."

"Good. I'd offer if she hadn't. Randl trusts him completely, and it only takes a second for Zaria or me to see he's worthy."

"Yeah—besides, nobody needs to be placed in that kind of danger without some sort of protection. We have more than enough problems as it is. Who's the pod'l-morph?"

"Someone who recently graduated from the ASD Academy. Randl asked me to ask Ildevar if we could ah, borrow him. Ildevar couldn't act fast enough to assign him to Randl's detail. His name is Rajeon Dare, and he's really, really good at what he does."

"His name has a good cadence to it. I hope I get to meet him, since he'll be working with Travis and Trent."

"I think that can be arranged. Eventually. Perri may go with Zanfield, as his fiancée, since Ylisis is engaged, now."

"Are they actually together—Perri and Zanfield?"

"I think Zanfield is working on it—slowly. She's had a lot of trauma in her life, and he knows to go slow with her."

"She's a good Fourth-level witch to have beside you," I conceded. "And her talent is power-scenting, so she'll know if anybody is placing spells they shouldn't."

"Good. Ashe and I will be helping Kay with the ones removed from those four worlds. Has Alrenardo already replaced Larvalis?"

"As of last night, while good old Larva was pupating."

"I suppose I should take him to SouthStar," Bree sighed.

"I'd suggest putting Renellia with him; she's already knocked up, so it won't matter if they're mating like bunnies while they're away."

"Maybe that will keep him from complaining," Bree said. "Is Renellia with him now?"

"Not yet. Nissa, Trik and Toff are waiting for us to take her before they go in."

"I can make the exchange," she offered.

"Sounds fine. Nissa complains that she doesn't see enough of her female relatives anyway."

"There aren't that many of us, you know." Bree grinned and folded away.

I had three daughters out of eight natural children if I counted Zaria, and two other adopted sons. One half-sister was dead long ago; I hadn't known about Breanne for a very long time. My own mother was dead, as was Bree's. Our grandparents were also dead, all the way around.

"Kifirin, the old you fucked up," I announced to the air.

"I know," he rumbled, appearing before me. "I cannot *Change What Was*, avilepha, no matter how much I'd like to."

"I sometimes wonder why Zaria only changed a little with those girls," I sniffed.

"Perhaps she was hoping that they'd steer onto the proper course, once she opened the way for them. You see that they went right back to their old habits, without a backward glance or a shred of guilt?"

"I see it, definitely."

"This wasn't to save their lives, as Zaria is prone to do. Therefore, the choice is theirs. They made it, leaving their mother to suffer. Before you say it, I understand my role in all this. You cannot make me feel more ashamed of that than I already do. It grieves me to think on that period of my life."

"Honey, you were as much under someone else's thumb as they were under yours," I sighed.

"I have done some time-bending recently," he said. "To examine many of my deeds during that time. No, I did not interfere anywhere," he held up a hand to stop my question. "What I did find is this, however, and I have no idea what impact it will have for the future."

"What did you find?" I was becoming worried.

"Quislus managed to hide some of Earth's vampires from me—when I brought what I thought was the full population away and allowed the worst of them to die. I did not wish you to have to deal with the criminal element on Le-Ath Veronis."

"Let me guess—there are still criminal vampires on Earth, squirreled away somewhere with no Vampire Council to hold them back."

"Not all of them are criminals," Kifirin shook his head. "I'd say that the good and bad are almost evenly divided."

"One bad vampire can make up for a whole lot of good ones," I pointed out. "In a human population. And, with no Assassins or Enforcers to hunt them, they can get away with almost anything. Damn. This doesn't sound good, and there's no time to go hunting them now."

"Yes. Exactly. As I said, I have no idea what this means for the future, but I fear that it won't be anything good."

"Well, at least we know, don't we?"

"Yes, for whatever good it does us. I fear we have passed the time of interference in all this."

"Yeah. Something to consider."

"M'hala, now you know what I have known for several months. We face larger difficulties, just as you say. Perhaps a few vampires on Earth will not be such a problem compared to that. After all, they have been there for several centuries, without an outcry. Perhaps they live in fear that they will be taken away, like the others were."

"Then we'll hope for that, huh?"

"Yes. Most certainly we will hope for that."

"Thank you for telling me."

"I have also informed Hanlekidus."

"Well, Hank should be the one to hear it first, I suppose."

"Since it was my initial mistake, under Quislus' hand," Kifirin dipped his chin in agreement.

"What an almighty asshole Quislus was, too. You know, sometimes I'd like to have your trick of blowing smoke—it's quite handy for expressing your feelings."

"I'm sure you could employ power to achieve it, although I have no idea how it would be received outside my presence."

"So, you're saying it's not a good idea?"

"I would suggest that it is not."

"Will you be available if I need you on this assignment?"

"I will always be available for you. You need only call for me. I will warn you to tread carefully in another's shoes."

"Good to know."

"Are you not curious as to why I give you this advice?"

"Well, I suppose, now that you mention it."

"A world will fall in love with real justice, if they see it in front of them. You are a justice that cannot be coerced or bribed, my love. I cannot say the same about many politicians or world leaders."

"Tell that to my detractors," I grumped.

"They are detractors because they cannot have their way in everything," Kifirin pointed out. "In most cases, it is because they wish to further themselves in less than legal ways."

"Don't get me started," I fumed, thinking this would be an excellent time to blow smoke.

"I can't wait to see what your sister does in your place," Kifirin struggled to hide a smile.

"Well, Bree straightened out a few folks last time. Maybe she'll do it again. I don't regret anything that she did on my behalf, including doing away with a few criminals."

"She also brought you back to us, by *Changing What Was*."

"Yeah. I remember that, too."

"I only bring this up because your mission is dangerous, m'hala. Never forget that. You have a habit of ah, throwing yourself in front of a speeding train."

"Have you been watching Old Earth movies? I'm so proud of you," I patted his arm.

"Tying helpless females to train tracks was apparently a desirable distraction, but mostly to motion picture writers and directors."

"Yeah, I'm not sure it's an effective way of knocking anybody off. So many of them were saved by the good guy."

"In motion pictures, I believe they were all saved." Kifirin wanted to laugh, I could tell.

"We have news," Connegar and Reemagar appeared simultaneously inside my suite. "Prime Minister Fallah has been assassinated on Corez."

CHAPTER 5

*L*issa

"Who is taking her place?" I strode into my office as if I were running a marathon.

"Her First Advisor, Haris," Bree was back, giving me necessary information. "It will require a switch between you and Rigo—he has a female assistant with him most of the time."

"Her name?"

"Jezra. The laws state that if the Prime Minister dies in the last third of their term, then the First Advisor rules until the next scheduled election."

"Do we know who killed her?" I asked.

"Not yet. I suspect that things were sliding out of control, because Fallah had begun making decisions that went against her previous policies. Haris isn't obsessed yet, but that could only be a matter of time."

"Was he involved in the murder in any way?"

"I doubt it, he was on vacation—on Murazal. He's currently on a ship back to Corez."

"Have we sent someone to ensure that he arrives safely?"

"He now has three guards he didn't have before," Bree acknowledged. "Hank may be one of them."

"Then I pity anybody who tries to pick a fight," I sighed. "Damn. Can somebody send for my bunch? They all need to know about this change of plans."

~

SouthStar

Zaria

"Slight change of plans," Ashe said as he took the poolside lounge next to mine. "Fallah of Corez was assassinated earlier, which puts her First Advisor, Haris, in charge. Lissa is taking his assistant's place, and Rigo will be First Advisor."

"I'm sorry to hear that; she was a decent person."

"I believe that's why she became inconvenient to those who obsessed her—she began doing things so differently that the change was remarked upon by many."

"No doubt," I whispered, shaking my head and holding my sudden anger back.

"Zaria, this may be a good thing," Ashe said soothingly. "If they attempt to place obsession, or assassinate either Rigo or Lissa, they won't expect either to fight back or be immune to their efforts."

"First, we have to make sure that the assassination was performed by the enemy, don't you think?"

"Well, that's true," he agreed. "I'll pass that along to Lissa and Breanne."

"This means Lissa has a second mystery to solve while she's there. At least it will be easier for her to navigate the State House and surrounding city, as a lesser employee."

"I'll make sure she's aware of everything we've discussed."

"Tell her she can contact me anytime if she wants. I'm sure her dreams are just as bad as mine."

"Val can place a healing sleep," Ashe reminded me.

"I'll consider it. Right now, I'm considering Scotch and a waterfall."

"So you've found our little oasis, huh?"

"It's nice, and the splash of falling water drowns out most of my concerns."

"The plumeria are blooming," he grinned at me before rising and walking away. I only noticed he was barefoot and wearing cargo pants as he retreated.

"Want company?" Bleek, Edden, Ilya and Tamp appeared as if called. Halimel misted in seconds later.

"Sure. Let's hit the waterfall. If I don't, I'll be haring off to Corez to figure out who killed Fallah."

Ashe

"Ah, Zaria's asleep, now. Energy sex has that effect," Ren informed me. He and I sat in my library; I had a glass of bourbon in front of me, which I'd filled almost to the brim.

We'd received information from Nefrigar, who'd heard it from Zaria. It troubled me.

"A world spirit actually called the Prophet *the god who always comes at the end?*"

"Yes. And the Wise Ones also have this information. They are quite tight-lipped about it, too."

"Are they hesitant to speculate, or merely refusing to say what they know?"

"Perhaps both. Their caution is legendary. Even my own son and grandson, Graegar and Garegar, refuse to tell me anything."

"Important stuff, then."

"I'd say so."

"If there's a god who always comes at the end, it makes sense that he'd have helpers along the way," I said.

"Agreed."

"Yet we're still not sure that D'slay and the Prophet are truly connected or deliberately working in tandem."

"Also true. As they are Sirenali, or have Sirenali connections, it is impossible to say unless we find solid evidence of collusion."

"Now there's a word," I shook my head at the complexity of the situation. "One that could fit perfectly, but evidence must still be found."

"Then let us hope we find it, one way or another, during these missions so many are undertaking. Only a Sirenali can place an obsession, therefore, we must find one and attempt to retrace their steps. Doing so can lead us to the real puppet master, if the Sirenali him-or-herself is not fully responsible."

"We also know the Prophet has rogue gods at his command, provided by his higher ranked, rogue-god father."

"And we have no idea of their ranking or strength, because they are also hidden by Sirenali."

"I'm beginning to think that all those other times, the God Wars may have been won, but the victors fell to cunning and deceit left behind by those they defeated. Otherwise, why would a world spirit say *the god who always comes at the end?*"

"A wise question. I have not the answer."

"Then I hope we find an answer soon. I'm getting worried. Lissa says that Valegar from the future came to take Zaria away for a little while. Now she won't speak of what she saw."

"I know this, as does my father, my uncle, and the Wise Ones, of course."

"So, no information from Graegar or Garegar, or from Hiragar, Tenigar or Meligar?" I named all five Wise Ones.

"Lips so tight nothing will get past them," Ren shook his head. It was a very human gesture; he often employed human gestures, if they fit his need. Most Larentii never bothered.

"Then they have a reason not to tell us, I suppose."

"They have not steered us wrongly as yet."

"And I don't expect that to change."

Queen's Palace, Le-Ath Veronis

Lissa

"Where did you get this information?" Rigo asked. I'd just told him that the ones who'd laid the actual obsession on Fallah may not have been involved in her death.

He, Drake, Drew, Winkler and Gavin had joined me for a private dinner in the arboretum, to discuss the mission.

"Zaria told Ashe. When he relayed her response, I recognized and agreed with her logic."

"The logic that there is no need to destroy a good servant?" Gavin asked.

"On the nose," I tapped mine to indicate his accuracy. "This means we may be searching for another killer, and it also means that another obsession could be laid, likely on the First Advisor. Right now, he's under guard as he's traveling back from Murazal, so we need to be there when he hits the ground."

"You're saying we must move our departure up considerably," Rigo said, the vampire non-expression firmly in place.

"Yep. Haris is scheduled to arrive tomorrow morning, our time. Hank will remove him from the ship just before it arrives, and Rigo will walk off it as Haris, First Advisor of Corez. As for the rest of us, we'll be waiting for him at the State House in Varalon. Ashe and Kay will have removed both Second Advisors and Haris' assistant, Jezra. Rigo, you'll be expected to make a speech regarding Fallah's death, coordinate the search for her killer, arrange a funeral and command proper days of mourning. Ildevar will make a very rare appearance at her funeral, just so you know."

"I will prepare something, tiessa."

"I know you will. All of you have appropriate attire, now, thanks to my Larentii and the Saa Thalarr. You'll find it ready for packing in your suites."

"This is a hell of a thing, isn't it?" Winkler's frown told me how disturbing he found all this.

"That's for damn sure."

~

Larentii Homeworld

Graegar

"All the connections are traced and verified," Hiragar set the clear memory stone on the marble table. Few ever saw where the Wise Ones met, under a roofless sky in the wilds of our homeworld.

Records of all our doings were transferred to Nefrigar in the Archives, once they were detailed and classified as finished. The section in the Archives was hidden, and only accessible by Nefrigar and by us. No other could visit unless we gave permission.

We had given no others permission.

"In all our long history, we have never done such," Meligar said softly. "I hope you understand how this has affected me."

"Be strong, brother. We must see this through."

"I know."

~

Hank Bell

If Fes and Farzi hadn't come with me, I may have lost my patience with this one.

"Where are we? I demand to see your superior," Doy Haris attempted to remove his arm from my grip. Rigo was already aboard the ship, which was docking at Corez's space station.

"All will be explained in time," Fes reassured the First Advisor. "This is to save your life, you understand. I doubt you wish to follow your own superior?"

"You are at my home, at SouthStar, upon Avendor," Ashe appeared from nothing, forcing Haris to move his jaw while no words escaped. "Fes is correct; had you stepped off that luxury star cruiser, things would have gone badly for you in a hurry."

"Whatever do you mean?" Haris found his voice and his indignation at the same moment.

"It means that shortly, without our interference, you'd likely be placed under a Sirenali's obsession and forced to do his will, just as Fallah was."

"I don't believe you."

"Shut mouth. Listen," Farzi snapped at him. He'd lost patience, just as I had.

"Perhaps he needs convincing."

My mouth refused to work, this time. Zaria had arrived in full Larentii mode. Her blue eyes bored into Haris' and he took a step backward.

When appearing like this, she caused my breath to stop. Yes, I realized that I was mated to her mother—one of them, anyway. Perhaps I should have the M'fiyah muted, for both our sakes.

At least I'm not her father, I kept reminding myself. I did know her father; he and I had a long history together—he'd often directed my deeds and actions, although he'd sent the shining ones at first, to pass messages along.

"We will keep you apprised of the events on Corez," Zaria informed Haris in a stern voice. "To go back there now is to commit suicide. The moment we relieve Corez of its trouble, we will place you in your position again and leave you there, without a backward glance."

"I suppose you'd better tell me what is happening, then," Haris mumbled. "If you can."

Much better, Ashe sent. *Now he can be reasoned with.*

"Sit down," Zaria told Haris. "This isn't a short story. But first, we'll allow you to watch the speech being delivered on Corez on your behalf."

~

Corez

Lissa

Only those of us who knew him could see Rigo's true appearance through the disguise he wore. As Doy Haris, First Advisor, he stood tall and dignified as he delivered a speech for the ages.

He finished with this; "I dedicate to every citizen of Corez my focused attention and unwavering determination to find the one responsible for Prime Minister Fallah's death. I promise that true justice will be delivered. This will not only be our last act of respect for a beloved Prime Minister, but also an act of respect for ourselves, as none of us should be willing to continue with anything less than our finest words and deeds."

We see the spy most of the time. Now we see the King, Gavin's mindspeech whispered to me.

Yeah. Let's hope we can get this sorted out without anybody else dying. Rigo just became a huge target.

~

SouthStar

Zaria

Haris wiped tears away at the end of Rigo's speech. "Who is he?" he whispered.

"That, dear First Advisor, is Rigovarnus the Great, former King of Hraede and an ancient vampire. Corez is in the best hands possible."

CHAPTER 6

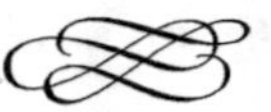

*S*outhStar
   Zaria

"It's easier to trade places while they're asleep," Ashe announced to all of us. Reah and her crew, Zanfield and his crew, and I and my crew were gathered in Ashe's library, waiting to take our places on several worlds.

Nissa, Toff and Trik were already in place on Hraede, as was Alrenardo. So far, nothing of import had come of that substitution.

"Some bending of time will take place to get you to the proper moment," Ashe continued. "Those you're replacing will be brought here, where Kay and I will see to their comfort and determine whether to remove the obsessions they bear, and when to do so. Zanfield," he turned to Zan, who now was a duplicate of President Ylisis, "Renegar will ensure that your crew arrives at the proper time. Remember, you are taking another's place and are required to act accordingly. Welcome, Rajeon. You are getting a trial by fire, I fear."

"I have been briefed," he replied. "I am eager for the assignment."

"Honey, it's dangerous, no matter how you look at it," I told him. "You were chosen because you have a talent for discretion and a feel for what's right."

"Travis and Trent told me about you. Are you truly Larentii?"

"In this incarnation, yes."

"They ah, also tell me that you're responsible for saving many of my kind, myself included, from the destruction of Siriaa."

"It was the right thing to do. I don't know how many pod'l-morphs died before I got there. I rescued those I could."

"I imagine that my family was among the dead; they did not come to SouthStar with the rest of us."

"Then I grieve for your loss."

"As do I."

"Someday, if you wish to know, I'll explain how and why pod'l-morphs were captured and imprisoned on Siriaa. The person instructed to choose which of those trees to employ for a particular purpose had no idea they were killing a sentient being."

"I will ask—someday. I have to digest what you've told me, first."

"When this is over, come see me," Tamp spoke up. "I somehow escaped the notice of the one who imprisoned all other pod'l-morphs. I searched for others like myself for centuries, with no idea what happened to them. I was preparing to give up my life when Zaria found me and gave me new purpose. And then she found you—and those trapped with you. She took me to visit that forest of pod'l-morphs, and I fell to my knees in joy."

"I do want to hear that story. Please."

"We have to survive this mission, first," I warned. "Then, we'll answer all your questions."

"Then I'll work toward that end."

"Everyone ready?" Ashe asked.

"I believe they're ready," I turned toward Ashe.

"Good. We're going, then."

I folded my own crew to the proper place and time.

Corez
  Lissa

Drake, Drew and I waited outside Haris' office for Rigo's arrival. Another assistant and the Prime Minister's staff waited with us. The Prime Minister's staff were hoping they'd be given employment with Haris, rather than being let go.

I see them, Bree told me as she looked through my eyes at the staff assembled in Haris' large reception area. *Those two standing together on your right despise Haris. Tell Rigo to send them elsewhere or terminate their employment.*

I'll do that. Anything else?

Nothing that stands out for now.

See anyone who'd be useful on Rigo's staff?

Three. Two women and the young man at the very back. They were the newest hires for the Prime Minister and won't mind handling the media and arranging meetings with other government officials.

Noted. I'll tell Rigo to keep them for sure.

Most of the others can be fit into slots in other agencies. Ask the new people to help with that.

All right. Thanks for the info.

No prob. Have fun. Be careful.

Rigo walked in surrounded by State House constables, who saluted him and marched away once he reached his office door. Drake and Drew, armed with seemingly ornamental blades and dressed in State House uniforms, took their positions on either side of Rigo and followed him inside the office.

"First Advisor Haris wishes to meet with the following people immediately," I announced. The entire crowd went silent and waited expectantly.

"Durese Salvi," I called the first woman's name. "Heercie Yongha," I called the second woman's name. "Farel Mikkuls," I spoke the young man's name. "Please join me and the Secondary Advisors in the First Advisor's office. Everyone else, return to your desks. You will be notified shortly regarding the future of your employment with Corez's government."

Murmuring began immediately as they shuffled away. Unwilling to take any chances, I placed additional shields around the reception area. I wanted no surprises while Rigo sorted out his new employees and diagrammed a course of action for our mission. Besides running the government, there was the public hunt for Fallah's killer and the secret search for those who'd laid the obsession on her.

I was the last one inside Rigo's new office, so I shut the door behind me. *Bree recommended you keep these three on as additional assistants, and they can help place most of the others in new jobs,* I sent to him. *She also said there are two who should be let go. When you fire them, place compulsion. Bree says they hate the real Haris with a passion, and that sounds like fertile ground for a conspiracy to me.*

Send them to me after this meeting is over. We'll see to that, first thing.

Murazal

Travis

I should have known Zanfield would leave nothing to chance. He'd studied Ylisis' words, movements and mannerisms carefully and carried them out to an exacting degree.

His hair was now a solid, auburn color, just as Ylisis' was, thanks to Perri's spell. We'd been deposited in the proper homes and suites where Ylisis' guards and assistants lived, and, when it was time for us to go to work, we went through the normal routines of breakfast and traveling to work.

Perri, as Ylisis' fiancée, lived in a separate suite at the Presidential Palace. It was easier to guard her if she were there, rather than in her own home.

Bro, you on the train? Trent sent to me.

I am—third car from the engine, I replied.

Be there shortly. In less than a minute, Trent walked through the open door, which shut behind him as he sat two seats down from me. This was the busy time for the train; it was loaded with people going to work.

The man who sat beside me had to be in his one-sixties and not far from retirement. A comp-vid held loosely in one hand, he read an article on Prime Minister Fallah's death, which included Rigo's speech after his arrival on Corez. The news outlets were buzzing about the speech; some speculated that there was little evidence to go on in Fallah's death and that Rigo's promise could be an empty one.

If they knew my mother, they'd back up in a hurry. Mom would solve this mystery if it were solvable, even if she had to bend time to do it. If she read the same article, that would be the same as offering a challenge.

I wondered how Kell, Kooper and Opal would deal with Mom looking into Fallah's murder, because the ASD could, by law, be asked to investigate the unnatural death of any world leader.

"You see this?" the man shook his comp-vid at me. "Even a blind man can see that Haris is involved in this somehow."

"I think the ASD will have the final say," I said evenly, not wishing to pick a fight.

"Hmmph. Bunch of helpless dinkies, in my opinion."

"Have you always felt that way, or has something recent convinced you otherwise?" I asked.

"Hmmph. That bunch stood aside and let the entire planet of A'pelur get blown to bits."

"Ah." I wasn't about to say that I'd personally been there until just before it did blow up, and there was nothing else to be done about it.

"Did you lose family or friends?"

"Hmmph. Oldest daughter married a damn idiot from there."

"What was her name?"

"Sharal. Sharal Sawin. Dead and gone, with not a bit to say farewell to."

Randl, I sent, *is there someone named Sharal Sawin on Sirena now? From A'pelur?*

She's here—her husband isn't.

Well, her dad is sitting next to me on a train, bashing the ASD because they didn't save her or the planet.

I'll make a note to have a visit with her.

Thanks.

"I'm sorry about your daughter," I told the man as our train pulled into the State House station. "What did you say your name was, again?"

"Didn't. Name's Tedri. Tedri Clurk. Work in the Water Purity Department at the State House."

"Tedri, I hope your day is a good one."

"Well, thank you, I suppose. Not often I talk to anybody about my girl."

I let him get off the train first, so I could exit with Trent.

He may not have talked to you if you were dressed in your uniform, Trent informed me as we stepped onto the decorative swirls of colored stone at the State House's landing. Conversation between the crowds disembarking from the train echoed against the hard surfaces surrounding us.

You heard that? I replied.

Yeah. Hope his daughter wants to see him, or he'll go to his grave thinking she's dead.

Randl will sort it out, now that he knows about the problem. Maybe we should convince Zanfield to invite him to a function or something.

Good idea.

We walked along a corridor in the State House, which led to a trans-vator going to the First Advisor's suite of offices on the top floor. Our wrist chips caused the security scanner to beep when we boarded the car, noting our arrival and granting permission to access the top floor.

The guard's office held desks, a bathroom, changing room and personal lockers, so we could dress in our decorative uniforms. We no longer appeared as Falchani and I was glad about it; no self-respecting warrior would dress in orange and green, with tassels hanging from the grip of their blades.

"Nobody's going to mistake us for anything other than the High Guard," Trent mumbled as he fastened the top buckle on his knee-high boots. "For real."

"Incentive to get in and get out, then," I reached out to smack his arm. Instead of the usual, dull, decorative blades the other guards carried, our swords gleamed, sharp and straight, in the artificial light of the changing room.

Our blades slipped into scabbards simultaneously. We preferred having swords at our backs rather than at our sides, but we'd been taught both ways, so it wouldn't be a hindrance.

And, as people would only see the hilts of the blades, they'd never know they were authentic weapons.

"Ready for day one?" Trent grinned at me.

"Yeah. Let's get this show on the road."

State House, Corez

Lissa

I followed Rigo; Winkler and Gavin followed me as we headed to the First Advisor's office for a scheduled meeting, first thing. Drake and Drew, already dressed in purple and green, like grapes with green leaves tossed in, stood outside the wide outer door, guarding it against imaginary intruders.

Nice outfits, I told them as we passed through.

Inside the conference room and to the right were several department heads, mostly from security and investigation units, waiting there for us. At least they'd had drinks and snacks available to them.

"My apologies for keeping you waiting," Rigo announced, although we were on time for the meeting.

You see them? I sent to Bree.

Yeah—nobody guilty in this bunch—not of the murder, anyway.

Good. Thanks. I can take it from here.

"We have the preliminary findings from the crime scene," a man to Rigo's right said, pushing a comp-vid across the opaque glass tabletop.

"I see," Rigo lifted the comp-vid and expertly flipped through the screens, which showed pictures and descriptions of forensic evidence.

"No indication of poisoning, although there are several poisons which cannot be detected," he mused while reading.

"There were marks on her body," a woman on the left spoke up. "No clear death wounds, according to the coroner, but marks, nonetheless."

"I'm looking at those now—she was bound, hand and foot—is that correct?" Rigo lifted his eyes from the screen to study the six officials around the table.

"Yes, that does appear to be so, but those were certainly not death wounds."

"Of course." Rigo went back to the comp-vid. "No asphyxiation, no injection wounds, no noted poisons. Have there been any other deaths similar to this one?"

"No, First Advisor. My department has carefully searched all records going back fifty turns. Nothing like this has been reported."

"Your name?" Rigo asked.

"Parak, First Advisor. I'm Assistant Director for the Records and Reports unit of the Department of Investigations."

"Good work, Parak."

"Thank you, sir."

"May I make an observation?" The woman to Rigo's left spoke again.

"Go ahead," Rigo nodded.

"It's no secret that Prime Minister Fallah had strayed from her usual ah, course, recently," the woman began.

She's Anila Milli, Chief of Investigations, I sent to Rigo.

"That is an astute observation, Chief Milli," Rigo told her. "One that has been remarked upon by others. Do you believe this may have resulted in her death?"

"I think it's possible," she replied. I could see that she was pleased the First Advisor knew her name.

"As do I. Regardless of straying off course in recent days, Prime Minister Fallah was a good public servant, and we will put forth every effort to solve this murder. Someone who committed murder is still among us and needs to be brought to justice. Is there anyone here who disagrees with that decision?"

"None, Sir," came from the man on the right.

Faram, Chief of Police for the city, I told Rigo.

"Thank you, Chief Farram," Rigo said. "Going forward, I expect all of you to work together and share information. This isn't a contest between departments or services. This is a quest for justice and must not be hindered for any reasons, including personal ones. Now, I have a special request for you, Chief," he told Farram. "I wish to visit the crime scene with the Second Advisors and my assistant. Can that be arranged today?"

"I was going to stop by on my way back to the station," Farram said. "You're welcome to accompany me."

"I think we'd all like to come, Sir," Chief Milli said.

"Then we'll go. Jezra, arrange for transport, please."

"I'll have it available in less than fifteen," I said.

"Very well. That will give us time to refresh ourselves," Rigo turned toward me.

Drew, honey, I sent to him. *Get us a bus to carry twelve to the crime scene.*

Where the First Advisor goes, we go, he pointed out.

I'm counting on it, I replied.

The hoverbus provided was quite plush and was normally utilized to haul visiting diplomats and their families. I doubt it had ever made a trip to a crime scene during its existence.

"Why or how the Prime Minister left the State House is still under investigation," Parak explained after Rigo questioned him. "We've watched every recording from every device, in and outside of the State House, with nothing to show for it. We've found nobody walking away or driving or taking the train," he added. "It makes no sense."

"Are there any wizards, witches or warlocks living on Corez?" I asked.

Parak blinked in surprise when I asked the question, rather than Rigo.

"Jezra has a mind for solving puzzles, Assistant Director," Rigo reassured him. "Answer all her questions, as she will only share the answers with me."

"Ah. Very well, then. I have done some research in that area, and have a list of names, although their past personal and work histories don't point to them as suspects. I'll send it to you now," he tapped on his comp-vid. In no time, I had a list of fewer than thirty power-wielders to go through.

None of these names make me itch, I sent to Rigo.

Folding space or skipping seems the only way she could have left the State House, Rigo observed. *Someone we don't know about, most likely.*

"I'd also like a list of names, with images, of all visitors to the State House, who had interaction with the Prime Minister within the past three months," Rigo told Parak.

"I'll have it for you this afternoon."

"Very good. Ah, we're here," Rigo announced as the hoverbus stopped, then slowly lowered itself to the wide walkway outside the brothel, where the Prime Minister's body had been found.

I hope there's still some scent left that hasn't been disturbed, I told Rigo as we stepped off the bus.

I worry the scene may have been contaminated by too many investigators, Gavin chimed in.

I feel the same way, Winkler noted. *The scene is muddied now, scent-wise, unless I miss my guess.*

Still, there may be something to be found, Rigo said calmly.

"We've checked the recorded images of all who came and went during the time of the Prime Minister's death," Parak volunteered as we walked inside the square, six-level, nondescript building which housed a legal brothel.

"Somebody was making a statement by dumping Fallah here," Chief Milli sniffed.

"I think the same," I told her. "Parak, are there any security cameras on the roof of this building, or trained on the roof of this building?"

"None on this building. I'll do a search of those surrounding it."

"I'll order satellite recordings if necessary, during the appropriate time," Rigo murmured.

"I'll go through employee records at the State House," I said. "When we get back."

You'll send them to Quin?

Of course, along with the visitor records from Parak.

Very good. If any of them have a whiff of Sirenali influence about them, we must know that quickly.

Right there with you, dude.

You call me dude?

I called you dude, dude.

I think I like it.

Gavin sure didn't.

I saw the corners of Rigo's mouth curl. Hah—I cracked an old vamp, and it felt like a victory.

The room was at the top of the building and undergoing renovations when the body was discovered. I walked in with Rigo, and the hologram of where the body was found still shone on the floor.

Paint containers and the reno-bot were in a far corner of the room; it hadn't even started putting color on the walls before the body was left there.

Rigo's head turned and his eyes met mine. Before anyone could stop us, we went straight for the paint-bot.

Randl would be helpful, right now, Rigo said as he and I sniffed around the paint-bot.

How would we explain what he can see? I asked.

No idea.

I may have another idea, but we'll get to that later. Let's do more sniffing, then go back and send those images to Quinnie Bee.

Too many people in here for me to sort through all the scents, Winkler informed me after only a few minutes.

Any evidence has been collected by forensics already—I'll look into that, Gavin offered.

I may do some time-bending tonight, if you guys want to come with me, I sent.

I want to come, Winkler said right away. *We can get information from the room before anybody else invades it.*

I will most certainly come, Gavin insisted.

As will I, Rigo agreed.

"The body was found in this pose," Parek showed an image to Chief Milli. "I think Fallah was killed somewhere less ah, hospitable."

"Than an empty bordello undergoing renovation? What do you have that supports your theory?"

"Forensics just found the tiniest spot on one of the Prime Minister's fingers—it was originally classified as a burn, but someone decided to look again, because if it were a burn, it would have to originate from a very small point of heat. What the assistant coroner found is that in this tiny instance, that part of the body was exposed to acid."

"How small?" Rigo demanded.

Parak handed his comp-vid to Rigo.

"What do you think?" He held the comp-vid so I could see the image displayed.

"It's like the tiniest droplet splashed right there, and only one, unless there are similar spots elsewhere?" I frowned at Rigo.

"No other spots have been found," Parak said. "The acid is a corrosive, obviously. Preliminary findings suggest berolic acid."

"Berolic comes in crystal form," Rigo said. "A single crystal, perhaps, somehow came in contact with her finger?"

"If it is berolic, then I assume so," Parak agreed. "I had no idea you knew so much about acids."

"Curiosity, mostly," Rigo said. "Who has access to berolic acid? It's a controlled substance."

"I'll do research," Parak promised.

"I hope you have employees who can help," I said. "Your duties are stacking up, Assistant Director."

"I have two assistants. They can trace sales of the acid while I tend to other things. The Director is on family leave with a new wife."

"Then I shall send a note of congratulations," Rigo said. "Come—I think we've seen enough for today."

Make sure I get a pic of the Director, then, I grumped to Rigo. *For now, nobody is above suspicion.*

Tiessa, I also wish to see this Director. His absence is rather convenient, after all.

We were on our way back to the State House when the news hit. Winkler held his comp-vid while Rigo and I watched; Drake and Drew had hands on sword hilts as we pulled into the designated parking slot.

Someone, somewhere, had leaked falsehoods to the media, and those reporting it hadn't troubled themselves to check the veracity of the information or their sources before running it.

Therefore, Rigo was placed under arrest by Chief Milli and Chief Farram as he stepped off the bus.

"Three witnesses from Murazal claim they overheard the conversation between the First Advisor and someone on his comp-vid," a reporter said as he consulted his own comp-vid while on camera. "We don't have the names of these witnesses as yet; we are working to obtain that information."

"Unverified, undocumented speculation," I hissed and waved off the screen with power.

"At least Connegar and Reemagar are with him, to make sure he isn't harmed in any way," Gavin muttered.

"If they hadn't volunteered, I'd have gone myself," I grumped. "Do we have anything from Zanfield, yet, regarding this information that somehow slipped off his planet?"

"He's currently engaged in a state function, but Travis and Trent say they'll get information somehow on where this came from,"

Winkler said, tapping his comp-vid to turn it off. He was just as weary as the rest of us regarding these accusations.

Somewhere at SouthStar, the real First Advisor should be more than happy that he wasn't on Corez right now. *Rigo, are you all right?* I sent to him.

Tiessa, I am fine, but weary of answering unending questions.

Place compulsion on the lot of them, then, to leave you alone.

I will if it becomes necessary.

If you don't, I will.

I will let you know. I can see Connegar and Reemagar nearby; the others here cannot. That gives me comfort.

Good. They'll make sure you're comfortable, at least—outside the stupid questioning, anyway.

Ah, Connegar just waved a hand and the questioning stopped. I believe I will be placed in a cell, next, Rigo informed me.

Good for Connegar. Let me know if you need anything.

I will be fine.

Okay, I have to go; Chief Farram and Chief Milli are requesting an interview with Winkler, Gavin and me.

Do not let them mistreat you, my love.

Oh, I won't. Count on it.

"You don't believe the First Advisor is involved in this murder?" Chief Milli was giving me her best intimidation techniques.

"No. If you knew him as well as I do, you'd never suggest such an outrageous thing."

Winkler and Gavin were being questioned in another room by Chief Farram, while I was the focus of Chief Milli. Their idea was to keep us apart and find holes in our story. Too bad they didn't realize we had mindspeech and were in constant communication.

Bree, too, was watching things through my eyes again. *Milli's confused about all this, because she knows darn well that nobody's produced actual witnesses or hard evidence,* she informed me.

"Chief Milli, there is a call for you from President Ylisis of Murazal," one of Milli's assistants poked his head in the door. "He says it is quite urgent."

"Very well. Send it straight to my comp-vid."

Moments later, I heard Zanfield's voice, although Milli believed it was Ylisis.

"Mr. President, thank you for taking the time to speak with me," Milli gushed. Well, somebody had a secret crush, looked like.

"I'm afraid I may be upsetting your plans a bit," Zanfield replied coolly. "We've tracked down the supposed witnesses who gave information to your journalists. It appears that these witnesses were created digitally, and their messages were distributed to the media on Corez."

"What?" Milli squeaked, and the timbre of her voice embarrassed her.

"I'm sending you the evidence now, Chief Milli. It didn't take long to ferret out the disinformation. Had your media come to me in the beginning, it may have prevented this entire, humiliating episode."

"Do you have the perpetrators behind this erroneous information?"

"I do not; I only know that the original message came from Corez, bounced from one of our satellites to another, and then was sent back to Corez as if it came from Murazal."

"You have all the evidence related to this?"

"Yes, of course. I have experts on my staff, here. It didn't take long to unravel."

Milli cursed softly. "I will review the evidence you send, and then decide whether we will release the First Advisor from custody."

"You should have checked all sources before arresting him," Zanfield snapped. "You'd have learned quickly that the charges were based on faulty information."

Damn, Zanfield is good at this, Bree's mindspeech whispered in my head.

"I'll get on this immediately," Milli sounded cowed. Bree was right —Zanfield really was good at this.

"Please inform me if there is anything else I can do to be of service." Zanfield ended the call.

"Well, bitch," I snapped at Milli. "Maybe you should tune up your resume after arresting somebody with no evidence."

Milli's eyes widened in shock. "Oh," I added, placing compulsion, "you'll forget I ever said that, too."

CHAPTER 7

*K*wark

Zaria

"If Zanfield had been obsessed like Ylisis was, he'd have supported the misinformation, rather than looking into the veracity of it. Haris would be hanging out to dry without our intervention," I told Edden, dropping a comp-vid on his desk with a sigh.

"Then at least we've interrupted one act of chaos," Edden leaned back in his chair and laced fingers behind his head. "My love, you look worried."

"You know more of this is likely in the works. We're just waiting for shoes to drop."

"Shoes to drop?"

"Never mind—just a figure of speech."

"Very well. You think something will happen here?"

"Of course I do. Edden, if anybody tries to put you or any of the others in jail with no real evidence, they're going to have one angry Larentii plotting revenge."

"I should warn them. I doubt many will realize that my mate can give them painful boils for the rest of their lives."

"Or send them to a place that they may believe to be the real purgatory—for as long as they can last there, anyway."

"Dearest, you are not so bloodthirsty, are you?" Valegar appeared beside me.

"No, but sometimes it's nice to imagine delivering pain, in return for pain given."

"I understand." Val drew me against him. "You are well acquainted with pain, my love."

"Yeah. That's why I only think these things and don't carry through with them. I know exactly what it feels like."

"I have the biotech conformer for you," Val smiled down at me. "Just in time for the birthday celebration tomorrow."

"Good. Bleek is sick to death of only using two hands," I sighed. "Where is it?"

"Wrapped and inside your closet," Val beamed. "I believe you can make it disappear the moment Bleek tries it on?"

"Honey, his real extra arms will become visible and the gadget will be transported to Sirena," I said. "Since he wants the damn thing."

"I believe he'll have his gift working exceptionally well in no time," Edden teased.

"No doubt," I agreed. "I'll alert the media."

"Please don't," Ilya and Tamp folded in, with Bleek in tow. "After the fiasco on Corez, I'm wondering which of us will be accused of the next crime."

"We were just talking about that," Edden said. "We have a royal dinner scheduled for tonight. We need to be visible to as many of the media as possible and watch carefully so that no guests meet with accidents or end up dead."

"Well, that would be an ideal opportunity, all right," Bleek grumped.

"We can't say for sure that someone will be targeted this quickly," I pointed out. "After all, somebody, somewhere, is likely having a fit over the failure to have the First Advisor take the fall for the Prime Minister's death."

"Probably did put a kink in someone's plans," Ilya agreed. "A big kink."

"Problem," Halimel misted into the room.

"What problem?" I whirled to face him.

"Alrenardo says there have been more ah, murders, and the counterfeit Order of the Night Flower is taking credit."

"Who and how murdered?" Ilya growled.

"Two of the Queen's attendants, and both were beheaded."

"So, real vampires, real, unsanctioned murders, and a fake organization," Edden pushed back his chair and stood. "What else does Alrenardo say?"

"He says both female attendants were killed elsewhere, then laid outside the Queen's suite door, so they'd be found either by her or one of her servants."

"Has anyone made any headway tracking these imposters?" I asked.

"Not yet. I've asked to have someone question our prisoner again, although I doubt it will do much good."

"I'd contact Lissa and Rigo about this, but they're still working their way out of the mess that happened on Corez earlier," I said.

"What do Nissa, Trik and Toff say?" Bleek asked.

"They're waiting for the coroner's final report, which they will filch a copy of to transfer to me," Halimel replied. "All three have volunteered to do undercover investigation for me if needed. We really must shut these imposters down, before they do more damage."

"This may be a ploy to draw the real Order out of the shadows, don't you think?" Valegar offered his opinion.

"I've considered it and am coming to believe it's true," Halimel nodded to Val. "Do they want to kill us, or capture us and force us to their will?"

"They may be hoping you're susceptible to a Sirenali's obsession," I said. "Or, they may want to experiment on you with it, to find out how old and how strong a vampire must be to remain invulnerable to them."

"Not a pleasant thought," Hal shook his head.

"Nope, and it could put a lot of vampires in danger if they learn anything at all. Face it, on record, Rigo is one of the oldest vamps in existence."

"As are most of us in the Order," Halimel conceded. "The youngest is four thousand years old."

"That would take strong obsession, I think, to get past that," Tamp said. "I often think that a pod'l-morph's immunity, along with our other talents, convinced Liron to force the race into tree-shape on Siriaa."

"Then maybe we should sneak in a pod'l-morph or two to help Alrenardo," I said. "Any suggestions?"

"Several have gone through training with the RAA and ASD," Bleek said. "I'm sure one or two would be suitable for the assignment."

"I will take this information to Ildevar Wyyld," Val offered. "He can contact you with suggestions, perhaps."

"Good enough. Tell him we need at least two to work with Nissa and her two mates on Hraede."

"I have a suggestion," Tamp began.

"What's that?" I turned to my pod'l-morph.

"I'll go to Hraede. I'm well-versed on subterfuge and intrigue. Get me to Alrenardo as a guard or something, and we'll sort this out. I dislike leaving you, but another of your mates can take my place here."

"How does that sound?" I asked Hal.

"I would prefer that to two unknowns," he agreed.

"All right, then. Who should we bring here to replace Tamp?"

"I suggest Gerrett," Tamp said immediately.

"Good thinking," I agreed. "I'll see if Randl can let him go for a while. Hal, would you like to come with me, so I can drop Tamp off with Alrenardo?"

"I'd be delighted."

Royal Palace, Hraede
Halimel

"It has been a while," I peered up at the carved and gilded ceiling of the King's suite, which was freshly conserved for perhaps the hundredth time.

"It's strange, sleeping in the palace again," Alrenardo agreed, slapping my shoulder. "I've barely convinced the Queen to speak to me, but she actually had a short conversation with me last night."

"Remember not to make her suspicious," Tamp said. "We don't want to alarm the entire planet—more than they are already," he said.

"What do you say?" I turned to Zaria. She was still staring at the gilded ceiling, as if committing it to memory. Perhaps she was; after all, she'd rebuilt an entire palace on Sirena from memory.

"Nice rooms," she lowered her eyes and smiled at me. Her smile alone could squeeze my heart and heat my blood. "Al," she spoke to Alrenardo, shortening his name, "if there's no other option, we can pull the Queen in on the ruse, and also place compulsion if necessary. I trust you and Tamp to make that decision between you, and don't forget to call on Nissa, Trik and Toff if a bit of wizardry would be helpful. They can be here in a blink if they're needed."

"If you can track those imposters while you're here," I said, "I'd appreciate the information."

"I think I'll ask Nissa to go to work on that now," Zaria said. "Nissa really wants to get into the intrigue."

"Does she have protection against a vampire?" Alrenardo asked. "We move swiftly—sometimes too swiftly for a protection spell to be cast."

"All three have Grey House protection jewels they wear at all times," Zaria replied. "Those will activate if anyone attacks them. Speaking of which," Zaria held out her hand, and a small box appeared on her palm. "This is for you, Al. Hal and Tamp already have one. Wear it always; it will react much the same as the Grey House protection jewels."

"Ah. I feel very fortunate," Alrenardo breathed as he accepted Zaria's gift. "Thank you."

Without hesitation, he opened the box and slipped the medallion over his head, tucking it beneath his shirt. "We will certainly keep you and Halimel informed regarding our search for the imposters. I dislike them destroying our long silence and vows of secrecy."

"As do I. I really want to know how they came by our information and had the audacity to pose as a murderous cult in our place. There is no sophistication in their methods, and no good or just purpose in them, either."

"Agreed," Alrenardo nodded at me. "Only the guilty shall be punished. That is a part of our creed."

"We'll leave you now—we have to get Gerrett and go back to Kwark. Let me know if you need us for anything. Ready?" Zaria turned to me.

"Of course."

She took my arm and folded space. In a blink, we landed on marble floors of the palace on Sirena. The rotunda where we were was currently empty. I chose that moment to take Zaria's face in my hands and kiss her—something I'd wanted to do for a very long time.

Zaria

"Wow. If I'd known you could kiss that well, we'd have done it before now," I blinked at Halimel when he stepped back.

"Sometimes the wait makes it sweeter," his brown eyes twinkled at my compliment.

"Unfortunately, a wait is what we'll have for anything else; we need to get Gerrett and go. Nissa, Trik and Toff have a pile of ash after one of our imposters just tried to kill them."

"Already?" Hal took my arm this time, pulling me toward the hall leading to Gerrett's quarters.

"Yeah. Gerrett's on the way. We'll go straight back to Hraede from here."

"Here," Gerrett appeared, his voice rough from disuse, and breathing hard as if he'd ran instead of folding space.

"Honey, I'm sorry we're rushing you," I told him. "But we're needed on Hraede."

"I know. Go," he urged me on with a gesture. Grasping one of his hands, I hurled us back to Hraede, bending time so we'd land in the proper place just before Sir Fangy-pants met his untimely end.

We had questions. I hoped he'd have answers.

~

State House, Corez

Lissa

He's out of the pokey and only slightly ruffled, I responded to Zaria's mindspoken question regarding Rigo. *Why do you ask?*

We have another vampire on Hraede who just tried to kill the King's mistress. I had to bend time to prevent his death. If you and Rigo want to hear what he has to say, I can arrange it.

Can you bring him here for questioning? We're currently in the First Advisor's private suite, while the Corezian press is going nuts pointing fingers at one another over the bad source of information and Security's rush to put somebody in jail for the same.

We'll be there shortly. If Rigo needs it, I can offer a bit of healing help.

I'll ask.

"Rigo," I turned to him. He'd just gotten out of the shower, and only wore pants. "Zaria's bringing another vampire who claims to be a member of the Order."

"How quickly?"

"How about now?" Zaria, Halimel and Gerrett arrived, with Halimel pushing a cuffed vampire before him, then shoving him to his knees before Rigo.

"Who the hell are you?" the vampire demanded.

"Shut it." My claws were out and at his throat before he could blink. "You're not worth the sock fuzz from this man's toenails, you runty toadstool."

"My love," Rigo spoke, his voice indicating the amount of patience required to do so, "my foot hygiene and his resemblance to fungi aside, I believe I'd like to ask this one who he is."

"Hear that?" I hissed in the vamp's ear. "We've had a really rotten day so far, so it'll be a pleasure to remove your head if you don't cooperate."

He's not obsessed, is he? I sent to Zaria.

No, but he is under compulsion, probably by the one you have in your dungeon. Gerrett can get around that, I think.

"Gerrett?" I straightened and backed away to allow Zaria's Sirenali mate access.

"Master vampire, you will answer all our questions honestly from now on," Gerrett commanded. Even I felt the vibration in Gerrett's voice as obsession was placed.

I think it resonates in parts of the brain, particularly in the amygdala, Zaria informed me.

Thank goodness we're immune, then.

In our copious free time, we should work on just that.

What?

Immunity. For everybody.

When we have free time.

Right.

"I'll have your name, first," Rigo growled.

The vampire cowered at his feet. "Erryl Fixx," he replied, spitting the name through clenched teeth.

"Erryl Fixx? The same Erryl Fixx who was the royal bastard of King Erdyl? The Erryl Fixx who disappeared two hundred fifty years ago?"

"Yes," Erryl whined.

"How did you learn of the Order of the Night Flower?" Rigo demanded.

"A man came to Naril. Told Naril of an ancient group of vampires who no longer existed. Called themselves Rith Naeri. We were to become their replacement. Sworden was the last of us Naril chose, and since he had little experience in killing, he was placed as Larvalis' advisor."

"Naril?" Rigo lifted an eyebrow.

"The eldest of us. We've known one another for two centuries. Not above a bit of larceny now and then, but not enough to get caught."

"Until now. Where is Naril? Where does he stay?"

Erryl rattled off an address in one of the elite subdivisions of the capital city.

"Who else is in the group?"

"I only know of Sworden and Alek. The other two Naril won't reveal."

"I've passed the address to Tamp and Alrenardo," Zaria said softly.

"Very good. Lissa, I ask you to send this one to keep Sworden company," Rigo sighed.

"Oh, that won't be a problem," I said. "I have more questions for him anyway."

~

Dungeon

Queen's Palace, Le-Ath Veronis

Zaria

Sworden watched me warily from his seat on the bunk in his cell. Hal, Gerrett and Lissa stood with me. Behind us, Merrill, Tony and several palace guards stood, keeping watch.

Sworden wanted to rush the bars and hiss at us, but he'd been placed under compulsion by Merrill, so his ass stayed where it was.

In a nearby cell, Erryl was making himself comfortable, which meant he was fuming over Rigo's instructions not to be a nuisance and only answer questions politely and truthfully. It really sucked to be him right now.

"What's the payoff?" I asked Sworden.

"What?" He pretended not to understand.

"What did you get out of this? Was there a payoff—or the promise of a payoff?"

"Speak truth," Gerrett's voice vibrated.

"I was promised wealth, fresh blood and a new home," Sworden rumbled.

"A new home where?" Lissa demanded.

"Le-Ath Veronis. We were also promised a way to survive in daylight, too, but I didn't believe that part."

"Did they say how that would be accomplished?" Lissa was now very interested in what Sworden had to say.

"A device," Sworden shrugged.

"Did they ever show you the device, or explain how it worked?"

"Said it attached to the back of the neck—I've never heard of such."

"It does exist, but it doesn't stop the vampire's desire to sleep during daylight, so you could be in full sun—but sound asleep," Lissa snorted. "Anybody could kill you while you were like that."

"Where were you promised a home on Le-Ath Veronis?" My arms crossed over my chest. I could see the answer in his eyes quite plainly. This was for Lissa's benefit.

"We were told we'd have the run of the palace."

"Well, you currently occupy a small section of the dungeon in that palace," Lissa hissed. "Try my patience and you'll die here."

I knew why she was so angry; Rigo had been locked up for the very supposition of a crime, and without proper investigation. Plus, she was exhausted. She hadn't been kidding about the rotten day she'd had.

Mom, I'm taking you back to Corez, I told her as gently as I could. *You need some sleep. So does Rigo, and he won't go to bed until you get there.*

She blinked at me before wiping a tear away. I'd never called her Mom before, and it served to put a better end to the past few hours. "All right," she nodded. "But if you so much as breathe wrong, I'll be back," she pointed a claw-tipped finger at Sworden. "I rule here. You don't."

I took the opportunity to fold space with her and the others, so she'd have the last (and best) word.

Corez

Zaria

"I left a doppelganger in your bed," I told Lissa after dropping her in Rigo's suite. "Just fold there when you wake up and it'll disappear. If anybody disturbs it, you'll know that, too."

"Thank you." Rigo, who stood by a massive window near his bed, turned to me and dipped his head. He and Lissa needed each other tonight; I recognized it easily.

"We'll go, now," I turned toward Hal and Gerrett. "I'll keep you posted if we hear anything from Tamp and Alrenardo. I really, really want to speak to Naril. I get the feeling that D'slay may have had something to do with this. I can't think of any other way that someone would release information about the Rith Naeri, unless there was a rogue god, a Sirenali or someone else quite powerful involved."

"You've already checked all the members, haven't you?" Rigo lifted an eyebrow.

"Yes. I hope you don't mind."

"No. I'm glad you did that, so we can eliminate all of us as suspects in this."

"We'll go, then. Let us know if you need anything." I folded Gerrett and Halimel to Kwark, so Lissa and Rigo could have time alone.

~

Royal Palace, Galk

   Vik

"They take their job quite seriously," Reah breathed a sigh as her suite doors shut behind her. She'd described the two guards who stood outside, armed to the teeth and unwilling to let anybody through who didn't have the Queen's permission.

"Were they here for the real Queen?" I asked as Reah pulled the platinum coronet from her hair and placed it on a table.

"No. Zaria sent them. She says Ocenosek and Cudworth are brothers and will guard us with their lives, so that's why they're at the door, now. Wyatt, Denevik and Bel Erland are with us during the day; these two will stand guard at night. The suite is protected—Zaria placed shields. If the palace implodes, this part will still be standing."

"I really wish we could find the ones responsible for the obsession; things are wonky around here," I growled

"No joke. Did you hear that fool, Addul Gurr, in court today? Asking for special favors as if he expected it automatically? Bel Erland *Looked*; only recently has he been attending court, but he got money for a stupid road on his property that nobody will use."

"It's a safe bet the money will end up elsewhere," I said. Everything the man said was a lie; Reah knew it, too, she just didn't say it.

"Addul Teran needed the funds more, and he got them. I wonder if whoever placed obsession knows somebody else is in charge, now."

"Probably, if they're bothering to check. I know Mom and Rigo have already had a run-in with that problem. Zaria says to watch everybody and stay on our toes."

"She's worried this is connected to that rogue Sirenali, isn't she?"

"Definitely. He's out to cause trouble, you can count on that. If he can disrupt hub worlds, then he can easily start wars. Frankly, I think this is only a subplot in his machinations."

"That's terrifying. What makes you say that?"

"Actually, Meerius and I both say that."

"Meerius?"

"A world spirit. We've bonded."

"Worlds have spirits?"

"I know it sounds weird, but they do."

"Kifirin has a world spirit?"

"Yeah. Zaria has bonded with him. She said to tell you if you wanted to know."

"Why—and how—did they bond with you?"

"They've placed themselves inside coins and have bonded with our bodies."

"Show me."

"Are you sure you want me to take my shirt off?"

"Yes, I want to see it."

"All right." I began unbuttoning my shirt and held it open. "He's here, on my chest. He says you can touch if you want."

"Meerius said that?"

"Yeah."

Reah approached cautiously, until she reached my side. Slowly she reached out to touch the coin adhered to my skin. An indrawn breath informed me they'd connected in some way.

"He said *greetings, Life Giver*," Reah breathed. "How does he know?"

"They are now communicating with one another," I shrugged my shirt on again. "That wasn't always the case, but they got tired of being destroyed again and again, in the recurring God Wars."

Your mate healed many worlds, Meerius reminded me.

"He says he knows you've healed many worlds," I grinned at Reah.

She also has brought vitality back to Kifirin, with her daughters.

"He ah, says you brought vitality back to Kifirin with your—our—daughters."

Kifirin is quite pleased with her.

"He says Kifirin is quite pleased with you." I hadn't seen Reah blush in a long time. She was blushing now.

"He knows this because he's talked with Kifirin?"

Yes. We are speaking, now.

"He says they're talking now."

"Incredible," Reah sighed. "I never knew. I thought that Kifirin—you know, the god, Kifirin, was in charge of the planet."

He and Hanlekidus are in charge of the surface and the beings upon it, in a way. The Kifirin I am speaking with is the soul of the world that is Kifirin.

"He says the Kifirin he's speaking with is the soul of the planet. Kifirin and Hank are in charge of the people on the surface."

"Interesting."

"Look, I think we're both tired," I told her. "I can answer questions later. We have an early day tomorrow, so unless there's something important, I'll go to my suite, now."

"All right. Good-night, Torevik."

"Good-night, Reah."

~

Reah

Tory was right; someone had taken notice of my actions the previous day. That's why a media conference the following morning went sideways.

"Why was Addul Gurr given funds two moon-turns ago for a road on his property, when no road was needed?" a journalist demanded. This wasn't the first time I'd been shoved into an unforgiving and career-destroying spotlight.

"I have previous records of Addul Gurr's attendance at court in the last five years," the journalist went on. "He has only attended once, for the biennial ball."

"You've neglected your research," Bel Erland stepped forward and intervened smoothly. "Any Addul is entitled to a request for funds, as long as those funds do not exceed the tax amount for any five-month period, once every five years, according to the law. There is no limitation placed on the use of those funds, perhaps by an oversight of the Council itself. Addul Gurr has not requested any funds for more than ten years. Therefore, the initial request was granted. The request put forward yesterday, by the same token and according to the law, was denied."

I watched as more than six journalists deflated. Someone, somewhere, hadn't checked the minutiae of the law before placing obsession and laying a trap within it.

Zaria is seeing this through my eyes, Tory informed me.

What does she see? I asked.

These journalists were tipped off in a similar way to those on Corez. There's definitely some collusion and conspiracy going on. I doubt you'd find anybody who could have spouted that bit of legislation off the top of their head, either, he added. *Zaria says it was buried in the language of a non-related law. If Bel Erland hadn't gone* Looking, *we'd be in trouble right now.*

Just as Rigo was in trouble two days ago. "Do you have other questions?" I asked the crowd of journalists.

"I'd like a copy of the law in question," someone raised his hands.

"You'll find it on your comp-vid, dated twelve years ago, fifteenth day of Leafling Month. Decision eleven," Bel Erland quoted. "It's buried in the language of that unrelated piece of legislation, on page six."

"What was the legislation about, that included this law?" A woman journalist asked.

"About water rights between Addularchies and Rezoarchies," Bel said.

"I'd like to prevent such things as unrelated passages being added to legislation in the future," I announced. "So that none of us are caught unaware again." *Where did they get this information?* I sent to Tory.

Zaria says she's got the same people on it as in Rigo's case. That means Dave, Sabrina and Perri are hacking into journalists' systems.

Good. I hope we hear something from them soon. These people wanted a scandal today. This one backfired. What will the next one be?

One more carefully researched, no doubt, Tory's mindspeech sounded grim.

"If there's nothing more, I have a meeting to attend," I announced.

When nobody said anything, I turned to go back inside the palace, my group falling in behind me. I may have flounced the official robe of gold I wore as I turned; I'd likely see it on the evening news reports if I did.

"That was a near-fiasco," Denevik breathed as we walked into the central dome area of the palace, marble tiles echoing beneath our feet.

"Bel Erland, you are a gift to me," I told my son. "Thank you for your wisdom in a crisis."

"Thank Dad and Grandpa for court etiquette—they taught me most of what I know. Being cool in a tight spot comes from you."

He gets his smile from you, too, Tory bumped my shoulder with his.

I bit back a laugh, something I hadn't expected to happen.

"I'm pleased to see you in such good humor, after a near-character assassination," Rezo Nilus, highest ranking member of the council, walked toward us. "Trust Addul Gurr to cause trouble after being away so long."

"I don't wish to take sides in this, Nilus," I held up a hand.

"However, I will have words with anyone who provided misinformation to the media."

"Do you have suspects in mind?" Nilus, his hands studiously behind his back, fell in step with us. Tall, thin and dark-haired, he resembled an old crow with sharp eyes and carefully-placed strides.

"None at the moment, but it will be looked into, I assure you."

One of Nilus' eyebrows lifted, but he didn't respond. "What is your stance on today's meeting?" he asked instead.

"I'm waiting to hear from all involved," I said.

"That isn't what I heard."

"Then I'm sorry you heard otherwise."

"I'm not. I'm waiting to hear from the others, too. Trade between the Addularchies and Rezoarchies has always been without tariffs and taxes. Placing those now could certainly result in ah—hardships for some."

"I agree. I still want to hear what brought this on, before turning it down flat."

Nilus laughed, this time. The sound was rich, smooth, and boomed throughout the rotunda as we entered the meeting chamber. *I hope we can get something to drink before this fiasco proceeds*, I sent to Tory. *I feel dry, suddenly.*

CHAPTER 8

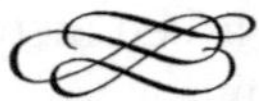

*K*wark
Zaria

"Reah just had her first run-in," I told my bunch at breakfast. "Honey, I sure as hell hope nothing goes wrong at this birthday party of yours."

"I'll just slap four knots on everybody's head. That should do it," Bleek grinned at me.

"The other bad news is that Kay can't get to the gist of the obsessions placed on the hub world leaders. They're all obssession-free at this point, but we don't know any more about it than we did before," I reported.

"Have you heard anything from Tamp or Alrenardo?" Halimel asked quietly while buttering a breakfast roll.

"They went to the address we had; looks like Naril hasn't been there for a day or two. They did find a missing man—dead of course. Seems Naril never learned the proper way to take blood, and the victim bled out after three major arteries were punctured and not healed afterward."

"Idiot," Halimel muttered. "Do they have the victim's identity, yet?"

"They're working on it, but there's nothing showing up in any of Hraede's databases."

"Not from there, then," Hal bit forcefully into his roll and chewed.

"Yeah. Don't worry, we'll get to the bottom of this," I soothed. "Unfortunately, unless we want to bend time and come back exhausted again, we have a full day planned here."

"I'm not willing to ask that of you," Hal turned dark eyes in my direction.

"Nissa is setting a tracking spell, which will only work if Naril doesn't bathe or change shoes," I told Hal. "If it doesn't work, we may have to ask Erland to set a scrying spell or get Kaldill Schaff to look for him. Wherever he is, he's hiding behind a Sirenali or a Sirenali's bone dust by now. If he weren't, I'd have had him, first thing."

"I've never considered asking the King of the Elves for help," Hal confessed.

"Last resort—it's a very intense process," I explained. "I read about it in the Archives. And, with Sirenali involvement, who knows if all that effort will be for nothing?"

"I suppose it's too much to ask to have things be easy for once," Ilya said.

"Yeah. I guess that's true."

"Look at us, so morose and all. It's my birthday," Bleek grinned. "Well, somebody else's birthday, but I'm celebrating on his behalf."

"I hear the cake is enormous," Edden stifled a grin.

"He can eat a lot of cake," Gerrett pointed out. He'd know—he'd baked enough of them, and Bleek was always happy to eat anything Gerrett made.

"Six lobes," Bleek grinned. "Have to keep those operating at full capacity."

"Would you like to unsaddle your high horse for a minute and talk to us peasants?" I teased him.

"I thought we were talking about my birthday."

"Honey, your real birthday is two months away and no, I'm not telling you anything," I held up a hand before he could ask.

"Just don't forget," he offered a cheeky grin.

"Nobody who's ever met you will forget you. What with six lobes and all."

"Yep, it's the first thing they notice." He made a show of placing all four hands behind his head.

Halimel turned his head to hide a smile.

We may have to shove Bleek in a cold shower; he's just too hot to handle today, I sent to Hal. He barked a laugh.

Murazal

Zanfield Staggs

"The reception to welcome the Ambassador from Nagulez is this evening," Rajeon read the schedule for me. "This afternoon, we're meeting with a group from the Shipping Federation after three Murazalian ships were attacked by pirates last year."

"Only three, and they're complaining? That's a low number," Travis observed. "Were there deaths involved?"

"One, and that was afterward—the ship's chief engineer had a massive coronary and died from all the chaos of being boarded and their cargo stolen."

"Anybody know what the cargo was?" Trent asked.

"I have the manifests," Rajeon passed a comp-vid to Trent. "I also have the flight plans and thought to pull the actual flight memory from each ship. There were slight deviations in each. The navigator claimed it was to avoid space debris in one instance. Another, it was a glitch in the nav-comp. Third time, to work around crowded conditions in the shipping lanes."

"Let me guess—each time they were hit, they were off course?" Travis snorted.

"Yep. The records indicate just that."

"Same company or different ones? Same navigator or different ones?" I asked.

"Different each time on both counts," Rajeon reported.

"You're really good at this," Travis told Rajeon. Rajeon grinned.

"If this is connected, and it could very well be," Travis turned to me, "then somebody has been screwing around with the navigators. They have free rein to make minor course adjustments without informing the Captain. A major change will have to be approved by the Captain or second-in-command."

"You're saying that each time, the ship was just enough off course to be hit by pirates?"

"That's the way I see it," Rajeon agreed.

"I think we need to interview all three navigators, then."

"I'll send a notice to the local ASD, but the navigators in question may not be on the planet right now. They're navigators, and they ship out regularly," Trent observed.

"We can work around that if we have to—I think we really need to see all three of them and as soon as possible. If we're forced to catch up with them on a ship, then Morrett has to come with us."

"I will come." Morrett, who'd remained silent during our early morning meeting, spoke. "If they have obsession or compulsion, I will know it."

"I think Travis, Morrett and Rajeon should go if it's necessary. That will leave enough of us here to fend off an attack if something happens," Perri suggested.

"Find out where the navigators are, right away," I said. "We need you gone and back before the meeting with the Shipping Federation."

"I have that information now," Trent tapped the comp-vid. "Two are here; one is on a ship bound for Lurjakk. The ASD is already gearing up to bring the first two here. I'm sending you the flight plan for the third's ship."

"I think we can hit that," Travis agreed. "Just in case, I'll notify Zaria."

"Get it done," I grinned at him. It was nice being in charge for a change. "Now, what are you wearing for the reception tonight?" I turned to Perri. "We have to coordinate, you know."

～

Travis

I'm sending Valegar, Zaria sent. *He knows the layout of the ship in question, so even if it's hidden by bone dust, he can aim for a specific section inside the ship and still get there.*

I didn't need to ask how that happened; Valegar had likely bent time to get to the ship when it was last in port. No Larentii would be seen unless they wanted it, and nobody would find a power tag placed by a Larentii unless they wanted it found. Valegar would get us where we needed to go, in order to have a personal chat with the navigator.

Seconds later, Valegar appeared. We'd borrowed an empty, inner office to make our departure and return; Perri and Zanfield would ensure it remained locked.

"Ready?" Val offered a rare smile.

"Ready."

Suddenly, we were on board the *Delineator*, where our navigator-suspect worked. Currently, he was on a sleep rotation while the ship's comp flew a course designated by him.

"Time to wake up sleeping beauty," I whispered. Rajeon and Morrett nodded their agreement. Val transported us to the navigator's berth, where we found Cadge Arra wide awake atop his bunk, both hands behind his head while he stared at the ceiling.

"Hello, Cadge," I greeted him, causing him to jump and scramble against the wall, his arms raised to defend himself from blows.

"Zaria says to bring him back with us. Now." Valegar made himself visible to Cadge. The subsequent, indrawn breath actually sounded relieved.

~

"Ordered by the Captain?" Zanfield questioned Cadge while the rest of us, Zaria included, looked on.

"He ordered me to take the ship off-course. Then he told me that I'd lose my license if I told anyone that he ordered it, and to write in the records that we encountered space debris, which caused the course corrections. He's been Captain for nearly sixty years. I've been a navigator for less than five."

"Where is he now?" I asked. "What's his name?"

"Captain Varber, and he's still with the fleet, although I heard he was making plans to retire."

"Did Varber have connections to the other pirated ships?" Rajeon directed his question to Trent, who was busy with his comp-vid.

"Nothing apparent," Trent reported moments later. "Different Captains each time. By the way, the other two navigators are waiting outside with an ASD escort."

"Bring them in," Zanfield said. "I'll be interested in their stories, too."

Zaria

Cadge is telling the truth, and he's terrified he'll lose his license, I sent to Zanfield and the others, while two more navigators were brought into Zanfield's borrowed office.

"Would you prefer that I stay?" The ASD agent asked Zanfield.

He can stay, I sent. *He plans to secretly record this portion of the meeting. I think he should do just that.*

"Please," Zanfield offered chairs to our new arrivals. "Now, let's get right down to business; we don't have a lot of time before the meeting I have scheduled with the Shipping Federation, who seem to want me to do something about the piracy occurring on their ships outside Murazalian-controlled shipping lanes."

"If these attacks of piracy were planned, as all of you are saying, what do you imagine was in the cargo that the pirates wanted?" Travis asked. All three navigators had similar stories to tell—the commanding officer in each case had ordered them to deviate from their original course.

"I have no idea," Cadge spoke first. "We were carrying farm-bots, seeds and seedlings—mostly trees—to restore a burned fruit and nut farm. I don't know why anyone would want to steal that."

"What about you, Nenn?" I turned to the second navigator.

"Nothing out of the ordinary," Nenn replied. "We were on our way back with a load of sand for glass. We also had three passengers that nobody was supposed to know about. After we were pirated, the sand and the passengers were gone."

We'll be back, Zaria told me. She and Valegar, who were invisible to the others, departed.

~

Zaria

Val and I bent time, arriving seconds before the pirates boarded.

Dearest, we cannot interfere with this event; you know this, Val reminded me as we watched the loading bay door open—from the inside.

I know. I didn't tell him that I might find what I wanted to know just by looking at a few of the participants. He probably knew it, too, but didn't voice his opinions.

On this ship, the Chief Engineer stood by after opening the door, while enormous barrels of sand were transported from one ship to the other.

The Captain issued a command for the remaining crew to stand down and leave the loading bay, because the pirates demanded it. Failure to comply would result in their deaths.

The Engineer is sweating and his heart rate is quite fast, Val reported.

That's because he figured out what's in those barrels, beside sand.

What is that, dear one? Val turned to me.

Uranium, I breathed a mental sigh. *No wonder he had a heart attack afterward. They weren't stealing sand. They were transporting an illegal substance, and ah, those three Sirenali, right there,* I added, as three women opened a hidden door in the last barrel and stepped out of it. The barrel was large enough for them to have supplies and makeshift beds. I imagined they'd gotten out a time or two, just for exercise.

Somehow, Nenn had caught them outside their temporary habitat and was threatened if he revealed what he knew. The women were escorted off the ship, their empty barrel came next, and the Chief Engineer, clutching his chest, manually shut the door behind them.

Shall we see who delivered the sand to the ship? I asked Val, who was now very intrigued. I paid no mind when the engineer dropped to his knees from the pain in his chest. *I think a visit to the Captain is the first place to start.*

When we visited the third ship, which was reportedly carrying organic fertilizer, it wasn't just the smell of cow dung that hit my nostrils. If Lissa were here, she could probably tell us how many and what type of cows had pooped, and just how many bodies were buried in each wooden barrel of the same.

My love, Val sent as the pirates boarded this ship to take its cargo, *do you see what I see?*

That this is the same bunch of pirates? Yeah, I see that, all right.

I have a plan, Val grimaced.

Honey, you're the one who said no interference.

They've forgotten that barrel hidden behind the broken-down loader.

So they have.

Shall we go stand there?

I think we should.

Val moved us quickly, and, as he knew it would, the shield around us also hid the barrel behind us. We watched as once again, the pirates exited the cargo hold and the Captain shut the door manually behind them.

I don't think he wants this barrel, do you? I turned my face up to Val's.

I can't say that he would; it stinks of excrement and decomposing human.

I'll take it with us, then. He'd appreciate that if he knew.

Travis, I sent, *have someone bring Captain Deherdt to the meeting. I believe he'll have something interesting to report to the delegates of the Shipping Federation.*

Opal, Kell, I sent next. *I really, really, need your help.*

~

Presidential Palace, Murazal
Zanfield

It was difficult, but we managed it. "Welcome," I stood to greet the delegates from the Shipping Federation. They'd been led into a small room often used by the guards. They were expecting to visit my office, instead.

Well, the actual meeting wasn't going to take place in the Presidential Palace, anyway. "I've had the meeting relocated," I told them. "We only have three hours, so we should get going."

"Where?" Darak, President of the Shipping Federation, demanded.

"Oh, you'll recognize the place. It's in a Shipping Federation warehouse, commandeered by the ASD. This meeting involves both visual and physical aids for your perusal, and a very unusual story to go with them. Shall we?" I urged them toward the door they'd just entered. "A hover-limo is waiting outside for us, and drinks and snacks will be provided."

Mumbling to one another, I took the lead and pulled them into the rotunda, where Travis, Trent, Rajeon and Morrett waited to escort us. No doubt, the real and very obsessed President of Murazal wouldn't have looked into this mess; he'd likely been told not to, and to make excuses. Instead, today would be quite the eye-opener, as Travis was fond of saying.

Still, it made me wonder who'd placed the obsession in the first place. As far as I knew, nobody had stepped forward to attempt it another time.

I'm still concerned all of this could be a trap, I sent to Zaria, who'd gone back to Kwark after arranging things here for us.

As am I, she returned. *Someone is watching, I'm sure of it, and if they haven't started figuring all this out by now, then they're more dimwitted than*

I think they are. Keep your wits about you and don't go anywhere alone. I've grown attached to you, for some reason. You're the younger brother I should have had and didn't.

You count me as family? I almost stopped in my tracks, which would have caused the President of the Shipping Federation to run into me.

Honey, I count you as family.

I have family, then, I agreed.

Of course you do. Now, go give those guys an eye full.

I intend to.

"What's this?" President Darak exploded as we walked into the massive warehouse, where a large crate and two barrels waited for us. One barrel was enormous—and gave off a stink that would cause a scent-impaired vetti-slug to cover his nose.

Travis, Rajeon and Morrett were already here, along with Kell Abenott and his wife, Opal Tadewi. Both held high-ranking positions in the ASD. Zaria had certainly put the effort into this investigation.

"Good afternoon, President Darak," Kell stepped forward. "I am Vice-Director Abenott of the ASD. This is Vice-Director Tadewi of the ASD," he introduced Opal. "At President Ylisis' request, we have investigated all three incidents of piracy on Murazalian vessels. It's quite interesting what we found."

"What's that?" Darak lifted his collar to cover his nose, so his words were garbled.

"Bring out the accused," Kell nodded to Travis, who issued the order verbally into his comp-vid. Moments later, two Captains and a Chief Engineer were brought out of the warehouse office, all three in power cuffs.

"We have conclusive evidence that these three, along with the deceased engineer, took bribes to order the pirated ships off course, so they could be attacked by the pirates who paid them," Kell stated without inflection. "As for the larger barrel, we've done an image scan, and know what it contains."

"Cow shit," muttered Darak. "I've checked the manifests myself."

"Ah, but what you don't know is what wasn't listed on the manifest. There is a body inside this barrel, President Darak. President Ylisis asked us to wait to reveal it at your arrival. You see that the seals are still intact, and the locks provided by the shipping company have not been tampered with. Whether the person inside the barrel died of natural causes or was murdered, we have yet to determine."

"They were smuggling bodies?" Darak's Vice President was aghast at Kell's words.

"Every barrel on board that ship held at least one body within the compost. This is the only barrel we were able to recover. At this time, we do not have information on where the other barrels are. As for the other shipments, we have no idea why the pirates wanted fruit and nut trees or farm-bots, but the last shipment wasn't only sand for glass."

"I can't wait to hear this," Darak grumbled.

"Uranium was packed within the sand. Now, you know as well as I do what the penalties are for shipping illegal substances, and in such large quantities."

"Mother Murazal be merciful," Darak's Vice President wailed.

"We've already questioned these three, and I'm sure we'll be asking even more questions—not only of those shipping companies, but many in your organization as well. If you have any knowledge of these incidents, or of the bribes placed, now is the time to speak," Kell ended his speech.

He'd glossed over the three Sirenali passengers that were transported. I'm sure Zaria requested it. That was something for us to investigate, rather than the ASD or the Shipping Federation of Murazal.

"Please, send images of what is found in that barrel," Darak was ready to gag, I could tell. "With your permission, President Ylisis, I'd like to take my associates and go."

"You have my permission. We'll contact you with further information," I waved them away. It was all Darak could do not to run out of the warehouse.

"We'll get the barrel sorted, and give reports to you and to Zaria," Opal stepped forward and shook my hand. "I don't think anyone could have filled in for Ylisis better than you."

"Thank you," I grinned and felt embarrassed at the same time.

"Keep up the good work, all of you," Kell sounded pleased. "Stay in touch, too, if you notice anything that we should know."

"We will," Travis agreed.

"Incoming," Rajeon shouted, and before any of us could react, he'd formed a tangled, diamond web about us and flung us out the warehouse door while the cavernous building and the evidence sitting within it was blown to bits.

"I think somebody didn't want us to see what was in that barrel," Opal complained. Someone had transported us to a nearby warehouse, where we were gathering our wits and looking for cuts and bruises from the blast. Kell had taken charge of our prisoners, who were shaken but unhurt.

I'd already been in contact with Security, their explosives experts and the fire brigade, ordering all of them to the scene. All told, Rajeon had kept us shielded quite well; we only had torn clothing, a few cuts and minor bruises to account for our nearness to the explosion.

Rajeon sat on an empty crate, head bowed and hands hanging loose after his amazing rescue; I imagine his heart was still beating triple time—mine certainly was.

"Where'd you learn that trick?" Opal knelt down next to him. "It's quite amazing. I only had a personal shield up," she added.

"It's something my father taught me," Rajeon lifted his head to look at her.

"You want a special agent's job with the ASD, you have it," Kell gruffed.

"We ah, Randl has dibs, through Ildevar," Travis said softly.

"If you decide not to work with the Formidables, come see me," Kell nodded.

"Thank you, sir, but Randl and I have an agreement," Rajeon dipped his head to Kell.

Thank the stars, I sent to Travis. Rajeon would be a wonderful addition to our crew.

"I'll bring in a crew to help investigate," Kell said. "Here's your ride back to the Presidential Palace."

The hover-limo pulled up outside the warehouse; Trent and Perri got out. That told me that both had gone over the limo completely, making sure it was safe before we got in.

"We'll see you soon," Opal called out as we limped toward the vehicle. I lifted a hand in a half-wave—shock was beginning to set in and we still had a blasted party to attend later.

Corez

   Lissa

Just a little banged up, that's all, Travis reported. *Mom, that warehouse was checked over roughly an hour before we held the meeting there. Kell and Opal's crew are sniffing around and checking all outside vids, but so far, they've found nothing.*

So the explosives had to be folded, skipped or transported in somehow.

That's our theory. We have a reception tonight, so we can't leave Zanfield without a proper guard to go looking for ourselves.

What does Zaria say?

She says that she'll do some checking on her end tomorrow—they have a party on Kwark tonight for one of her mates. He's about to have four arms.

Bleek probably appreciates that.

I'm sure he does. I'm worried about all of us, at this point, after today's surprise.

Do you need Karzac to come—for any of you?

It's not worth calling out the big healing guns for bruises and shallow cuts. Rajeon's diamond web kept us from getting knocked around by the blast.

I'd like to see that, actually. Tamp can do something similar, though.

I'm really glad it's an available option. Look, I have to go. The reception is about to start and Trent, Rajeon, Morrett and I are Zanfield and Perri's guards.

Keep your eyes open, hon. Somebody is gunning for all of us, now.

Yeah. We know that for sure.

~

Queen's Palace, Kwark

Zaria

"They may be going to plan B across the board, now that they've figured out something's wrong," I said, fitting the coronet on my hair, which was piled high on my head.

"Plan B?"

"Their first attacks were to discredit us, or those whose places we took, I think. The next attacks are focused on killing or doing harm." I turned to Edden, who stood behind me at a dressing mirror. "And, since they now know we're not the ones they obsessed originally, they're upping their game to get rid of us."

"If we could find the ones who placed the obsessions," Edden's arms folded around my shoulders, while he leaned in to kiss my bare neck.

"Honey, I think those three Sirenali women I saw aboard that ship could have something to do with all that. I mean, how easy would it be for a woman to approach someone at a function or something, and let obsession drop out during what looks like a normal conversation?"

"Not hard at all," he sighed and pulled away from me. "Men will be flattered in many cases, while women will see another woman as non-threatening. Especially if she's passed the guards into the function."

"Exactly."

"We can go back to the point where each hub world leader began to stray off course and look for any parties, receptions or large meetings they could have infiltrated."

"I know." I let my shoulders sag at the thought of endless hours of work.

"My love, you are weary," Edden observed. "I say we make this event a short one."

"Suits me," I replied. "Come on, the others are waiting."

We walked out of the Queen's suite together, joining Bleek, Gerrett, Ilya and Halimel, who stood outside the door.

"Shall we go find the enormous cake everybody's talking about?" I straightened Bleek's collar. He smiled and leaned down to kiss me.

~

SouthStar, Avendor

First Advisor Haris of Corez

To provide needed information, and for a semblance of balance if not peace of mind, we were given access to important events on our homeworlds. I'd already witnessed the accusations and imprisonment of the one who'd taken my place, before he was released and the word got out that the accusations were manufactured.

President Ylisis of Murazal had been shocked by what he'd seen occurring on his home planet only today. If his replacement and those around him hadn't been there and prepared for attempted murder, he'd have died in an unexpected explosion.

He sat in a chair not far from mine, now, elbows on his knees and eyes not leaving the monitor screen, as if he were afraid to do so.

Now, Queen Ilise of Kwark watched with us, as her replacement and those of her five husbands made their way to the ballroom for a birthday party. Like Ylisis, her eyes never wandered from the images we watched.

"This is terrifying," Ilise mumbled. "We know something is about to happen, and all I want to do is shout a warning."

"I know," Queen Myriae of Galk whispered. "If our replacements are killed, where will that leave us?"

"Hold onto hope and strengthen your faith that all will be well at the end," Kay and Ashe joined us in the large media room. Ashe spoke; Kay smiled at us.

Yes, we'd all heard of the reclusive owner of SouthStar Groves on

Avendor, in the Campiaan Alliance. I couldn't help thinking that he was much more than most of us imagined in the past.

As for Kay, she'd somehow taken away the affliction we'd arrived with; Ashe called it obsession. I didn't want to insult our hosts by being too inquisitive; so far, everything they'd done served to keep us safe. Had we been faced with the events taking place on our home planets, surely we would be dead or in prison by now.

"Look—there's my ballroom," Ilise pointed out breathlessly.

All of us turned back to the screen. "How does she look exactly like me?" Ilise asked.

"Move in closer," Ashe commanded. I blinked—the micro-cameras transmitting the images moved in obediently, until they were so close to Ilise's replacement we could see the tiniest diamonds crusting her necklace.

"Someone's poisoned the food," the replacement Queen told her escorts. "Edden, if you'll make a brief speech, I'll neutralize the drug they've used."

"Power," Ashe finally responded to Ilise's question. His voice was deeper than normal and held such force that it took my breath away. I jerked my head around to look at him; his eyes had gone dark and stars fell through their depths.

CHAPTER 9

Queen's Palace, Kwark
Zaria

"Slow acting poison," I told my bunch as we retired for the night. "Should take effect three hours before sunrise. Now, I'll be interested to see who comes to check on us early."

"I can set perimeter spells," Ilya offered.

"Do it, and record images of anybody going in or out of the royal suites. I'll have shields up, too, in case anybody else has ideas to hasten our demise."

"I'd like to know about that if it happens," Bleek cracked knuckles on all four hands.

"As would I," Halimel nodded to Bleek. "If the poison hadn't been neutralized, it wouldn't be just us dying from it."

He was right. Every guest who'd attended had gone home with an invisible Larentii tag, so I'd know if they were attacked further. I'd carefully checked, too; nobody at the party was involved in the poisoning. I'd looked at everyone still working in the kitchen; they hadn't known either.

I'd look in on the head chef in the morning, and any of his assistants who'd left before the party started. If none of them were involved, then someone with power, personal or paid-for, had placed the poison.

I was going to find out who that was, but first, I needed rest. More than anything, I wanted to fold away from Kwark and sleep in a safer place. I doubted my rest would be peaceful here—if I got any at all.

"Go on to bed; we'll take care of things from here," Edden gestured toward my bedroom.

"Fine. I'll know if anything happens," I reminded him.

"We know," they chorused.

Royal Palace, Galk

Reah

I stood at the wide window in the Queen's private study, arms crossed tightly over my chest and barely seeing the beautiful, decorative garden outside. I still fretted over the Council meeting the day before, disturbed by the argumentative mood that had taken the Council and divided them almost equally. My vote was the one deciding the entire affair, leaving trade on Galk tariff-free.

"Half the Council is in a snit; the other half is breathing sighs of relief," Wyatt reported. He'd quietly canvassed the mood of the Council after the bill to place tariffs on trade between fiefdoms failed spectacularly—by a single vote.

There wasn't any need for those tariffs, and those who'd suggested it knew that. They were only looking to fatten their own coffers, at the expense of others. The end result, of course, was an increase in prices for the regular citizens of Galk, and that would only bring harm to the entire planet.

After all, if locally made goods cost more than they could pay, they'd have to do without and let the local stuff rot; they couldn't afford to do otherwise. Eventually, it could lead to the shutdown of factories and farms on Galk, and putting citizens out of work.

That could lead to recession and depression, and, as Galk was a hub world, the infrastructure would be neglected and the spaceport itself fall into ruin. A hub world in the grip of poverty and chaos meant shipping companies would suffer, and goods normally brought into port here would no longer be transported to satellite worlds.

Shortages and hardships caused wars, just as Lissa said. Galk didn't need richer nobles. The planet needed more responsible ones, with an eye on the long game rather than the shorter-sighted one of instant gratification.

Ultimately, Galk could lose its membership in the Alliance, and it could take down many satellite worlds with it.

Was that the enemy's ultimate goal—to divide and conquer? To leave all of us on our own and battling a hidden threat we couldn't find?

I hear you, dearest, Nefrigar's voice sounded in my mind. *You and the others are now on the front line of that war and must not fail in your quest to stabilize worlds that could bring about a terrible catastrophe.*

You can see the end result if we fail, can't you?

Yes, dearest.

I hadn't heard him come in, but Tory's arms settled around me from behind. He knew how upset I was. *Don't let this bother you,* his words breathed into my mind. *We have to stand strong, without calling them all difiks. At least not in public.*

I snorted a laugh and the dark mood was broken.

Tory moved away, then, taking his warmth and comfort with him. I hadn't realized until then that I'd appreciated his intervention.

"What's on the agenda for today?" I turned toward Wyatt. "Where's Bel Erland?"

"Bel Erland is having tea with Rezo Nilus," Wyatt replied.

"Why aren't we all having tea with Rezo Nilus?" I asked.

"Because we ah, don't want to show favoritism. Rezo Nilus was the force behind the opposition to the tariffs."

"And if we hadn't been here, he'd have lost that battle, right?"

"That's the way I see it."

"So, we shouldn't have tea with Rezo Nilus." I sighed and turned back to the window.

"At least not for a few days," Wyatt counseled.

"Of course. Out of curiosity, why is Bel Erland having tea with Rezo Nilus?"

"He's worried that Rezo Nilus may be a target for the enemy's obsession. Everybody saw how close the vote was, yesterday. One or two more obsessions will guarantee a re-vote."

"How many re-votes do they get?" I flung out my hands in frustration.

"Only uh, one," Wyatt said. "And only when the vote involves all Addularchies and Rezoarchies. It has to be held within four days, with further arguments from both sides beforehand."

"Can my life get any worse?"

"I'll order tea." Tory strode toward the door, long legs eating the distance in less than three seconds.

"Thank goodness for tea," I sighed and slumped a shoulder against the window frame. "We can have a hot drink and dainty cakes while a hub world goes straight to Jufaleh."

∼

Royal Palace, Kwark

Zaria

I dreamed I woke in the middle of the night. I also dreamed that a Larentii sang to me—the song that will make anyone fall asleep. It should have been a Larentii I knew to dream about. Instead, the song held a timbre I'd never heard, and was followed by soft words, saying *sleep, little swan.*

Regardless, when Ilya woke me two hours before sunrise on Kwark, it was to let me know that the head chef and the chief steward were the ones who'd attempted to break into the suite.

Actually, the chief steward had keys to the suite, but, as he had no talent to subvert a powerful warlock's spell, he still couldn't get the doors open.

Both men were very surprised to find Bleek, Gerrett and Ilya standing behind them as they quietly discussed how to proceed.

~

"What should we do with them?" Ilya asked. I paced inside my sitting room while two men, restrained by a warlock's power and unable to move, sat on chairs looking quite guilty.

"They were duped—for a truckload of credits," I snapped, more at the chef and the steward than at Ilya. "They were led to believe that we'd only suffer indigestion from the additions to the cake, and only to the top layer, which was reserved for me and my husbands."

"Except that the entire cake was poisoned," Bleek crossed all four arms over his chest and glared at our prisoners.

"Who did they allow into the kitchen?" Edden asked.

"Someone who called himself Ethan Looms. Not sure he's the ultimate culprit, though. He may just be a middle man, and someone else paid him."

Zaria? Travis' voice interrupted.

Travis? What's wrong? I could tell by the tone of his sending that something was certainly amiss.

The ah, body in that barrel had Prophet's disease, and now we have three ASD investigators quarantined.

"Fuck," I said aloud.

"What's wrong?" Ilya stepped toward me.

"The barrel that was blown up in the warehouse on Murazal held a body infected by Prophet's disease. Now they have three investigators who are afflicted with the same malady."

"Do you think we need to?" Edden breathed without finishing the question.

"Yeah. I think we need to. Shall we take our perpetrators with us? I think they require a lesson or two in what it is they almost accomplished last night. We'll have to put Ethan Looms on the back burner for now."

"Get up, you're coming with us," Ilya growled at our captives.

"Who will take their places?" Edden asked.

"I'll ask around," I said. "On the way to Murazal."

"That'll take two days," the head chef thought to point out.

"Oh, I forgot," I retorted, letting my disguises fall. It's amazing how often people's mouths drop open when they're faced with a real Larentii.

"Well, you drooling son of a reptagator, do you have any other comments?" Ilya pulled the man to his feet. "If not, we'll be there in seconds."

~

"We sent all the remaining debris to Tiralia," Opal reported when we arrived at the remains of a former warehouse. It still looked like a pile of rubble, but it wasn't the original pile of rubble. Opal had replaced the tainted stuff.

"If we need to examine it further, I can *Pull* it away from there," I said with a sigh. Nearby, the chef and steward stared and blinked at where we were and what we were saying.

"Those two the ones who tried to kill you?" Kell stepped toward them and showed them his fangs.

"Yes, but they're only the last ones in that line," I said. "We have to track down the one who paid them, and then the one or ones who paid before that."

"We can ask Fes to fill in for the cook," Opal looked thoughtful.

"Fes Desh? You think he would?"

"If it's not for a long time," Opal replied. "As for the steward, well, Lynx might like a change of scenery."

"You think you can arrange that?"

"I think I can. Lynx already said yes."

"At least something is going right, then," I shook my head. "I'm going now to visit those three in the hospital. Who wants to come with me?"

~

"False alarm," the physician declared after a third set of tests came back negative. I'd *Changed What Was* for three men, when I shouldn't have had to.

"We're still looking for those responsible," Opal spoke quietly beside me as doors were opened on quarantine wards and three men walked out whole and healthy.

Opal and Kell had used their positions with the ASD to gain access to the floor in question, and then requested that more tests be run after I'd done what I could for the men infected.

"They'll be released now, and we'll send them home for a few days," Opal said. "This was a huge scare for them and their families."

"It was a scare for the entire planet," I grumped. "Thanks for getting Fes and Lynx for me. We have to go. I'll drop our miscreants off somewhere so they can't try to poison anyone else."

～

Royal Palace Kitchen, Kwark
 Fes Desh

"This came for you," a cook's assistant handed an envelope to me. My hand tingled when I accepted the rare paper packet, telling me there was something wrong with it.

"Come with me," I instructed the assistant, before grabbing him by the collar of his white coat and dragging him toward the head chef's office.

"Who else touched this?" I demanded after shutting the door. The young man's eyes widened at the veiled accusation in my voice.

Yes, I looked just like his former supervisor, and he was terrified of the man.

"I—it was delivered by your friend, who dropped by the other day. You know, that uh," he struggled to recall a name. "Athan? Ethan? Yes, Ethan. That friend."

"Has anyone else in the kitchen touched it?"

"N-no. Ethan handed it straight to me. He said you'd know why and left."

Zaria? I sent. *We have a problem in the kitchen.*

"He doesn't know anything, and I've neutralized the acid on his skin. Nothing else in the kitchen was affected by it." Zaria sounded weary. She looked weary, too, but I didn't express the obvious.

She'd let the kitchen assistant go back to work, after Halimel placed compulsion for him to recall only that the envelope was passed to the head chef.

"We have to find Ethan Looms, and soon," Ilya growled. "If he has more berolic acid, I want that disposed of, too."

"Then you get to look for him, I think," Zaria said. "Let me know if you need help."

"I'll go with Ilya," Halimel offered.

"Good," Zaria waved a hand. "Fes, I just had your duplicate walk into the kitchen and have a heart attack. I'll change your appearance to be your own replacement."

"I'll make sure the news is distributed, right after the royal physician makes the call and has the body removed," Edden offered.

"Good. Awesome. What's next on the agenda for me?" Zaria sighed.

"An afternoon meeting with six ranking members of the Council."

"Yippee. Bleek, will you come with me?"

Bleek, I sent, *if she so much as wobbles on the way, take her back to her suite and call off the meeting.*

I will, he promised. *Be assured of it.*

Zaria

I was tired.

Again.

The walk to the meeting hall would take ten minutes, because it was in the opposite wing of the palace. I never wanted to fold space so badly in my life, but I was determined to make it. Once there, I could set Zaria two-point-oh on autopilot and maybe nap for a while. Bleek would alert me if something came up that my faux persona couldn't handle.

We'd reached the far wing when I suddenly felt dizzy. Before things went dark, however, I heard many voices, some of them I certainly didn't recognize.

~

Larentii Archives

Nefrigar, Chief Archivist

"Do not chastise him. The child made his own decision in this. Valegar is not to blame."

Kalenegar studied me for several moments, although he knew I spoke the truth. Valegar could only make his own decision in this; the child overrode that decision and broke out of the shield himself.

"The child could be female."

"Yes, it certainly could. The odds are not in favor, as you well know."

"The question remains, will Zaria continue with her quest?"

"Are you willing to attempt to stop her?"

"No." Kalenegar held up a hand—a very human gesture.

"Zaria will be well aware of what her limits are from now on, I think. And, if the Mighty give permission, she will have Larentii guards about her at all times, Valegar included."

"Have you chosen a surrogate father, yet—to help with the pregnancy and teach the child afterward?"

"I have only learned this quite recently; there has been little time to make choices. There is something else to be considered, here."

"Which is?"

"That Zaria, in her own peculiar terminology, will be pissed."

I didn't add that Zaria had gotten pregnant in the future, rather than during present times. This meant I needed to speak with the Mighty, to determine whether the child should be born in this time or in the future, when he was conceived.

Father, Wisdom says the child needs to be born in this time, Valegar reported. *He said that the child understood in the future that he needed to come back—to free his mother for more important work in the years to come.*

Then tell Wisdom to come tell Kalenegar that himself; the Head of the Larentii Council is standing here with me in the Archives, looking much like a dark blue thundercloud.

He says he will come now.

Only a moment after Valegar sent mindspeech, he arrived with Wisdom. The name Charles no longer fit him, although some still called him that.

"So. There is a reason," Kalenegar lifted an eyebrow at Wisdom.

"Yes, there is an important reason, and the child knows it."

"I don't suppose you will tell this reason?"

"Of course not, and it isn't only because I don't know all of it. This is his journey. Telling anyone about a small part of it could change everything."

"The Larentii are well aware of what interference can do," Kalenegar replied stiffly.

"And that's why I haven't sought the whole story," Wisdom challenged. "The child knows something important and has made his presence known."

"Regardless, Zaria is four months pregnant. Now, and for the next seven months, do we have your permission to send Larentii to protect Zaria?" I asked the question foremost in my mind.

"Of course. The Vhanaraszh belongs to all of us."

Before I could ask him to explain, Wisdom vanished.

"I suppose we can interpret that any way we want, then," Valegar sighed. "I will go back to Zaria—she should be waking now, and no doubt will have a few words for me when she does."

"Underneath it all, she will be complaining about the situation, child. Nothing more," I reminded him.

"To quote Zaria, I will say, *says you.*"

Royal Palace, Kwark

Zaria

"It appears that the child circumvented Valegar's hold on him, and ah, made the journey to you, in the future," Renegar attempted to explain how things were.

"So I'm supposed to have words with the baby when he's born? I knew I shouldn't have stayed in the future as long as I did."

"How long did you stay?" Renegar inquired.

"Six months." I didn't hide my frustration; Ren already knew I was pissed.

"That explains why you're four months into the pregnancy," he dipped his head in a nod. "I was attempting to work that out."

"But a Larentii child requires eleven months to be born. That means another seven months," I grumped.

"It also means you will continue to tire easily, if you go on at this current pace. I hear that the Larentii have been given permission to help you in your self-assigned duties."

"Wisdom gave permission, I heard him say it myself," Valegar appeared, looking ashamed and contrite.

"Honey, I hear you didn't have anything to do with this. Sure, I feel like yelling, but it won't do any good to yell at you."

"I beg you not to have ill feelings toward the child," he knelt beside the bed and took my hand.

"I—can't. I'm sure he felt his reasons were sound ones. At least I know why I've been so tired since I started this mission."

"Someone will bend time whenever you need rest, to ensure that you get enough sleep and sunlight. Those things are important to both of you."

"Because the baby needs sunlight to develop properly." I shut my eyes and lay back on the pillows stacked behind my head.

Bleek had placed me on the bed and called immediately for help. Help had arrived in the form of Renegar, who'd then informed Nefrigar and Valegar of the situation.

The entire Larentii race likely knew by now.

At least they weren't hauling me off for sequestering; I figure they knew better than to try that.

"I see a lot of time-bending in the next seven months," I sighed.

~

Corez

Lissa

"Of course it wasn't planned," I hissed at Gavin. "Somehow, the baby decided—in the future, no less, that he'd hitch a ride to the past and be born now."

"How are the Larentii dealing with this?" Rigo asked softly. "Will she be risking too much to continue with this mission?"

"From what I hear from Connegar, she'll have a battalion of Larentii around her at all times, ready to jump in and do anything for her—if she'll let them."

"I hope they don't try to smother her," Winkler remarked. "She's quite independent and may not like so many surrounding her."

"I know. I'm still trying to come to terms with this, and I'm not personally involved."

"Except as a grandmother," Rigo told me.

"Yeah. Except for that."

"Have you asked to be included in regular reports?" That question came from Winkler.

"Connegar has volunteered to be one of the Larentii with Zaria. He has a great deal of experience with Larentii in the womb and can communicate with them. He's an ideal choice and will keep us informed."

"Good." Winkler visibly relaxed. He was worried about Zaria. Did he know that she'd been the catalyst to rescue him from the past? Perhaps he did know on some level and felt even more protective as a result.

I think she'll be taken care of, I sent to Winkler. *We have to believe that, anyway.*

Well, if they ever need a wolf to help, then tell them I'll make myself available.

Lissa? Merrill sent.

Merrill? I was surprised to hear from him.

Conner, Kiarra, Adam and I have volunteered to help out—with Zaria and with whatever needs doing. We'll fit ourselves in here and there, and not just in Zaria's court. We can be anywhere at a moment's notice, without being too obvious about it, he added. *On another note, I think the entire pod'l-morph nation has offered to help, if it will aid Zaria in any way.*

I wasn't surprised about the pod'l-morphs—Zaria had saved them from extinction on Siriaa. If D'slay was behind all this mess, he had a growing number of enemies determined to separate him from his life if he threatened her in any way.

Well, there's an idea—they can hide in plain sight anywhere, I replied.

I believe Ashe is considering which ones are suitable to send. I'll let you know when some are sent your way.

They need mindspeech, I warned. *Even if it's only temporary.*

They'll have what they need for this task. This will give us eyes in many places.

Yes, it will. They may be needed, more than we know. I suggest we start with the worlds experiencing unrest—and the other six hub worlds. We need suitable spies in all those places, and someone to gather their reports and distribute them to the necessary people.

We'll be on that in an hour, Merrill promised.

Presidential Palace, Murazal

Travis

"I'm only authorized to give you temporary mindspeech, until this mission is over," Opal informed Rajeon, as she placed hands on either side of his face. "If it's deserved, perhaps one day it can be given permanently, but that will have to come from someone else."

"I'm grateful," Rajeon told her.

"As are the rest of us," I said. "This way, we can communicate without leaving anyone out."

"There, it's done," Opal let her hands drop. "Go forth and have mindspeech," she smiled.

"Is Zaria really, well, with child?" Zanfield asked what we all wanted to know.

"Yes. Expect a flood of Larentii helping out, and there may be more pod'l-morphs scattered throughout, too. They'll act as extra eyes and ears. Ashe is choosing from a list of volunteers, now."

"Will she be all right?" Zanfield was concerned. I think we all were, we just didn't say it aloud.

"I think the Larentii will make certain of it," Opal reassured him. "Children aren't common for them, and each pregnancy and birth is a cause for rejoicing."

"Then let's hope for a successful mission and an easy birth," Trent said.

"I have to go, now. I don't need to remind you to take care; many things are moving within the universes, and some of them are carried on ill winds," Opal advised.

She was right—Randl said almost the same thing. Things were moving, and we had to separate the bad from the good and then do something about it.

It's why you and I are bonded, Vallon reminded me. *As my twin, Hallon, is bonded with Trent. You have walked between time with the Soul of the Worlds. That is also why we chose you.*

Royal Palace, Galk
  Reah

"I connected with Quin," Bel Erland reported. "She says Rezo Nilus isn't obsessed. I believe a complete change in his opinion would be far too obvious. If the re-vote is demanded by the Council, it'll probably mean that one or two who were on the fence will be obsessed to change their votes."

"The Council is requesting a tally for a re-vote," Tory held out his comp-vid. "You have to register your decision in the matter, but you only have one voice in this, same as any other."

"I know." I took the comp-vid from him and tapped my decision against a re-vote. "I have no doubt that at the end of the day, we'll be looking at all the Council, to see who's been obsessed. We won't have much time to track the one placing the obsession, either, before the re-vote is cast."

"I'll start working with Quin on it," Bel Erland said and stalked toward the door.

"He is so much like his grandfather Erland it's shocking," Tory murmured.

"And very much like who he was in his former life," I looked up at Tory. Wizard Bel had been a very good spy, and Erland could fit in anywhere and convince anyone to trust him while he learned everything there was to know about them.

Bel Erland was certainly showing his heritage.

"I can place compulsion if it's necessary to change votes to offset any ah, obsessions," Wyatt cleared his throat.

He could. Like his father, Wyatt was a King Vampire, but he didn't employ that legacy often. He felt it gave him an unfair advantage. In this case, his ability could be more than a blessing.

"Stay in contact with your brother, then. I don't want anything to happen to either of you."

"Mom, we'll keep you in the loop." Wyatt grinned as he turned to mist and went in search of Bel Erland.

"Ocenosek and Cudworth told me this morning, before they went off-duty, that they've notice unusual activity with the cleaning crew at night," Denevik informed me.

"What sort of unusual activity?"

"Moving of statuary and other art pieces, in the rotunda and in other locations inside the palace."

"It could just be changing displays," I said. "Museums and other places do it on a rotational basis, so all the collection can be seen. I'm sure there's a massive room filled with that stuff here somewhere."

"With your permission, I'd like to follow up," Denevik said.

"Of course. You'll let me know what you find?"

"Yes, Granddaughter, I will certainly let you know." He gave me a smile, then; one I hadn't seen in a very long time.

I thought to ask as he turned to go, "What are you going to do first?"

"Ask Cudworth and Ocenosek more detailed questions—they'll wake for a meal in three hours. I'll join them."

"Call Tory or me if you need help."

"I will."

I watched him walk out of the study, leaving only Tory with me. I wasn't worried; if he and I couldn't handle an attack against us, our alter-egos most likely could. "Tell me about what happened on A'pelur," I said, taking his hand and leading him toward a sofa against the opposite wall. "I want to hear about the Prophet's attack and how it was circumvented."

"Our ranos rifles' charges ran out and the weapons were worthless, except to bludgeon the corpses attacking us," Tory began as we settled on the sofa. "That barely helped, as the dead would rise up again and attack a second time."

"How many—of these corpses were there?" I breathed, confounded on how anyone could force the dead to leave their graves and attack the living.

"Thousands. Tens of thousands. If we hadn't been protected by these," he withdrew the gold medallion he wore around his neck for me to see, "most of us would have been infected by the Prophet's disease, because those corpses were filled with it. Every time we fired our weapons and a corpse exploded, the disease was blasted into the air."

"That's terrifying," I shivered.

"The Prophet is terrifying," Tory replied. "If Randl hadn't come at the last, and if Meerius hadn't joined me," his voice trailed off.

"I'm glad you made it out of there. I'm glad you didn't die," I sighed, leaning my head against the back of the sofa and closing my eyes.

"Why?"

"Because I still love you, you difik."

CHAPTER 10

*R*oyal Palace, Hraede
Phrinnis Tampirus

"When did you get this?" Queen Mephista asked Alrenardo, as she fingered the fronds on the cheefuu palm that I'd become. My roots were coiled in sandy soil in a giant, decorative pot inside the King's private quarters.

I feared Alrenardo, disguised as King Larvalis, may have been too attentive to the Queen recently, and that had precipitated her visit to his suite following a banquet the night before.

"Someone suggested that I needed more greenery in my private space. I believe it was good advice."

"So, you're starting with the largest, and working your way down?"

"One might think so. When I asked for a small tree, this is what was delivered," Alrenardo gestured toward me. "I had no idea the lengths my subjects will go, just to provide me with plants."

"So, you're having more delivered?" She lifted an eyebrow at him.

"Are you joking? Look at the thing," he shook his head. "What will they bring if I ask for something shorter? An entire flowerbed?"

Mephista barked a laugh at his words; I could tell that hadn't occurred before in any of their conversations. In truth, I doubted that any conversation between Larvalis and Mephista was more than stilted tripe until Alrenardo's arrival.

We have eyes on Naril, Nissa broke into Alrenardo's and my thoughts.

Alrenardo turned swiftly in my direction, sizing up the situation with the speed of an ancient vampire.

Where? He included me in his reply to Nissa.

He's with a delivery van at the back door of the palace kitchen. He's also wearing extremely dark goggles in full daylight.

"Stay here; you will not recall my disappearance," Alrenardo placed compulsion on Mephista. Her eyes widened but she didn't move. As I returned to myself, Alrenardo pulled me into his mist and raced toward the ground floor of the palace.

Nissa

Illusion spells, I mentally shouted at Toff and Trik while I spun a shield around Alrenardo, Tamp and Naril. Both vampires were now circling one another, fangs and claws out, red eyes alight as they sized one another up. My hastily-constructed shield kept them invisible to the other workers unloading the delivery truck.

I hoped Alrenardo knew to keep Naril alive if he could; we needed information that only he might have.

Naril ignored Tamp—to him, the pod'l-morph was a much lesser threat than another vampire. Naril lunged toward Alrenardo; Tamp chose that moment to show Naril what his talents were.

"Alrenardo went back to his conversation with the Queen. Tamp, as you can see, is the one who latched onto Naril." I explained what I knew to Aunt Bree, who stood next to me in Mom's palace dungeon, where a diamond-thorned Tamp held onto a wriggling, uncomfortable Naril.

"Well, well. What's Naril been up to, lately?" Bree stepped forward until her eyes locked with his; she could read him as easily as Zaria or Quin could. I waited to hear what Bree saw in him.

After only a few seconds, Bree gestured toward an empty cell. The door opened when she exerted only a bit of power. "Toss him in," she told Tamp.

Tamp's thick, diamond vines and thorns moved, before shooting Naril into the cell like a cannonball. Naril hit the back wall, rolled and came up cursing as Bree closed the cell door with a heavy clang.

"You won't make your meeting," Bree told Naril casually. "But somebody will. If you'll come with me?" She nodded to me and to Tamp, who'd returned to his humanoid shape.

Naril was still hissing and cursing when we were folded away by Bree. "I'll have somebody go down and lay compulsion," Bree sighed as we landed in the library. "Naril is supposed to meet with the one who signed him up to form a new Rith Naeri. I'll have someone bring drinks and snacks while I figure out who to send back with you."

~

State House, Corez

   Lissa

Of course we want to go, I responded to Bree's mindspeech. *Rigo really wants to know who's behind this. It's his reputation, after all.*

   Are you available to go now?

   We have a few minutes. I can bend time to get us back. Get another cell ready, in case we need it.

   I have one waiting. She rattled off the name of the tavern where Naril arranged to meet his contact.

   Rigo needs to be wearing really dark goggles, she sent an image of what Naril had looked like in his. I imagine the device on his neck and those dark goggles had ensured he'd be awake and unfried during daylight.

   I'll make sure he's presentable, and I'll be right beside him as mist.

   Good. Let me know if you need anything.

Oh, rest assured, I said. *We'll be there on time, as requested.*

"Rigo," I turned to him. "I have to make you look like Naril, dark-colored goggles and all." I set about transforming the former King of Hraede before folding us to a tavern on that planet.

We had a meeting scheduled.

"It will be all right," Rigo mumbled, squaring his shoulders and preparing to walk into a foul-smelling tavern in a suburb of the capital city. As mist, I floated next to him, waiting for him to cross the street and enter the low, squat building.

Near the door and leaning against the side of the building, Tamp stood as if waiting for a friend. Just as Rigo took his first step forward, Nissa came walking toward Tamp. He offered her his arm and they went in ahead of us.

Keep your eyes open, hon, I told her.

We're on it, Mom, she replied.

The scent of soured beer and vomit hit us as we reached the door; it was apparent that cleanliness wasn't a priority in this fine establishment.

I moved to hover over Rigo's head, waiting to see whether the one we were supposed to meet was already here.

"Take the empty booth at the back," a server hissed as she handed a beer to Rigo and brushed past him.

As instructed, Rigo headed for the booth in question. A hooded figure sat there, wearing a cloak so dark it blended with the stained wainscoting of the wall. I got a sniff, which sent alarms ringing through my brain.

Sirenali, I hissed at Rigo. *Female,* I added, before slapping the toughest shield I could around her and shouting for Nissa and Tamp to follow us back to my dungeon.

"Well, she's not gonna talk to us like that." Bree's arms were tightly crossed as she studied the Sirenali, who'd gone scaly-fangy on us, while hissing and clawing at the bars of her cell.

She'd discovered quickly that she couldn't fold herself away; my shield wouldn't allow it. Therefore, she was refusing to cooperate.

"Can you see anything in her?"

"I can't see past the obsession another Sirenali placed on her," Bree grumped. "I think she's some sort of hybrid—susceptible only to certain Sirenalis' obsessions, while still being able to place her own."

"You think the Prophet's behind this—or D'slay, or both?"

"No idea, but it has to be at least one of them, right? What I'm surprised about is that she didn't obsess Naril."

"You think that's by design? Were they waiting for Naril to be followed, so they could see who came in after him?" I'm sure they told her to place obsession on whomever it was and bring them into the fold as a double agent. Somebody may be waiting outside the tavern, watching."

"Tamp and I can go back," Nissa offered quietly.

"No," I said immediately. "We need a mister. Rigo, who's available in the Rith Naeri right now?"

"Yan can go." Rigo didn't like sending another in when he wanted to go himself.

"I can get him there," Bree offered, "if you two need to go back. If I learn anything from scaly britches, here, I'll let you know."

"Thanks, Bree." I gave her a quick hug and folded back to Corez with Rigo.

Tamp

"Yan can take me inside his mist. I can be quite useful—and discreet when needed," I told Breanne.

"Fine. Nissa, go on back to Hraede. I'll send Tamp with Yan."

"You called for me?" Yan appeared in the dungeon with us—he'd misted in. His full name was Yandiveri, but he only went by Yan.

"We have a tavern to visit on Hraede," I told him. "I wish to be included in your mist when we investigate."

"Are you ready?" Bree asked.

"Yes," Yan replied. With barely any effort, Breanne sent us back to Hraede, and straight to the tavern in question. We searched the areas surrounding the bar and found nothing. *Had our spy gone inside?*

The barmaid sent Lissa and Rigo to the proper table; shall we start with her? I sent to Yan. He and I hovered as mist near the tavern's ceiling, studying the patrons and employees of The Black Boot, which was as close to appropriate as I could imagine. The place smelled of sweat and stale beer to me.

I'll have to wait until she goes to the back to place compulsion, Yan replied.

Just get me close; I'll see if there's anything she knows, Zaria's voice sounded in our heads.

As instructed, Yan moved lower until we faced the barmaid, who was pouring beer into tall mugs behind the bar.

She was obsessed, Zaria observed. *Show me the others there.*

We went to three tables with nothing noteworthy from those patrons. The fourth table, however, Yan and I felt Zaria's mental shiver. *Wait until that one leaves, follow him out and grab him,* Zaria instructed. *We'll come get him from you.*

We? I asked.

Well, at least three Larentii and I will. Show me the others while you're waiting. We'll see if they need to be picked up, too.

Royal Palace, Kwark

Zaria

Connegar, Daragar and Valegar were coming to Hraede with me, while leaving two other Larentii behind, in case my doppelganger was required. They could recreate anyone they chose if it became necessary.

"I shall take us," Connegar smiled as I looked up at him. He was quite tall—taller than Val or Daragar.

"Come," Valegar lifted me in his arms. "I will ensure that none think to attack you."

"Fine," I grumbled against his shoulder. He chuckled, which caused his chest to rumble beneath my ear.

Connegar folded space; soon, we stood outside a smelly tavern on Hraede, waiting for a certain criminal to depart. Tamp and Yan, as mist, would be right behind him.

We're outside, I sent to Tamp. *You'll be able to see us, but nobody else will.*

Good. He just finished his last beer and is waiting for his credit chip to be scanned. How are you feeling? he added.

Fine for the most part. I've been feeling queasy today, but that could be anything. At least we're in sunlight right now, so that's a plus.

Still an hour or two of sunlight left, he replied. *He's getting up. We'll be out in a few.*

Tamp was right—the man walked out of the tavern, probably slower and more wobbly than he went in.

I have a shield around him, Daragar reported.

I've created his duplicate, which will continue walking down the street for a little way, Val said.

I've gathered the misting ones, Connegar added.

In moments, we landed in Lissa's library, where the man vomited inside the shield Daragar constructed.

If he hadn't been inside a shield, one of Lissa's priceless, Serendaan rugs would have been ruined.

Temporarily.

~

"He hasn't been obsessed, but he's seen D'slay," I paced in front of Ethan Looms. "You sure get around, don't you?" I stopped in front of him. "What with working with D'slay and all."

"D'slay?" Ethan frowned at me.

"Oh, that's right. He didn't tell you his real name, did he? As long as the money's good, you really don't care."

"What was he doing in that tavern?" Tamp asked.

"He was there to witness the obsession of Naril and whoever followed him in, by scaly-pants in the dungeon downstairs," I said.

"Who do we have here?" Bree appeared, looking like herself rather than Lissa.

"Ethan Looms. Ilya and Halimel have been looking all over Kwark for him."

"The one who tried to poison you?" Bree was now glaring at Ethan.

"That's the one. Doesn't look like much, does he? Almost barfed on Lissa's rug, too."

"Had too much beer, after the ones he was watching disappeared right in front of him. He wasn't sure what to tell his boss," Bree nodded. She'd seen the same thing I had—that Ethan was getting drunk after a mysteriously failed mission.

"You can stop wondering where they went; they're both in the dungeon several floors beneath your feet," Bree told Ethan. "It's where you'll be after we finish picking you apart."

Ethan shifted uncomfortably in his chair; he wasn't sure what Bree meant about picking him apart. He was imagining physical torture. Frankly, my queasiness had ramped up and I wasn't in the mood for anything of the sort.

"Where was D'slay when Ethan saw him?" Ilya had folded in, bringing Halimel with him.

"On Kwark." I shook my head and immediately regretted it; the movement made me dizzy.

Val, I don't feel so good, I sent.

"We'll be back," Val announced, and, with Connegar and Daragar, we folded away.

"Honey, where are we?" I blinked my eyes open to see Val's worried face above mine.

"A beach on the Larentii homeworld," he said. "You needed sunlight, and, as this was a sunny, cooler place at the moment, it also serves to cool your body temperature, which was rising above normal."

"Here," Connegar, who was somehow sitting behind me, placed sunglasses on my face so I wouldn't be blinded by the sun overhead.

"At least my stomach feels better," I sighed.

"The child was pulling too much energy," Val murmured. "Connegar has spoken to him about this. It may be that you'll need much more sunlight than you've been getting."

"Huh? Is that normal?" I tilted my head back so I could see Connegar's face again.

"I believe it is normal for this one," Connegar smiled at me. "Stop worrying; all will go as it will."

"Do we need to get back?" I asked.

"Why do you ask?"

"Because I'm comfortable," I replied. "I think I'd like another nap."

"Dearest, we will bend time. Sleep as long as you like," Val leaned down to kiss me, then began trilling to help me sleep again.

Larentii Archives

Nefrigar

"Valegar and Daragar are with her. You should begin your preparation to record the child's journey now," Connegar reported.

"You've spoken to the child?"

"Yes. Let me say this, and this only; Zarigar will come early, and his talents may be such that we haven't seen them before."

"Some Larentii children do come early—it is out of concern for their mothers, who may not be prepared to deliver a fully-developed Larentii. We tend to be large when we're born," I stated the obvious.

"Zarigar is certainly concerned for his mother, but that is not the whole reason. As his paternal grandfather, you will see this for yourself soon enough."

Connegar's words concerned me. "Do you believe Wisdom had something planned when he ah, arranged DNA to produce Zaria?"

"I hesitate to assign specific reasons to anything the Mighty may do, but I am cautiously optimistic about this. This isn't only Valegar's child, and since Zarigar has a Larentii mother, he will certainly draw much from her."

"As it should have always been," I agreed. "Ferrigar is no longer with us, but he still has much to answer for since he affected the entire race with his selfish decisions."

"Kalenegar and all the Wise Ones disagreed with him at the time, and yet he made his choices anyway," Connegar conceded. "I was not alive, then, although I have gone back to observe."

"As have many others. It is not an easy thing to witness, as you know. I, too, attempted to reason with Ferrigar, but he would not listen."

"He was only thinking of the pain he felt—at what he saw as his daughter's defection from the race."

"Now, her Larentii blood is diluted and scattered throughout the Grey House wizards, who are more talented than any others," I pointed out. "Even Ferrigar eventually saw them as kin, although he only knew a few of them well."

"At least the talent has to be deliberately awakened in any child born," Connegar stated. "It keeps the talent pure and belonging only to Grey House."

"For which the Larentii race as a whole should be grateful. Have you told Zaria yet that the child will come early?"

"Not yet. I believe she will determine that soon enough on her own."

"Tell my son to take care of her and the child—they are both precious to me and to the entire race."

"That goes without saying, but I'll tell him anyway," Connegar smiled before disappearing.

~

Royal Palace, Galk

Reah

"What do you mean, Rezo Nilus has disappeared?" I sounded frantic, because I was.

"It had to be sometime between when I had tea with him and the dinner hour. I've already contacted security, and they're checking every recording device in and out of the Palace, in addition to contacting anyone who is remotely connected to him. He doesn't have any family here; his wife died two years ago, and his son is off-world in the military," Bel Erland reported.

"Put Lissa and the others on alert," I snapped.

"On it," Wyatt told me.

"Has Denevik reported back, yet?" I asked Tory.

"Not yet. Want me to find him?"

"Please. Maybe he saw or heard something while on his quest."

I watched as Tory sent mindspeech, then *skipped* away without telling me where he was going. So far, he hadn't taken advantage of the news that I still loved him—beyond a hug or two. I could tell he was processing everything, however.

This Tory—I wish he'd been the one with me all along, rather than the broken High Demon who couldn't be fixed—until Zaria remade him by *Changing What Was*. I saw no prejudice in him—no petty jealousy. What I did see was loyalty—and love. The final choice would be his—to remain my mate or dissolve that part of our lives completely.

I'm bringing Denevik back with me, Tory reported. *He has a few things to tell you.*

~

"I had to ask the Larentii filling in for Zaria for help; she was sleeping when I contacted her," Denevik said. "But we got all the statuary evacuated and exact replicas set up without even the slightest hint of what was happening."

"How in the name of Jufaleh did they sneak in bodies infected with Prophet's disease?" I demanded. "Where is the night crew now? We have to question every one of them."

"Cudworth and Ocenosek are determined to round them up when they come on duty, and they'll investigate whether any are now missing."

"Did they even know what they were handling?" Tory asked. "Do they know they could be infected, too?"

"This is worse than I could ever imagine," I breathed a troubled sigh.

"It may be worse than that," Tory pulled me against him and whispered into my hair. "Prophet's disease can spread faster than wildfire and can be transmitted through sex. We don't think the Prophet knows that last part, yet, and we sure don't want him to find out. Don't worry, High Demons are immune, as are pod'l-morphs and a few others."

"Explain that to me—what, exactly, is Prophet's disease?"

"It's a way of spreading obsession through an infection," Tory pulled away to face Denevik. Frankly, I wasn't ready for him to stop hugging me. "Whenever one person gets infected, it can spread through sex, or through autopsy if the one infected dies and the medical examiner doesn't take every precaution. It can be carried from the deceased's organs into the air and breathed in. Or, if the body explodes, which is a favorite method for the Prophet to infect others, it'll infect anyone the infected bits get near."

"Why would he want so many infected?" Denevik asked.

"For control. Most people don't know they're infected, until the Prophet crooks his finger and they can't help but do his bidding."

"That's," Denevik searched for an appropriate term.

"It's fucking scary, that's what it is," Tory said. "Now you know what Randl and the rest of us who work with him are fighting against. If we fail, the entire universes will fall under the Prophet's rule."

"And you think D'slay is a minion in the Prophet's army, don't you?" Denevik asked.

"Yes. They're connected in some way. We're still trying to work that out."

"Where were the bodies and sculptures sent?" I thought to ask.

"To Tiralia. Right now, it's the dumping ground for this stuff."

"I want to be in on the questioning of the night crew," I stated flatly, expecting Tory and Denevik to argue with me.

"I was hoping you'd say that," Tory nodded. "We need another guli."

Kabbuc Mountain, Mardir
D'slay

"It isn't lost if we know where it is." I almost lost patience with the one who identified himself as Alken Wilker. If only he knew I had a wizard under my thumb, one far stronger than he had ever been as a warlock.

"They weren't supposed to find the bodies. It is our choice when to detonate those artifacts and release the disease. We took your word when you said the barrel on Murazal was a mistake, but this—it is too much. So far, the only thing you've done right is to kill the chef on Kwark—the royals are still alive."

"Yes, but I have information you don't have," I snapped at Alken. "The real Queen was obsessed by me, as were many on the other hub worlds. The only reason those royals are still alive is that they aren't the actual royals. We have powerful operators standing in for two Queens, the First Advisor, the President and a King. I have no idea where the real leaders are, but those in place now are certainly not the real thing."

"Powerful operators? Who are they? Do you even know, or are you trying to buy time? My superior will not be pleased by your failures."

"Finding their identities is only a matter of time; I am working toward that goal now. Should your superior, as you call him, desire to watch even bigger heads topple, then sit back and enjoy the show."

"You have three weeks," Alken growled before terminating the secure communication.

"Hear that, Toad?" I turned to my wizard, who cowered in a corner. "You have three weeks to find the information for me. Fail to do so and you will certainly regret it. You still have a few bits of unmarked skin for me to flay."

~

Royal Palace, Galk

Reah

Are any of them obsessed? I asked Bel Erland.

Quin says those three at the back are the only ones. She says six others were paid by those three to make the changes, although they had no idea what they were actually putting in the rotunda.

Standing at the doors in the very back of the meeting room stood Ocenosek and Cudworth, with hands on the weapons hanging from their belts. Both were tall, muscular and looked quite able to fend off an attack from three obsessed servants.

I hoped it wouldn't come to that; I wanted them to submit to cuffing peacefully, and that included the six others they'd paid to cooperate.

Anyone else involved in any part of this? I asked Bel Erland.

No. A few noticed the changes, but thought they'd been ordered by someone higher up the chain of command.

Good. Call out the names in question and ask them to stay behind. Send the others back to their stations.

"The Queen wishes to speak with the following employees," Bel Erland began. "If your name isn't called, you may leave and resume your duties." He then announced nine names and dismissed the others. Six of those staying behind began fidgeting in their seats.

The other three sat still as stone. Somehow, that concerned me a great deal. "I think we need to get those three out of here," Wyatt whispered.

Without waiting for my reply, Bel Erland cast a spell that flung all three to Galk's smallest moon, where they blasted a very deep crater upon detonation.

CHAPTER 11

oyal Palace, Galk
  Reah

The six who'd been paid tried to run the moment the other three disappeared.

That was a mistake; Ocenosek and Cudworth had them gathered and sitting again in no time, some of them slightly ruffled and showing purple bruising.

"Where are the others?" One of the prisoners demanded.

"They were carrying explosives," Tory stalked forward, a drift of smoke escaping his nostrils. "They were commanded to kill all of us. Now, aren't you glad we had a warlock to move them away from here?"

"They're—dead?"

"The explosives detonated," Bel Erland confirmed. "And there's a rather large crater on Smallmoon to attest to that."

"What we really want to know from you six, before we place all of you in custody for conspiring against the Queen, is whether you know anything at all about Rezo Nilus' disappearance." Tory's long arms crossed over his chest as he glared at the captives.

Quin says they aren't involved, and the three who are now dead were obsessed, so she couldn't get past that, Bel Erland reported.

"I didn't know he was missing," another captive spoke.

"Truth," I sighed and shook my head. "They don't know anything. We're back to the beginning on finding our missing Rezo."

"The longer he's missing, the worse it may be for him," Denevik stated quietly. "I'll help get these six to the lockup and arrange for the proper authorities to charge them with their crimes."

Royal Palace, Kwark
Zaria

"I feel better," I told Ilya and the others when Valegar brought me back to the palace. "Rested, at least."

"You're beginning to show," Bleek grinned. "I like that."

"Honey, Val has that part disguised to anyone except those who know already."

"There's a missing Rezo on Galk," Edden sighed. "They can't find him anywhere, and he's a pivotal point in a scheduled re-vote."

"That's not good. Val, will you take us to Galk?"

"We will take you to Galk," Val smiled as Connegar and Daragar nodded agreement.

Reemagar would have to pretend to be the Queen of Kwark for a while longer, but he was a student of, and reveled in court politics, so I doubted it was a hardship for him.

"The last time anyone saw him was when Rezo Nilus invited Bel Erland for tea yesterday morning," Reah paced inside the Queen's study.

"What time did you leave him?" I turned to ask Bel Erland.

"Half-past eleven bells; we were in his office in the western wing, talking about the re-vote and discussing who might change their votes if pressure were applied."

"I suppose you wish to bend time again?" Val lifted an eyebrow.

"I think I can handle that part," I told him. "I haven't done anything except sleep for a day and a half."

"We will bend time," Connegar said. "That much we can do. Anything needed past that should be left in your hands, as the Vhanaraszh."

"I'd like to come," Reah said.

"Then let's go," I told her. "Time's wasting."

Connegar took us back to the time indicated, to find Bel Erland saying good-bye to Rezo Nilus. The moment Bel Erland walked out the door and shut it behind him, Rezo Nilus disappeared, as if he'd been jerked away with power.

Reah shouted her protest beside me, but it was cut off as something happened that none of us expected, including the Larentii surrounding us.

Reah

The moment we landed in that dim, filthy building, it was to find a tortured Rezo Nilus hanging from cruel chains while two men nearby prepared to shoot him with laser pistols.

Without hesitation, Zaria flung out a hand, rendering both men to winking sparks as she separated their particles. Changing to my larger Thifilatha, I gently released the chains hanging over a hook above Rezo Nilus' head.

"We're in the future," Zaria hissed as she began healing Rezo Nilus before I'd even disengaged him from his chains.

"What?" I looked down at her in alarm.

"I don't know how we got here, but this is the future—three days in the future. I have no idea how this happened," she added, sounding slightly frightened.

"We do not know either," Connegar and Valegar helped lower Rezo

Nilus to the floor so Zaria could tend him. He was unconscious, with cuts, bruises and signs of burns all over his naked body.

I watched Zaria heal the worst of the man's wounds, before nodding to Valegar. Val lifted Rezo Nilus in his arms. "We can go back now; he's stable," Zaria said. Realizing I was still Thifilatha, I changed back to myself and expressed agreement.

Daragar took us back to my study, where and when we'd left it.

"He needs more healing," Zaria said immediately when Bel Erland shouted his relief at seeing Rezo Nilus.

"Where should we take him to recuperate?" I asked.

"I'll take him to Quin," Zaria said. "She and I together can make him whole, and she can help him with any psychological issues that may stem from this torture."

"Did you get a look at those two men before you killed them?" I asked.

"I can discuss that with you later. Val, will you take us to Avii Castle?"

"I will take you," Daragar said. "It will give me pleasure to see my Quin."

"Let's go," Zaria sighed. "I put him in a healing sleep, but he needs food and more healing quickly."

I watched Zaria and her Larentii bodyguards disappear, taking Rezo Nilus with them. I hoped for a full recovery, but after something like this, healing the mind could be a tricky business.

"If anybody can get him on his feet in time for the re-vote, Zaria will," Tory came to me. Without hesitating, I put my arms about him. He obliged by holding me tightly. "We have to create a cover story for Rezo Nilus," I mumbled against Tory's chest. "And we still have to figure out if anyone else has been obsessed or pressured to change their vote."

~

Avii Castle, Le-Ath Veronis
  Zaria

"You're safe and with friends," I told Rezo Nilus, who stared at Quin's red wings as if he'd landed in a bizarre fairy tale.

"I've heard of the Avii, and I've seen images, certainly, but this is beyond my imagination," he sighed. "Who rescued me? The last I knew, my captors intended to kill me after the vote was cast."

"I and a few others rescued you," I told him. "The vote hasn't been cast, yet," I added. "It's a bit complicated, too. You have one more day to rest and recover before we take you back. For now, your Queen is determining what sort of tale will account for your absence. We are still looking for those who pulled you away; the two men who were preparing to kill you didn't have that kind of power."

"If you don't mind my asking, how did you rescue me?"

"Like this." I became my Larentii self. "Three other Larentii assisted me."

"I have never been important enough to be rescued by Larentii."

"Don't sell yourself short," I told Rezo Nilus. "We're trying to keep hub worlds from falling into chaos and ruin. If that happens, well," I shrugged and became Zaria again.

"It means the entire Alliance could fall into chaos and ruin," Rezo Nilus muttered.

"Exactly."

"Is it possible to get out of this confounded bed? I feel fine," he said.

"Of course. All you have to do is get up and walk wherever you want," Quin smiled at him. "I will warn you, you are in a room connected to the library in Avii Castle. It is quite high up, with a multitude of stairs to consider if you don't have wings."

"Breakfast is on the way, too," I told him. "If you want, you can eat on the balcony outside this room."

"Is it sunny there?"

"It is," Quin acknowledged.

"Then I'll have breakfast there."

"How is he?" Lissa appeared inside the room.

"Queen Lissa?" Rizo Nilus breathed. "I never thought I'd meet you in person."

"I'm here," she said. "May I have breakfast with you? We really need to talk—about Galk, Kwark and a few other hub worlds."

~

"You're actually the one in charge of Galk, as the highest ranking member of the Council—the real King and Queen of Galk are in a safe place on Avendor. Three other hub worlds are in the same predicament; we've replaced the leaders, because the leaders had been obsessed by Sirenali, and that isn't a good thing."

Lissa's explanation brought a few eyebrow-lifts from Rezo Nilus; otherwise, he remained silent and processed the information carefully.

"Who is acting as the Queen of Galk, then?" he finally asked

"The Queen of Kifirin," Lissa replied. "One of my mates is acting as First Advisor on Corez, and I'm there with him, making sure nothing goes wrong."

"I'm on Kwark with six of my mates and two other Larentii," I said. "My brother is acting as President of Murazal, and a former King of Hraede, who is now a vampire, is in charge of Hraede."

"Why are you telling me this?" he asked.

"Because we find you trustworthy, and someone should know what's going on, don't you think?"

"Who is actually in charge of all this? Someone must be," Rezo Nilus pointed out.

"I suppose I am. When I found out what was happening, and that hub worlds were in danger and their leaders obsessed, I pulled in others who weren't susceptible and could take care of themselves in most situations."

"There are some not susceptible to Sirenali obsession? I must have misunderstood when I researched it a few years ago."

"There are some races who can't be obsessed. High Demons are one of those races. Very old vampires are immune, sometimes. Pod'l-morphs are immune. The powerful are immune, and the Larentii are certainly immune," Lissa replied.

"Powerful?"

"You may think of them as gods," I explained.

"Again, I have no idea why you're explaining this to me. It may be better if I didn't know."

"Because I interfered, and saved your life," I told him. "The only thing I can do now is make you a member of the Hierarchy, unless you want to be vampire."

"Hierarchy?"

"A low-level god. You won't be able to have children, but you already have a son. You'll also be immortal, and able to do some amazing things. Of course, you'll have to fake your death after this mission is over, but at least you can choose which way you'll check out."

"What do I do after that?"

"What all the Hierarchy does. You'd be amazed at just who you may know that are members."

"Such as?"

Lissa raised her hand. "The Queen of Kifirin is also a member, as are those looking after the leaders of the hub worlds."

"But what about you?" Rezo Nilus frowned at me.

"I have a different role to play and am not bound by the usual rules the Hierarchy abide by, and such is my daughter, here." I leaned over to hug Quin.

"It's a bit of an explanation. If you join the Hierarchy, you'll understand it better," Quin smiled at him.

"I should have died." Rezo Nilus absorbed that information. "What does becoming a member of the Hierarchy entail?"

"I can confer that status," Lissa told him. "You'll sleep afterward, and when you wake, you'll be younger and more powerful than you've ever been. You can disguise yourself to look as you do now, and if you need help with anything, send mindspeech. I can guide you."

"I'll have mindspeech?"

"Yes. You can communicate with Queen Reah at any time, once you've transformed."

"And if I turn down this opportunity?"

"Then I have to take you back and allow you to die at the mercy of those two men. The re-vote will occur and go the wrong way, and Galk will eventually become a casualty to those who wish the Alliances to fall."

"I'm ready whenever you are," he told Lissa.

"Finish your food, I kept it warm for you," she smiled at him.

"I can keep my food warm?"

"And your tea and your blankets on a cold night."

"Even the air around you—or keep it cool if it's hot," I said.

"Thank you," he nodded to Lissa. "Very much."

Royal Palace, Hraede

Tamp

"I want you to see something in the Hall of Kings," Alrenardo coaxed the Queen, after sharing breakfast with her. She was suspicious, but not nearly as much as she would be if King Larvalis had been the one to ask.

I wasn't sure this was a good idea, but he was right; she deserved to know what we were dealing with.

I'd sent a message to Zaria, letting her know of Alrenardo's plans; she responded by sending a medallion for Queen Mephista. It would protect her from many things, but obsession was at the top of that list.

Alrenardo was falling for Mephista—there was no doubt of it, and she was warming up to him—Larvalis had never made her laugh. Alrenardo did so every day.

I pretended to be a discreet guard behind both as they walked toward the Hall of Kings. With the medallion securely in my pocket, I waited for the outcome of this revelation. If she reacted badly, compulsion would be laid and that would be the end of it. If she were intrigued or reacted in a positive way, then the medallion would be offered and her protection assured.

There were still two Rith Naeri pretenders somewhere, and as they were vampires, they could get past most people who stood in their way.

Nissa, Toff and Trik were on guard constantly; if the Queen accepted her medallion, I would take her and Alrenardo for a visit, and let her know that the real King and his mistress were elsewhere and kept safe.

Not that Mephista would miss either of them, in all honesty.

"I always get shivers when I walk in here," Mephista confided in Alrenardo as they passed the high, decorative doorway in the Hall of Kings, where statues and paintings were kept of all the Kings of Hraede.

"Which is your favorite?" Alrenardo pulled her hand into the crook of his arm.

"I love Rigovarnus the First, of course. But after that, I adore Halimel, Yandiveri and Alrenardo."

"You do, eh?" Alrenardo beamed at her. "What is it about Alrenardo that you adore?"

"They called him Alrenardo the Just for a reason," Mephista sighed. "It's as if he could sort a lie from the truth, and sided with those who deserved justice, rather than taking the part of another because it was the popular thing to do."

"Yes," Alrenardo agreed. "Even though many offered him great wealth to agree with the other side, at times."

"Did that really happen? I've studied his writings and the history of the time. That was left out of it."

"It really happened, but it was left out of the history at his request."

"Why?"

"Because he often had help in determining the truth in the matter and did not wish to reveal how he came by it."

"Then how did he come by it?" Mephista asked, sounding breathless. She loved a mystery, it appeared.

"The Rith Naeri."

Her eyes grew round in disbelief. "That's—they are a myth," she scoffed. "A child's tale. That's why these recent problems cropping up with perpetrators claiming to be Rith Naeri are considered false."

"They are false—fake Rith Naeri, in fact," Alrenardo said. "Their crimes, however, are very real. That is why I and my guard outside this hall are diligently investigating them. With help, of course."

"You brought me here to tell me I may be in danger, didn't you?"

"Yes. That is certainly one of the things I wanted you to know. I am doing all I can to protect you and felt you should know everything."

"Who else is helping with the investigation?"

"Several factions, of which the real Rith Naeri are one."

"You're joking. I—I'm not sure I believe that."

"My dear, the first thing you should know is that I am not Larvalis. He, his lover and a few others affected by the enemy we hunt are somewhere safe. I am Alrenardo the Just, and an ancient vampire. That is how the Rith Naeri survive—all of us are former Kings of Hraede, and all are vampires, now. Rigovarnus the First is the one who made me vampire. If you wish, I can arrange a meeting, or take you to Larvalis, who can confirm that he has been elsewhere these past few weeks."

"How can this be?" Mephista took a step backward; her voice trembling with her question.

We need help, I sent to Zaria and Lissa.

~

"How long has he been under compulsion?" Mephista watched Larvalis on a comp-vid screen—he was confined to a large suite in Ashe's palace with his lover. "I knew about her," she shrugged off Renellia's presence. "I knew about Sworden, too, but had no idea they were working against the Crown."

"Renellia didn't know about that," I said. "But as she's pregnant, we thought it best to take her out of harm's way."

"This is so much worse than I imagined it could be," Mephista hung her head and rubbed her forehead. She was getting a headache, that was plain to see.

"That really is Alrenardo the Just," I nodded to Al. "I am mated to Rigovarnus the First, actually. He goes by Rigo, so there's no reason for you to link him to Hraede unless someone tells you."

"Who better to run the planet than a former King," Mephista lifted her eyes to mine. "No wonder he makes me laugh—he isn't Larvalis."

"He won't ever be Larvalis," I said. "You can trust him with your life. Now, I believe Tamp has something for you." I nodded at Tamp, who pulled the small box from a pocket and offered it to Mephista.

"What is this?" Mephista asked, accepting the small box.

"Protection," Tamp explained, pulling his own medallion from beneath his shirt. "It will protect you from obsession, compulsion, and harm from any other. Wear it always and never remove it."

"Where did it come from?" Mephista lifted the gold medallion from its box and held it up to the light.

"A Larentii made it just for you. If any other tries to wear it, they will die." Alrenardo stepped forward, lifted the medallion by its chain and settled it over Mephista's head. "This means I cannot place compulsion on you, nor can any vampire. If you wish to scream at me and call me names, I cannot stop you." He gave her a lop-sided grin.

"Of all your jewels, that is the most precious," I told her. "The only person who will ever tell you to remove it is Zaria, who made it."

"That's not a Larentii name."

"No—the Larentii call her Corinnelar."

"May I be of assistance?" Connegar appeared next to me.

Mephista's mouth hung open for several seconds before it snapped shut. "This is real?"

"It is most certainly real. Zaria does not bestow medallions lightly."

"What is Larvalis saying about all this? Is he still under compulsion?"

"He doesn't want to go back," I answered truthfully.

"Hmmph. Sounds just like him, all right."

"Are you ready to go back, my dear?" Al asked her.

"I suppose. Can we sit down, have a drink and discuss this further? I find all this unsettling."

"Of course, my Queen." Al dipped his head to her.

"Then I'm ready to go back." She looped her arm with his, nodded to me and prepared to be transported.

I sent Tamp back with her and Al; he was a capable bodyguard and she should know that.

"Things are getting more complicated by the minute," I looked up at Connegar. "How is Zaria?"

"Sleeping in the sun again. The child is pulling energy away from her at a rapid rate."

"She isn't in pain, is she?"

"Just weary, because her energy is being expended at three to four times the normal rate."

"She shouldn't be doing this at all, then," I shook my head at Connegar.

"We feel that there is a part she must play in this, my love. Otherwise, we would exert every effort, convincing her to allow someone else to take her place."

"What are you not telling me about this?" I asked. He was holding something back, I was sure of it.

"The Wise Ones have become involved. I cannot say where they are, exactly, but they have never done this sort of thing before. That, in itself, corroborates my opinion that Zaria must remain involved in this."

"Honey, you're scaring me."

"Do you think I and the others are not concerned? Zaria and the Wise Ones are most precious to the entire Larentii race. We cannot lose even one of them."

"Does anyone else know? Outside the Larentii?" I rubbed his lower back as I looked up at him.

"No, and very few Larentii are aware."

"This is a little overwhelming," I admitted. "I wish we had more time to discuss this, but I've already left Rigo and the others alone too long. I have to get back to Corez."

"At least the Queen of Hraede is safer, now, and Rezo Nilus will awake a more powerful being, as deserved."

"Small accomplishments, considering everything else. So far, we've had it fairly easy. I get a feeling that trend may not continue for long."

"I think the same. I also must go back. Tread carefully, my love, and call if you have need of me." Leaning down, he gave me a warm kiss that tasted of sunlight, then folded back to Kwark.

I'm on my way back, I sent to Rigo and the others.

About damn time, Winkler growled. *We've got more trouble brewing, and it's not pretty.*

"What do they mean, we're not honoring our trade agreements?" I demanded shortly after I arrived in the First Advisor's office.

"Apparently Prime Minister Fallah wrote this new law, signed it and then forged Haris' signature to push it through the Campiaan Alliance," Rigo growled.

"We can straighten this out through Teeg," I began.

"Except that the entire Campiaan Trader's Guild is now refusing to do business with Corez and its satellite worlds," Winkler snapped. "Teeg can't force them to do business with anybody."

"The obsessed Fallah did this?"

"Yes."

"Great. Can we prove that isn't the First Advisor's signature, rendering it ineffective?"

"That's all we have to go on, and most people will see that as an attempt to cover up a crime."

"No wonder they killed her—there's no way now to prove that she was having ah, issues, or that she forged his signature. Now it's his word against a dead woman's."

"The trouble, of course, comes down to the fact that as Corez is quite close to a hub in the Campiaan Alliance, they get much of their grain, meat and vegetable shipments from farming worlds there," Gavin laid out the problem in a nutshell.

"So, if we can convince them to trade again, the prices will no doubt be higher, because they've been insulted."

"Exactly."

"And if Teeg intervenes on Corez's behalf, and forces the prices back down again, there will be unrest starting there."

"That is what we believe," Rigo sighed. "The media is awaiting my announcement, actually, and we've made no headway in finding Fallah's killer. No doubt they'll point that out, too. I will tell them that my signature was forged, which is the truth, but I think I will also step down, in favor of one of the Second Advisors. Perhaps one of you," Rigo indicated Winkler and Gavin, "will be able to renegotiate a trade agreement."

"There's always compulsion," Gavin grumped. "I hope you want the job," he turned to Winkler. "I detest that sort of thing."

"Don't look at me," Winkler frowned. "I didn't sign up for that, either."

"I have an idea," I said. "Which one of you wants to stand in for Rigo? You graciously resign as First Advisor, and Rigo, disguised as one of you, takes charge until a new Prime Minister is elected."

"We can try that," Winkler agreed. "See how far we get, until the next roadblock."

"Rigo would be better at renegotiating the trade agreement anyway, with my help," I said. "Rigo, honey, how quick do you want to do this?"

"Call the outlets. Tell them we'll have an announcement in an hour."

"I'm on it," I said and grabbed a comp-vid off Rigo's desk to deliver the news.

~

Royal Palace, Galk

Reah

"I can't tell you how pleased I am to have you back, Rezo Nilus," I told him. Zaria and her Larentii guards delivered the newest member of the Hierarchy to my private study.

"Now we only have to present a logical excuse for my absence," he grimaced. To others, he'd resemble the man he was before; I could see straight through Zaria's disguise to the man who now looked to be in his prime—taller, straighter and with a regal bearing.

"We're going back," Zaria told me. "Lissa is dealing with yet another emergency. All we've done so far is put out fires that keep cropping up."

"I hear that," I agreed. "We've found two more obsessed Council members, and those are two votes which will be changed in favor of the opposition."

"What are your plans?" Zaria asked.

"I don't know. Bel Erland and Wyatt are talking to anyone and everyone on the Council willing to listen, so they can lay out the truth of what this re-vote means."

"I'll send Gerrett." Zaria's voice was flat.

"I will bring him," Valegar told her and disappeared. He and Gerrett reappeared moments later.

"Who will replace Gerrett on Kwark?" I asked.

"I will fill that role," Valegar replied.

"Somebody has to keep Bleek reined in," Gerrett teased.

"I have no worries concerning the Blevakian. I have worries concerning the two men who attempted to murder Rezo Nilus," Val smiled at Gerrett.

"Honey, do what you have to," Zaria leaned in to give Gerrett a swift kiss. "We have to go."

Royal Palace, Kwark

Zaria

"Did you see anything in those two men before you separated their particles?" Edden set a cup of green tea in front of me. Somewhere, Reemagar was giving a speech on the Queen's behalf, and looked exactly like her, down to her choices in jewelry and dresses. Any other day I might tease him about fashion, but not today.

"D'slay has a wizard he refers to as Toad," I sighed and leaned back on a wide sofa in the Queen's suite. "Both those men saw him, and it appears that D'slay has the wizard obsessed and is constantly torturing the man. That's all those two saw, so that's the only information I have to go on. For now, I don't know his real name or anything else about him. D'slay is using him to do some of his dirty work, no doubt."

D'slay didn't obsess the two men?"

"You only have to pay those who are already predisposed to do the worst thing possible anyway."

"Ah." Edden took a seat next to me.

"How are you doing?" Ilya walked in, followed by Halimel and Bleek.

"Feeling tired appears to be a constant," I replied. "Val is taking Gerrett's place; Gerrett is needed on Galk. They've got a serious problem with obsession going on, and so far, have nobody to pin that crime on."

"Do you think D'slay is popping in and out?" Bleek asked, sitting on my other side. With one hand, he lifted my cup of tea and placed it in my hands.

"He could be, but there are still two Sirenali women out there. The third one who showed up on Hraede is in Lissa's dungeon."

"Sirenali can fold space," Edden pointed out. "Why were three riding with that shipment of sand and uranium?"

"To protect it, perhaps?" Ilya suggested.

"That's my thought on the matter. They didn't want anybody knowing what those barrels actually contained, so they were there for damage control."

"Why didn't they use their talent for folding space to take those shipments where they needed to go?" Halimel asked.

"Because, as a general rule, Sirenali can only transport themselves. There may be a few who can transport others, but transforming heavy objects or other people is generally beyond their capability. I believe D'slay may have had help when he transported Irina away."

"Did the obsessed wizard help him do this?" Edden asked softly.

"He may have. The only way to find that out, however, is to go back to Russia a few centuries ago."

"Sirenali cannot bend time," Valegar appeared to join our conversation. "Between that time and this, there is no indication that he was active anywhere. If he cannot bend time, where was he and what was he doing?"

"Then he had help bending time, too? That would take another powerful being to accomplish that," Ilya said.

"This is really starting to worry me," I breathed. "I feel sick." I transported myself to the Queen's sumptuous bathroom and coughed up everything I'd just drank into her platinum-plated toilet.

CHAPTER 12

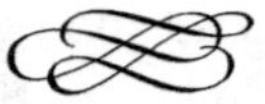

*R*oyal Palace, Kwark
   Ilya

This pregnancy is hitting her hard, I replied to Tamp's inquiry about Zaria. Even Connegar says Larentii females don't often experience nausea of any kind. She drank half a cup of green tea and then lost it all.

Could it be because most Larentii don't eat or drink like the rest of us do? They rely on sunlight to feed themselves.

They say it shouldn't have that sort of reaction. She's really showing, too. If she were human, I'd say she was at least seven or eight months along. The Larentii here have taken to surrounding her whenever she's outside the royal suite, and all of us are helping her in and out of chairs, as of this afternoon.

It may be easier on her if she stayed in her Larentii form, Tamp suggested.

She stays that way, now, whenever she's out of the public view. More and more, Reemagar is standing in for her, and they are in constant communication regarding what should be said or done in every situation. Connegar won't come out and say it, but I believe the child is growing at an accelerated rate and her body is having trouble adapting to the sudden changes.

Is there a reason for that?

I have no idea. We're keeping watch while we're waiting for the next disaster to happen.

As it surely will, Tamp agreed. *Have you heard from any of the others?*

More problems on Corez; they're still trying to pin crimes on Rigo, looks like, and the police are too busy doing the enemy's work for them to hunt for Fallah's murderer. Queen Reah has her hands full with a re-vote scheduled for tomorrow, because several members of the Council have been obsessed to change their votes and they still can't track down the source of those obsessions.

Anything new with Zanfield and his crew?

Haven't heard anything in the last few hours. I fully expect that to change, however.

We're still searching for the two missing members of the false Rith Naeri. No new murders have cropped up, but they probably know we captured the others and aren't anxious to join their brothers-in-crime.

Or waiting for the proper moment to strike, I said. *My concern is for Alrenardo; he is the weakest of the impersonators, as he has little past his vampire abilities to protect himself. That leaves a burden on you, my friend.*

Don't sell Al short; he hasn't survived for millennia by being stupid or incapable. Besides, he wears one of Zaria's medallions, as does the Queen.

Keep your eyes open, then. I feel as if the enemy has only been toying with us thus far and is saving the worst for when we least expect it.

We are keeping watch, and I will report anything unusual here. Staying in contact will be of vital importance, I believe.

Kabbuc Mountain, Mardir

   Toad

Some days, I feel almost strong enough to shake off D'slay's commands. He watches me closely, however, and if he imagines that his obsessions are loosening, he replaces them, and then strips off layers of my skin with a cruel, flaying knife.

I wish I could dampen the pain completely, but he commands that I feel it. Therefore, I do feel it, and the memories of it between times is far from pleasant. At least I no longer scream in pain; he has stripped so much of me away I've become somewhat impervious.

Long ago, I stopped cursing my mother, or the one who fathered me in a drunken dalliance. Had I been older and wiser, I'd have gotten away from my mother, who gave me to the first stranger who offered money for a six-year-old boy.

When Irina was still alive, she kept D'slay away from me much of the time, as I was forced to help her through too many pregnancies that would have terminated early with the child's death if I hadn't.

The last pregnancy was the one in which she developed the disease. I did not mention it to D'slay. When Irina died, I was flayed again, because he was angry—with me, with her and with the children he was forced to hand to others to raise.

Since then, he has driven me—and himself—to the breaking point. Only recently have I realized that he is also under another's command, and nothing he can do will relieve him of that burden. That gives me two masters rather than one, and I can only dream of escaping both.

I can only imagine what life I might choose for myself should I manage to break free. So much of the time, I think of how it could feel to help instead of harm, and to be myself and make my own decisions.

Such are the ways of dreams—that they are as intangible as fog, and often just as obscure in the full light of day.

"These are our targets," D'slay stalked into the room with a comp-vid in his hands, which he shoved in my direction.

I took it from him carefully; I was tortured when one accidentally broke earlier. Somehow, my broken fingers had healed straight, rather than crooked as D'slay left them.

The first image was one that surprised me, as he bore the likeness of an ancient King of Hraede.

"It's not a resemblance, that's really Alrenardo the Just," D'slay snapped at my hesitance. Yes, I could see past the disguise to reveal the real image beneath it. "The next image is much the same, only it's the real Rigovarnus the Great. He's second on our kill list."

I thumbed the next image to see another disguised former King of

Hraede, only this one was acting as First Advisor on Corez. "Those are two of the real Rith Naeri," D'slay began to pace in front of me. "They've managed to destroy most of my replacements; only two remain. But, as you and I know, we saved the best for last."

Dipping my head in a half-nod, I thumbed the third image onto the screen before my breath and my hand stilled.

"What is this one?" I finally found my voice again.

"We haven't determined what she is," D'slay resumed his pacing. "We'll kill her, just like the others. Keep going, so you'll know all your targets."

Reluctantly I tapped the image, replacing it with the next one. "We can't truly see who that one is, either, but she should be easy enough to kill, as the next one will be."

I revealed the last image. "Zanfield Staggs?" It was a stroke of genius to replace President Ylisis of Murazal with Staggs, as they had much in common.

"The same. Once we get rid of him, we'll take everything he has, since there are no heirs."

D'slay intended to steal everything from the wealthiest citizen in both Alliances. I didn't tell him he would have his work cut out for him; the image before Staggs' was of a High Demon, and most of D'slay's tricks wouldn't work against *her* kind.

That's why he didn't know what she was—he couldn't see it. Perhaps he wouldn't understand until she killed him for his trouble. My only hope was that she didn't kill me at the same time.

Before then, I'd return to the likeness now burned on my brain— that of the dark-haired, blue-eyed woman, who could stop my breath with a brief glimpse of her image.

State House, Corez

> *Lissa*

"Are you ready to do this?" I frowned at Gavin, who'd volunteered to stand in for the First Advisor and resign his position—after stating that it was to move Corez past the recent difficulties and allow someone else to take charge until the next election.

Gavin now looked exactly like First Advisor Haris Doy, while Rigo wore the senior Second Advisor's resemblance. Rigo, as the Second Advisor, would then take over for the resigning First Advisor. He'd be elevated temporarily to the First Advisor's position, until things could be sorted out.

At least I hoped they could be sorted out. I'm sure if the real First Advisor learned of any of this, he'd be having palpitations over it.

Gavin would be ushered out of the State House, where he'd be flown (supposedly) to his estate in the country and stay there until things became normal again. Frankly, I was beginning to wonder what normal actually was, and whether it would ever show its face in the Alliances after this fiasco.

As for Teeg and the Reth Alliance, we already had them halfway agreeable to re-signing the trade agreements, with only a few concessions to make them a bit happier with the deal.

Some compulsion may have been laid on a couple of people to get there, but for now, I wasn't about to become squeamish about it. We were lucky nobody else had died in the process, given what else we'd had to deal with.

"You fold space to get back here from Haris' country house," I straightened Gavin's collar before he went out to speak with an angry, rebellious crowd. "I'll have a shield up, and you should have a shield up, too. Somebody could be waiting for the opportunity to do you in, just as they did Fallah."

"Cara, stop worrying; I will be fine," Gavin gave me a slight frown.

"Fine. Go out there and get screamed at, then."

"I love you," he said, leaning down to give me a quick kiss.

"I love your ass, too. And most of the rest of you."

"You do not love all of me?" He pretended to be upset.

"Yes, I love all of you. Can't let you get a big head about it, now can I?"

"I suppose not. Remind me to take you to dinner and give you flowers when we return home."

"I'll hold you to that."

"Very well, then." Gavin squared his shoulders before walking through the door to the balcony, where official announcements were often made. Drake and Drew weren't far behind him, watching for any mischief to occur while Gavin gave the speech Rigo wrote for him, claiming his innocence and the reasons it would be better for him to step aside to put Corez back on track.

I was glad when it was over, and Rigo stepped forward to promise the crowd that Corez would be in good hands until the upcoming election, where it would likely be that a new First Advisor would also be chosen.

We're getting in the hover-chopper now, Drake sent as Rigo concluded his speech. *We'll be back in about an hour.*

All right. Keep your eyes open. Somebody could be waiting to do away with the First Advisor.

We're on it, he replied.

"How was it?" Rigo asked as he joined me inside the First Advisor's study and the balcony doors were shut behind him.

"It went as well as could be expected, I think," I told him. "Gavin got booed through the whole speech, so it didn't matter what he said. You only got booed a few times, and that's probably as normal as you can get in this situation."

"We have Teeg on the comp-vid; he has an agreement drawn up and ready to sign," Winkler told Rigo.

"Any changes since we last talked?"

"Only one, and it's not much—they want a credit for any packing containers we keep."

"How many do we keep?"

"Roughly one per cent—Corez doesn't like getting cluttered up with that stuff."

"The monetary impact?"

"Three million credits per turn."

"Fine. I suppose three million is a small price to pay to dissolve this wart on the Alliance's ass," Rigo sighed. "Shall we sign?" He turned to me and offered his arm. I took it and walked into his office to sign a document that shouldn't have had to be signed to begin with.

~

Royal Palace, Galk

Reah

"My Queen, it appears we are deadlocked." Rezo Nilus, as the ranking member of the Council, brought the news to me, along with his comp-vid count of the votes tallied. It was tied—that meant the enemy had gotten to one more member whose vote we'd counted on and hadn't discovered until it was too late.

I had to *Look* to see what needed to be done to break the tie, and almost smiled. The King was the tie-breaking vote, and no doubt the enemy was counting on him to cancel the Queen's vote, as they were always at odds with one another.

"Fetch the King," I turned and ordered Cudworth. He dipped his head to me and turned to leave immediately.

Five minutes later, amid whispers, coughs and the usual noise made by mostly old men in expensive garb, Tory walked into the Council chamber.

"The vote is yours, my King, to decide the tie on the tariff issue," Rezo Nilus bowed to Tory.

Tory turned toward me, his face expressionless. On one side of the chamber, the ones voting for the tariffs drew in expectant breaths.

They'd counted on this—someone had told them, perhaps. I was determined to get to the bottom of this before the day was over.

"The King votes against the measure," Tory snapped and stalked out of the chamber. Cudworth and Ocenosek closed the doors behind him.

"Those against the measure carry the vote," Rezo Nilus announced while tapping on his comp-vid. The chamber erupted in shouts and chaos.

~

Presidential Palace, Murazal
    Travis

"We're opening a new terminal at the space station today," Rajeon informed Zanfield. "It's one of those events where your wardrobe choices will certainly shine," he added.

"Perfect," Zanfield grinned. "Perri, what shall we wear?"

"Purple?" Perri asked.

"Purple it is. How much time do we have to dress?"

"Half an hour, so you should start now," Rajeon replied.

"I think we can manage that." Zanfield offered his arm to Perri, who took it and actually smiled at him.

"There will be a special docking of the Royal ship in its new berth after the dedication," I said. "And a cocktail party onboard following that."

"It's as if I'd planned this myself," Zanfield waved a hand and walked Perri toward her suite.

"He gets more and more into Ylisis' character as time goes on, and I thought he'd nailed it when we first got here," Trent, who stood next to me, whispered.

"I think we're only now seeing that our Zanfield is a perfectionist," I agreed. "Not that it's a bad thing," I added.

"At least we don't have to match his outfits to stand guard," Trent chuckled. "I'd have run away screaming at the yellow outfits they wore two nights ago."

"He doesn't need the competition," I teased. "This way, he and Perri are the standouts, and I'm good with that."

"Yellow isn't my color," Morrett declared as he and Rajeon followed Zanfield and Perri. "Purple isn't my color, either."

Trent snickered; he and I fell in behind Morrett and Rajeon and followed them toward Zanfield's suite.

State House, Corez
    Lissa

"Shouldn't Gavin be back with Drake and Drew?" I thought to ask after two hours had passed. Rigo, Winkler and I had spent that time sending out press releases and answering questions regarding the new trade agreement with the Campiaan Alliance.

"They said an hour, and it's long past that," Rigo's brow furrowed as he considered the passage of time.

Drake? Drew? I sent. *Gavin—where are you?*

They didn't answer.

"I'm not finding them," Winkler slid off his perch on a corner of Rigo's desk, concern on his face.

"The hover-chopper is parked outside the First Advisor's home, but they're not there," I breathed, trying not to panic.

"Let's go," Winkler grabbed my arm and folded space. When we reached Haris Doy's country manor, it looked as if a hurricane had passed through. Windows were broken, half the roof had been swept off and servants were standing outside, some of them weeping. Amid the wreckage, there was no sign of Gavin or my twins.

Now it was time to panic.

Gemma Village, Hraede
Nissa

"It's nice here," Trik said. He, Toff and I sat at an outdoor table at a local restaurant, having an afternoon snack before picking up groceries for the house.

"May I join you?" Tamp walked toward us and pulled out the remaining chair at our table.

"Sure. What's new at the palace?" Toff asked.

"Al and Mephista are having a late lunch," Tamp said. "I didn't want to interrupt them."

"They seem to be getting along quite well," I said.

"Better than well. It worries me a little."

"In what way?"

"What if they don't want to separate when this is over?"

"That could be a problem," Trik said, absently turning his mug of tea on the tabletop.

"Somebody in charge will have to make a decision, I suppose," Toff shrugged. "Is there any indication how much longer this mission will last?"

"No idea. We're sort of at a standstill at the moment, since we can't locate the last two members of the false Rith Naeri."

"Too bad Ethan Looms didn't know more than he did," Toff observed. "He apparently knew some of the others."

"I get the feeling they may have saved these last two because they're the worst of the lot," I said.

"It concerns me as well." Tamp breathed a sigh as our wait-bot arrived to take his order. "Black Mountain tea," he requested. "Hot, with honey."

The bot hovered away to fetch the tea while we continued our conversation.

Honey, Mom's voice interrupted. *Your uncles Drake, Drew and Gavin have disappeared. We can't find them anywhere.*

Presidential Palace, Murazal

 Travis

Trent and I would step off the president's shuttle first, followed by Zanfield and Perri. Rajeon and Morrett would disembark last, as the rear guards.

Ready? Zanfield straightened his purple suit, lavishly decorated with gold trim.

Trent tapped the code to open the shuttle door, where steps would form so we could walk regally onto the platform of the new section of Murazal's space station. In unison, Trent and I stepped downward, then separated on the deck to allow Zanfield and Perri to join the guests selected for the unveiling.

Clicking our heels together, we signaled the official arrival of the President and his fiancée. Rajeon and Morrett were supposed to follow them, and then Trent and I would close ranks and march into the main hall of the new structure behind the others.

Except Rajeon and Morrett didn't disembark.

In fact, they were no longer on the shuttle.

They'd disappeared into thin air and panic rose, threatening to choke my breath.

Where are they? Trent, true to his Falchani training, didn't twitch a muscle as he sent anxious mindspeech to me.

I don't know. Morrett? Rajeon? I called out to them. There was no answer.

Travis, Trent, Gavin and your fathers have disappeared, Mom sent. *We can't find them.* She sounded almost hysterical.

Mom, Trent's sending quavered, *Rajeon and Morrett just disappeared off the shuttle. We don't know where they are, either.*

~

Royal Palace, Galk

Reah

"Where's Tory?" I hadn't found him inside his suite or mine, and he hadn't answered my mindspeech.

I'd aimed my question at Cudworth and Ocenosek, who appeared just as worried as I did. "We cannot find Denevik, either," Cudworth whispered.

"We haven't been able to find Vik or Denevik," Wyatt and Bel Erland appeared at my side, both sounding out of breath.

"We tried mindspeech, and they're not answering," Wyatt added.

"So have I," I admitted, feeling more frightened than I had in a long while. "Where could they be?"

"Vik was headed toward his suite when he left the Council chamber," Cudworth said. "He told us on his way out the door."

"There's no evidence he even made it here," Bel Erland said after running a quick scry.

"Can you tell where he disappeared?" I asked my warlock son.

"Hold on, let me reverse the scry," he held up a hand and closed his eyes. When he opened them again, he didn't speak for several seconds. "Denevik met him in the hall leading to his suite. They disappeared from there—just—vanished."

"This leads me to believe they are prisoners hidden by bone dust or a Sirenali, or," Ocenosek didn't finish his sentence.

I understood his meaning, however. They could be dead, and we might never know what happened.

We have problems, Travis sent mindspeech. *Mom says our dads have disappeared with Uncle Gavin, and Rajeon and Morrett are now gone. We can't find any of them.*

We've lost Tory and Denevik, I replied, not bothering to call Tory by his other name. His brothers would know who he was.

Nissa, Trik and Toff have disappeared right in front of me, Tamp reported. *Vanished without a trace.*

~

Royal Palace, Kwark
　Zaria

Even in Larentii form, the pregnancy was so uncomfortable I was barely able to stand it. The child had grown huge inside my womb, and any movement he made was painful to me.

Lately, he'd been moving a lot. Connegar and Valegar were constantly singing to both of us, in an attempt to get the baby and me through this difficult time. The baby had to be feeling just as confined and cramped as I did, and I worried that he'd have a tough time making his way out.

Larentii females never pushed—the baby would crawl out on his or her own.

Contractions?

Those were just a suggestion that it was time to vacate the premises. Any attempt to push or force the child out could be seen by the child as a threat, and, as Larentii were born powerful, it could end up harming one or the other if the child fought back.

"Honey," I told the baby while rubbing my belly, "just hang on, we'll get through this."

He stirred in reply.

"My love, there have been ah, complications," Ilya and Valegar appeared beside me. Ilya was the one to speak; Val looked worried. A worried Larentii was never a good thing.

"What's wrong?" I asked, while the baby moved again.

"People have disappeared, and nobody can find them."

"Who?" Suddenly, I felt terrified.

"Vik, Morrett, Gavin, Drake, Drew, Nissa, Toff and Trik," Ilya reported. "We worry there may be more, and there is no explanation for the disappearances or where they could possibly be."

"Come, sit down," Valegar took my arm. I was far too tall at this point for Ilya to do so. Connegar arrived at that moment to assist Valegar. Together, they placed me in a comfortable chair, enlarged several times over to accommodate a tall, heavily-pregnant Larentii.

I started rubbing my belly again, to comfort myself as well as the child. Surely he could feel my distress at this unexpected and troubling news. *It'll be okay*, I sent to him as well as myself. It *had* to be okay. That was my brother, my sister and two brothers-in-law, in addition to a mate, two friends and three adoptive uncles missing.

Why hadn't my medallions activated? Morrett and Vik wore theirs —they'd never take them off for any reason.

As for Nissa, Trik and Toff—they wore protection jewels made by Grey House—had those activated and we hadn't known it?

"Was anyone with Nissa and her husbands when they disappeared?"

"Tampirus," Valegar nodded.

Tamp? I sent. I admit, I may have sounded more than frightened in my mindspeech.

My love, what is it? he asked, sounding concerned.

You were with Nissa, Trik and Toff? Did their protection jewels fire?

If they did, I didn't see it happen. They disappeared so fast, there was no flash of light or anything else to indicate the jewels activated.

Was anyone else around?

Just a flustered wait-bot, delivering tea. Shadow Grey is here, now, tearing the thing apart using power, to determine if it was spelled by someone.

Shadow was Lissa's mate and Nissa's father. I could only imagine how desperate he felt at his only child's disappearance.

How much power would it take to pull powerful Grey House wizards away? *It can't be a spell,* I told Tamp. *Two High Demons are missing, and no spell would have worked against either of them. That's not what's happening here.*

Then it has to be one of the powerful. Tamp was sounding more alarmed than before.

The only ones I know of are those aligned with the Prophet, I replied.

We've suspected his hand in this, along with D'slay's, Tamp agreed.

Tell Shadow to put the bot back together. There's no spell to find. Whether it passed information to someone else, however, remains to be seen. We need an engineer rather than a wizard on this. Call for Sabrina. If she and Dave can't figure this out, it didn't happen.

I'll send the message.

Keep me advised.

I will.

"What did he say?" Ilya asked.

"He says there was no indication that their protection jewels fired, and I didn't get any warning from Vik's or Morrett's medallions."

"Terrible news," Edden appeared inside the Queen's suite. He seldom folded space, preferring to arrive somewhere in a mundane manner instead. "The King of Karathia has disappeared, as has the Founder of the Campiaan Alliance."

Heaving myself out of the chair, I wobbled for a moment after rising so quickly.

That's when my water broke and my child disappeared.

CHAPTER 13

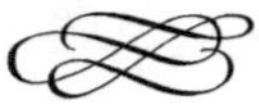

*R*oyal Palace, Hraede
 Tamp

"I'm surprised they're not hurling accusations at me right now, because my erstwhile mistress has disappeared, along with her guards." Alrenardo paced inside the King's suite while Mephista and I watched, helpless to do anything about the current situation.

"They may be biding their time, just to make you more miserable— or Larvalis more miserable," Mephista amended her initial statement. "Please slow down; we have to think logically about this, and plan what to do whenever their plot unfolds."

Tampirus, we have more bad news, Ilya interrupted the conversation. I'd never heard the stoic, Falchani-trained warlock sound so worried.

What happened? I asked.

Rylend Morphis and Teeg San Gerxon have disappeared, as has the child from Zaria's womb. Now, Connegar reports that the Larentii Wise Ones have gone in search of the child and can no longer be reached by any means of communication.

"Fucking, ass-riding hells," I cursed aloud.

"What is it?" Alrenardo stopped pacing immediately and stared at me.

"The King of Karathia, the Founder of the Campiaan Alliance and Zaria's child have all disappeared. The Larentii Wise Ones went to search for the child and have also disappeared."

"This is terrible news," Mephista dropped onto a nearby chair, her face in her hands. "Can anything save us?" she implored, dropping her hands and begging Alrenardo.

"We still have many who hold power," he attempted to reassure her. Stepping to her side, he knelt beside her chair and placed an arm about her. She leaned her head against his shoulder and wept.

What should we do—is there anything we can do? I sent to Ilya.

Lissa says stay where you are and watch for the unusual or any signs of the missing. She and Zaria worry that the rogue gods aligned with the Prophet are now making their presence known—in the worst ways possible.

How is Zaria taking this?

She is terrified for her child, but is forcing her way through this and working to keep her mind clear, in order to search for solutions and causes. We may have to ask for volunteers to replace those who've been taken. I hear there has been some recruitment among the Saa Thalarr. I will report any updates as I hear them.

Thank you. Has there been any word from the Three?

I have not been informed of it, if there has been.

I swear, if I find D'slay or the Prophet, I will make them wish they'd never been birthed.

D'slay, perhaps. The Prophet has power and rogue gods at his beck and call. I think only a few could ever be strong enough to oppose him.

Royal Palace, Kwark

Zaria

"There is very little healing necessary," Valegar soothed as Connegar ran his hands over my abdomen. "It appears the child was ready to be born when he disappeared."

"I think that, too," I agreed. I felt weary again, and knew I needed sunlight in addition to the healing efforts. "Sunlight?" I asked, the word sounding rough from a dry throat and mouth.

"Dearest," Valegar held out his hand, where a glass of cool water appeared.

"Yes, thank you," I sighed before shivering. He helped me hold the glass so I could drink—the water felt like heaven entering my system.

"Sunlight it is," Connegar removed his hands before folding the three of us to the Larentii homeworld.

"The sunlight here is always best for us," Nefrigar appeared on the brightly-lit hillside where we'd landed. He knelt in the grass beside me while Valegar propped me up and removed my clothing with a thought.

None of us mentioned the child as Valegar began to sing me to sleep. I went willingly; I needed the rest and all the strength I could gather to deal with the dark clouds piling up on our horizon.

～

Prophet's Compound, P'loxett
Alken Wilker

"Why would you think I'd understand what he said any better than you?" I snapped at Qatti. "All I heard was three, one, and he's too useful to murder right now."

I'd been sent to collect D'slay and bring him to the Prophet, who wished to speak with him. Where we were was hidden, even from D'slay. I suspected it was to keep him from revealing the location to any of the powerful, should he be caught and interrogated.

Qatti and I had overheard a snippet of the conversation, and now she wished to grill me over it.

Gillen was on another mission for the Prophet; I no longer asked where or what. I didn't need to know; my life depended upon that very ignorance at times. Qatti knew it too—after Gillen hit her the third time for asking.

Soon after, the door had slammed behind us as we left the Prophet's private quarters, and a sound shield dropped into place. We would get no further answers, and D'slay would kill me himself if I asked questions after taking him home again.

More than anything, I wanted to be done with all this—P'loxett, the Prophet, D'slay, terrible food and only chill, barren quarters to sleep in. We weren't allowed in the far end of the compound, where it was rumored that gardens and groves were being tended, but if that were true, the food never reached any of us.

We relied on prepared or preserved meats and vegetables, and much of those were just as tasteless as they sounded.

"Are you just going to sit there?" Qatti demanded as I made myself as comfortable as I could on hard, metal chairs in the hall outside the Prophet's quarters.

"I have to take him back, you know," I said. "You, on the other hand —aren't they expecting you elsewhere?"

"Fuck you, Alken," she whirled away from me, angry in an instant. I watched her as she stiffly marched away; I'd hear complaints from Gillen before long, no doubt, about insulting his wife.

If he bothered to return. If I were him, I'd do everything in my power to stay away as long as I could. I was tethered to the trips from P'loxett to Kabbuc Mountain on Mardir, and then back again.

Gillen was often gone for days, if not weeks, as was one of the Prophet's close associates. I knew nothing of that associate and didn't ask anyone else about him, Gillen included. That one held a power all his own; I'd seen him use it. It wasn't a wizard or warlock's power, either; I'd recognize it if it were.

The Prophet called him P'loxett, exactly the same as the planet he lived on. I still couldn't determine why. I only knew P'loxett was angry most of the time, and I stayed as far away from him as I could.

D'slay came storming out of the Prophet's quarters then, looking just as angry as P'loxett did on most days. I rose quickly; no need to anger this one on the return trip to Mardir.

Kabbuc Mountain, Mardir

Toad

Only a little more, and I felt I could break free. A little farther, and I'd loosen the bonds D'slay placed upon me.

Only a little farther; I felt the restraints opening, almost felt the freedom of slipping away from this small room where D'slay kept me.

Where would I go first? I reached out with my mind to find something beautiful.

Peaceful.

An image appeared, of lovely groves of trees. I knew those trees; they produced the most delicious fruit I'd ever tasted in my life. Yes. I would go there first, and eat my fill before finding another refuge.

Where D'slay and his overlord would never, ever find me.

"There you are, Toad." I jumped from my seat in a corner of my room. I'd wedged myself tightly into it, so it might feel like arms comforting me while I attempted to break free of my constraints.

D'slay was back. I watched as his mouth moved, saying the words that would bind me again. I wished to weep, but my tears had run dry long ago.

~

Hraede

Gillen Wilker

"Dig the hole here," P'loxett commanded. Already, I'd formed sixteen perfectly round, narrow holes, in which he'd dropped sixteen small vials of glowing liquid before ordering me to fill them in again.

I knew not to ask what those vials contained. I also knew not to ask how many vials there were, although I wanted to. Digging as deeply as he wanted, with the holes as narrow and perfect as he commanded, required much of my power. It drained me to control the spells to P'loxett's specifications.

"We have three more after this one," P'loxett informed me. "Gather your strength; it should be sufficient to finish this now. Afterward, we will visit D'slay's conscripts."

I hoped they'd have food and a bed for me; I didn't care whether

P'loxett was hungry or not. He hadn't been doing the work here; I'd done it. Again, questions crowded my mind, but I kept them to myself. No reason to aggravate P'loxett and our mutual overlord, the Prophet, by speaking out of turn.

Evening fell before we finished the project, after which I was exhausted and famished. "This is where you'll take us," P'loxett produced a comp-vid from a pocket and handed it to me.

On the screen was an address and an image of the small, secluded home near a forest. Praying that food and rest were in my future, I employed the last of my strength to transport us there.

"This is Je'Dik Dis'Rai." Kault, a vampire, introduced his companion. I'd never seen anyone like Je'Dik before; wide-bodied and sturdy, he wore dark goggles even at night, dressed in fur and skins over his armor-plated bulk, and looked as if he could stop a speeding hoverbus with one hand.

"These are the last two of the false Rith Naeri," P'loxett grinned at Je'Dik. "What one can't destroy, the other will."

"We specialize in assassinations," Je'Dik spoke, his voice the grating rumble of metal scraping over sharp rocks. "If we are sent to kill someone, they die. Kault is a mister and gets me wherever I want to go. After that, it's easy."

I didn't answer with sarcasm as I wanted; instead I dipped my head in a nod to both. I'd seen the forces brought against the Prophet on A'pelur. If we hadn't escaped when we did, we could have been destroyed.

I never pointed that out to the Prophet, either, as he'd saved our skins when he pulled us away. I wasn't naïve enough to imagine our enemies died when the Prophet destroyed the planet.

He hadn't claimed victory, either, so he understood they were still hunting him. Now, he and D'slay were taking a different tack in this war. I had no idea where it would all lead and, like all the other minions, was far too afraid to ask.

"We're here to kill the King," Kault informed me, sounding haughty and sure of himself. "Or the one parading around as the King. May get the Queen, too, if she's anywhere close. That will certainly put Hraede in a panic. After the work you and P'loxett did today, things will only get worse for this world in the days to come."

"We have food," Je'Dik grabbed my arm when my stomach growled involuntarily. "Fill your stomach, go to bed, and by the time you wake, our business should be done."

~

Royal Palace, Hraede
Alrenardo

Call it a weakness if you will, but she kissed me first. I may have told her she was beautiful as we fell onto my bed. I also may have confessed my love when we moved together.

She may have felt the same, if the number of yeses she shouted counted for anything afterward. Then, drowsy and replete, I settled her head on my shoulder and lulled her to sleep. I was feeling sleepy, too, but jerked fully awake when my medallion sent an electric shock through my chest.

Someone was here.

Someone silent as death. Turning to mist, I gathered Mephista to me and floated us above the bed.

I knew Queen Lissa's talent of seeing other misters when she was mist herself. Somehow, she'd given that same gift to me. I could see him hovering not far from the bed, no doubt wondering how his quarry had disappeared in front of him.

This, in all likelihood, was one of the last two members of the false Rith Naeri. Was he tied to the night, as I once was? Would he fly away before the dawn, where we couldn't find him again?

I should have known better. It took him a short while; he was an old mister, who took much longer to become mist and then change back again. Patiently I waited, while Mephista still slept inside my mist.

I still had time to put her somewhere safe before dealing with this attacker. *Tampirus*, I sent, *I have a misting vampire in my suite at the moment. I have Mephista safe within my mist, but I need to place her somewhere safe.*

On my way, Tamp replied.

Give her to me.

A Larentii appeared on the far side of the bed and held out his arms.

Do not fear, he added, as I reluctantly left Mephista in his care. *They will not see me, and I will protect her from the noise of the fight.*

At least he knew there *would* be a fight. I had no intention of letting this vampire escape. Tamp, as a vine of sharp crystal or diamond, burst through the door at the same moment the vampire coalesced completely, revealing the passenger he carried at his side.

Tamp

For thousands of years, Alrenardo had survived by not hesitating, which his adversary did. Registering his surprise that Alrenardo was also a misting vampire—one who could change far faster than he could, the vampire blinked. That was all the time Al needed to destroy his opponent.

Only slightly behind on my reaction, I swiftly encircled the other attacker with my thorny vines. He screamed as a thorn punctured skin between armor plates.

In hindsight, we should have attacked the vampire's companion first, but we didn't understand who or what he was at the time. Instead, Al removed the vampire's head before he could defend himself, and we both felt the massive pull as the stocky, armor-plated companion was jerked away from me by a hidden hand.

"What the hells just happened?" I demanded, coming back to myself after the unexpected disappearance. The dead vampire was already turning to dark dust atop the costly rug on the floor.

"I have no idea," Alrenardo drew in his claws. He was naked and didn't care. When the Larentii appeared to my sight and handed a sleeping Mephista to Al, I saw she was also naked.

Things had just gotten more complicated than an attempted murder, and I would have said it was next to impossible.

Before.

"Thank you," Al dipped his head to the Larentii, who smiled and disappeared. I'd never seen this particular Larentii before, but I didn't point that out.

Al settled the Queen back in his bed, covered her up and then led me out the door so we could talk.

"I'd say we only have one false Rith Naeri left, and he got jerked away by somebody else," I snorted, once Al moved me away from the doorway.

"That tells us he can't mist, isn't a vampire and has a scent I haven't encountered before," Al blew out a breath and leaned against the wall.

"Maybe some clothing?" I suggested, tactfully pointing out his nudity.

"Oh. I forgot," he waved a hand in dismissal before turning to mist again and going back inside his suite. A few seconds later he reappeared, wearing trousers and pulling on a shirt.

"Do you think they'll send that armored bastard after us again?" I asked.

"No idea. I get the feeling he's important in some way, though, or they wouldn't have hauled him out of here so fast."

"At least I punctured him somewhere before he got away. Did you recognize the vampire?"

"Kault. We've hunted him in the past. Never knew until now he was a mister, although we did realize he was an assassin for hire. Always did his business, then disappeared. Haven't seen or heard from him in roughly two hundred years."

"Well, we've seen the last of him now," I pointed out grimly.

"Yes. I'll inform Rigo of his demise."

"Do you have enough information to give a good description of the other attacker?"

"I will give what I noticed in only a brief glimpse. Perhaps you can augment that by giving a description from an alternate angle."

"Are you all right?" Lissa and Rigo appeared close by. It made me more than glad that I'd convinced Alrenardo to get dressed.

"We're fine. The vampire is dead, but his associate was pulled away, somehow."

"Randl?" Lissa spoke to the air. Randl appeared immediately and placed his hands on the remains of the door to the King's suite.

"It has the stink of the Prophet about it," Randl proclaimed after several moments passed. I understood he was looking with the inner sight he had to determine what happened. His eyes might be blind, but he was anything but.

"Do you think he'll try again?" Rigo asked.

"He knows we'll be watching this place from now on; he may shunt this project aside in favor of a different one next time, although this certainly tells us he has assassination on his mind. I can present a description to Kell and Opal," Randl added. "If they wish to place a price on his head."

"I'll let them make that decision," Lissa released a troubled sigh. "We should get back to Corez before somebody comes looking for us."

"Rigo will be a target," Randl told her.

"Tell us something we don't know already," Lissa replied and disappeared with Rigo.

"I need to make plans in case this cross-breed attacks again," Randl said.

"Cross-breed?"

"He's half Krelk. The other half, well, I'm afraid to say what that could be." He vanished while Al and I blinked at one another.

⁓

Army of the Eagle Warlord, Falchan
Drew Tatsuya
Why were we dumped here, two hundred years in the past, and without the ability to fold space or anything else to get us out of here? Drake sent.

At least we'd been dropped inside an empty tent, three hours before dawn. Most of the camp was still asleep, and I was grateful that our *Looking* skills hadn't been removed as well. Whoever designed this punishment for us understood that this could be worse than killing us. I still couldn't imagine who, besides one of the powerful gods, could remove power like this.

"When's the last time you fought with a sword?" Drake asked Gavin, who'd worn a deep frown while remaining silent since our arrival.

"I still have these," he growled, allowing his vampire claws to slide out.

"Nobody here is going to accept that," Drake pointed out the obvious. "The Warlord could order your death because of it."

"Then I will hide claws behind a blade in each hand," he snapped. "Problem solved."

"We've arrived just in time for a massive battle," I reminded both. "The enemy will attack just as the army rises for the day."

"Who wins?" Gavin demanded.

"Falchan, but the Warlord and his General are killed, along with two-thirds of the troops. Falchani history refers to it as the Battle of Dry River."

"So, whoever put us here is counting on our deaths, too?"

"Probably," Drake scowled at Gavin's conclusion. "This battle will last most of the day; those attacking us have been drugged and are crazed and formidable because of it. That means they won't feel the blows as they would in a normal fight. Kill with your first strike, if possible."

"Go for the head, then," Gavin slid his claws out to their full length and studied them. "Where and when we are, I suppose we are no longer members of the Hierarchy. This disturbs me greatly."

"Right there with you, dude," Drake agreed.

~

Capitol Square, Murazal

Nissa

"We're two years in the future," Toff pulled me into an alcove behind a crumbling, looted restaurant. Trik slid in behind me; there was a riot going on in the street adjacent to our location.

"How did we get here?" I hissed. Someone shouted obscenities at the rumbling crowd in the streets, before a shriek forced me to cringe against Toff.

We'd learned quickly that we couldn't fold space, because we'd tried after being set down at the back of the seething riot going on. It was all we could do to escape through the crush of bodies and the anger radiating off them.

In two years, not only were there food shortages, but the Presidency and the State House had failed and crime had run rampant.

"It doesn't matter how we got here—how do we get away?" Trik pulled one of my hands into his and held it against his chest.

"You can't reason with a mob," Toff informed us. "I think that's what the shriek was about. I heard someone trying to convince the crowd to join together. They're only interested in their own survival at this point."

"Can we still cast a spell?" Trik asked. Beneath my hand, I could feel the rapid beating of his heart, and realized it matched mine.

"One way to find out," Toff replied grimly. "I'll try an invisibility spell. Maybe we can get out that way."

"I smell smoke," I quavered. "They're setting fire to the buildings around us."

"It'll be all right," Trik soothed as fire bloomed with a roar and smoke poured into the sky overhead. "Look—Toff just disappeared."

"Thank the Mighty," I breathed while Trik and I cast invisibility spells for ourselves and began to run through the maze of alleys and rubble to escape the angry throng.

State House Gardens, Corez

Vik

"What just happened? My comp-vid shows that we're seven years in the future," Denevik shoved the device back in his pocket.

The gardens were overgrown behind the State House, and a closer inspection revealed that windows were broken or missing from the back of the building. Toward the front, half the building had collapsed. A fog-like haze hung about the place, too. "Smells musty—like a tomb," I muttered.

"Are those rocket blasts, or did something else cause all this damage?" Denevik focused on the rubble spilling from the building's sides, like a disemboweled beast.

"I don't think anybody lives there, now," I sighed. I didn't add what we were both thinking—how had we been tossed into the future? It made no sense. *Meerius?* I sent.

The spirit of Corez is dying, Meerius replied, his sending mournful. *She has been attacked and is suffering—I do not know how. I am having difficulty trying to reach any of the others.*

Has that happened before? That a world spirit sickened enough to die?

Never. We have always survived in some way. This is more than tragic. What can we do?

I don't know, but I think we need to get to the bottom of this.

"Denevik," I spoke aloud. "I think we have work to do."

"What work? And where?" he demanded.

"No idea, but I'd bet Zanfield's trillions it isn't here." Turning, I stalked toward the gateway into the gardens, smoke drifting from my nostrils. The garden wall had also been damaged, much like the building behind me. Somebody, somewhere, would explain to me what had happened.

I just had to find them, first.

~

Royal Palace, Kwark
  Rylend Morphis

Teeg and I landed in the Queen's study together; if we hadn't, we might have attacked one another in that ghostly place.

At least it was ghostly now—four years in the future. We'd discovered that by *Looking*; our ability to fold space had been negated in some way.

"You think you can charge this thing?" Teeg handed a comp-vid to me. It had a layer of dust on it that indicated nobody else had touched it for at least six months.

"Only way to find out is to try," I shrugged, taking the device and calling up the power to give the solar battery a boost.

Seconds later, the screen illuminated. "Here you go—good luck on cracking the safety protocols to get into it."

"Leave that to the engineer in the room," he grumped before tapping through a set of symbols.

"I thought you went through architectural training."

"That was before engineering school."

"Right."

I realized we were badgering one another to get around the elephant in the room, as Mom always said. The elephant of course, was how the hell we'd been pulled away and slammed into the future —one that didn't resemble anything of the past we'd just left.

And why Kwark? It made no sense at all.

In the past, Dad was probably going crazy, because I'd disappeared right in front of him. That would ensure Mom would be notified nanoseconds later and she'd freak, too.

And then double-freak when she found out Teeg was also missing.

"Here we go," Teeg grimaced as he pulled up information on the comp-vid. "This isn't good." He thumbed through section after section, image after image. "Civil war," he lifted his gaze to mine. "Famine. Outbreaks of unknown diseases."

"The apocalypse? Fuck," I breathed.

"Sure looks like it," Teeg went back to scrolling through the comp-vid. "Here's my question—what are we supposed to do now? We can't fold space and we never could bend time."

"I think we ought to get to the bottom of this," I said. "If we do manage to get back to our own time, at least we'll know what's coming. Maybe we can stop it, then."

"Or, maybe the enemy brought us here to die. Have you considered that?"

"Dude, I'm not going to give up until I *am* dead. Now, are you coming with me, or are you staying here and waiting to keel over?"

"Lead the way," Teeg gestured with a hand. "I'm not sure we'll be able to find anything at all, but you're now in charge of that."

"Right." I strode toward the doorway; the door was hanging off its hinges, as if pulled away by a giant hand. I wasn't going to think about that right now.

Definitely not.

~

Royal Palace, Galk
Rajeon Dare
Most of the palace was rubble. Morrett and I stood at the crumbling edge of the throne room, looking down at what used to be the ornate, front steps of the ancient building.

"Five years," Morrett shook his head. "This happened five years from when we were taken."

"You know that how?" I frowned at him.

"I *Looked*. It's a skill Zaria gave me."

"How did this happen? Did your skill tell you that, too?"

"It's hidden. I couldn't get to it. I wish we had a comp-vid."

"Can't help you there. Normally I carry one, but the dress uniform didn't have a suitable pocket."

"Same here." Morrett shook his head at the devastation surrounding us. "How can something of this magnitude happen so quickly?" he added.

"I've seen worlds fall in far less time," I sighed. "Can you get us away from here?" I knew Morrett could fold space.

"I cannot fold space; I've already tried."

"That's—unnerving," I said.

"Can you still transform? Your vines can get us down there if you can," he pointed to the open ground around the cracked marble steps.

"Let me see." In seconds, I had become a thick, ropy vine, without thorns. I didn't wish to puncture my companion in any way, so I built a seat to carry him, then grew downward until I touched dry grass.

That's when I learned how dead Galk actually was.

It was as if the soul of the planet had died, leaving nothing living behind.

CHAPTER 14

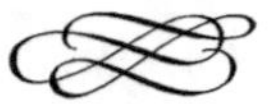

oyal Palace, Kwark
Zaria

My dreams were filled with love and comfort. I had no idea how or why, but I leaned into them when they came—a silent reassurance that all was not lost.

When I awoke the doubts always crowded in, but Valegar, who was just as bereft as I, stayed busy with the problems at hand.

The biggest of those, obviously, was finding D'slay and removing him from the playing board. The disappearances of so many others had to be dealt with, too, but even the strongest among us couldn't find them by *Looking*. That meant interference of some kind, and I disliked that a great deal.

Lissa, who'd had mates and children disappear, was tough on the outside, falling apart on the inside. I imagined that Roff, Toff's father, was quietly crumbling back on Le-Ath Veronis.

As for Morrett and Rajeon, I was very concerned, and couldn't imagine why they'd been taken when they had little connection to any of the others.

Except for you and Randl, a small voice informed me. Randl had approached Rajeon, even before this mission was offered. They'd reached some sort of understanding regarding Randl's mission to destroy the Prophet.

Somehow, all this tied together, and we were at a loss to connect the puzzle pieces into a whole picture.

"Dearest, are you well?" Valegar came and wrapped his arms about me as I stared blankly at the artfully arranged sculpture outside a window.

"I don't know," I breathed, feeling hopelessly lost. "I feel numb most of the time."

"As do I." He settled his chin atop my head and held me close. "My dreams say not to worry," he went on. "But those fade in the light of waking."

"I know," I whispered. "Sometimes, it's just—too much."

"It is difficult to take on the pain of others, is it not, when you are also suffering?"

"I think that is an accurate assessment."

"If only there were the tiniest of clues to inform us," he buried his face in my hair.

"I worry that they're swallowed up in bone dust, and are suffering," I said, as the first tear slid down a cheek. "Morrett has already been through so much, as has Vik and Rajeon. Trik, too, and Toff."

"If our child survives, will he also be damaged?"

At Val's question, I sobbed. This was what I'd been trying to avoid —thinking about the baby. How could anyone do this? It defied reason. Only once before had someone attempted to take Larentii children, and the Larentii race had arisen and destroyed an entire world because of it.

"Does he know how much we love him?" My voice quavering, I shuddered against Val, who was also weeping.

State House, Corez
  Lissa
"Of course I wish to go. I cannot trust any of you to find anything,

including Prime Minister Fallah's murderer." Rigo, now masquerading as Second Advisor Doril, snapped at Chief Milli.

Doril wasn't known for his steady temperament or reluctance to speak his mind. Rigo was now able to vent his frustrations against those he considered foolish or out of their depth.

We'd already been to the crime scene shortly after it happened, but had been called back to the State House to make a statement regarding the incident. Therefore, he and I had invited ourselves to the initial investigation of the crime scene at First Advisor Haris' country manor. Chief Milli tried to tell us we weren't needed. Chief Farram, who stood nearby, grasped Milli's arm and pulled her away from Rigo's wrath.

"I'll make arrangements for transportation," Assistant Director Parak intervened before Winkler could growl the order. At least Parak wasn't as offensive as the other two and was actually helpful most of the time. I wondered how much trouble it would be to send Milli to the Records and Reports unit and put Parak in her place. I had no doubts that he could do her job better than she could, with both eyes shut.

"We'll ride in a second vehicle, with Assistant Director Parak," Rigo informed Milli, his voice stiff and formal. "Please arrange it, Assistant Director," Rigo nodded at Parak.

"Of course, Second Advisor." Parak tapped on his comp-vid for a few seconds. "The vehicles will be waiting out front in ten," he said, shutting off his device. "Is there anything else you need, Second Advisor?"

"No. Thank you, Parak. We will meet you at the door at the appointed time. Until then, I have something to attend to."

Winkler, who stood nearby, acting as Second Advisor Miko, fell in behind Rigo as he headed for the door. I followed Winkler into the hallway, and then went on until we reached Doril's private office, a few doors down.

"Fucking hells," Winkler growled once the door was shut behind us. "Milli and Faram would argue with a leafing tree in the springtime."

"They'd probably fine it for growing leaves without permission," I agreed.

"Exactly my point," Winkler grumped. "Thank you for getting us a second vehicle," he told Rigo. "Parak is decent. The other two decidedly not. Even their scent offends me, now."

"Honey, we have to play nice in public," I reminded him. "The media will probably be there, waiting for us."

"Too bad they don't realize that Haris is alive and well on Avendor. I'd like to see how Ashe treats them when they show up and make demands."

"I think they'd likely find themselves on a deserted planet somewhere, with no way to get off," I said. "He isn't in the best of moods since everybody disappeared. Ashe says that he, Charles and Bree have *Looked* for the missing and haven't come away with even the smallest clue."

"If Wisdom found anything, would he tell us?" Rigo lifted an eyebrow. "If he finds any usefulness in the disappearances?"

"Good question. I don't have an answer," I shook my head. "We have to go or we won't get away ahead of Milli and Faram."

"Let's go, then."

"You say it was more like an earthquake, rather than an explosion?" Parak tapped notes on his comp-vid after Rigo questioned one of Haris' servants.

"I thought it was, because I've been in an earthquake before," the woman replied. "The others haven't, so I felt I ought to say what I think."

"Good observation," Rigo told her. "I don't feel a bomb can be ruled out completely, but the evidence certainly supports your view."

"Thank you for listening," the woman replied. "The local police discounted everything I told them."

"It will not be discounted now. We will also go over any recorded images that can be found of the incident. What troubles me most is the disappearances during the event."

"I worry about the First Advisor. He is a reasonable man and the best employer I've ever had. All of us are now concerned about losing our jobs, since the First Advisor's son is in the military off-world."

"That is understandable," I broke into the conversation. "If you do find yourself unemployed, contact this code," I handed her a small card. "Someone will get back with you."

"Thank you." The woman brushed moisture from her cheeks. "If you need to ask more questions, I'll be here as long as they let me stay."

Renee, I sent to my scheduling assistant on Le-Ath Veronis. *If we get a message from Cloudea Yonde on Corez in the future, find a job for her, all right? We'll pay travel expenses if she accepts the offer.*

On it, Renee replied promptly.

You've already arranged to hire her, haven't you? Winkler hid a smile.

You know it.

Cloudea nodded to me as she rose to walk out of the interrogation tent. She'd already talked to Milli and Faram. They'd dismissed her theory, too. No wonder we didn't have Fallah's murderer in jail, yet.

Quinnie Bee, I sent, *will you pull up recent images of Anila Milli and Chok Faram? Take a look and tell me what you see in them.*

I'll get back to you shortly, Quin replied. *I ah, haven't heard from Mom. Is she okay?*

Honey, I think she and Val need some time to grieve. They have no idea what happened to their child, and that has to be more than awful for them.

I understand. Thank you for telling me.

"That's the last of the witnesses," Parak shut off his comp-vid. "Shall we examine the damage to the home and surrounding grounds?"

"Yes, definitely," Rigo stood and stretched. The chairs we'd been given weren't the most comfortable, and the tent fabric had flapped in a brisk breeze the whole time we'd sat there, asking questions for nearly three hours.

My guess was we'd gotten more answers and taken better notes than the ones who were in charge of the investigation.

My thoughts were confirmed when we exited the tent, only to find Milli and Faram clumped together with several members of their team across the lawn, drinking tea and having casual conversation.

None of that conversation had anything to do with why we'd come here; Rigo, Winkler and I could hear it clearly from where we stood, although they imagined we couldn't hear anything from that distance.

Winkler growled when Milli referred to Rigo as a hard-assed number-cruncher.

"Is something wrong?" Parak asked.

"Nothing for you to worry about," I told him. "We've done our job—that's all that's necessary. Let's go examine the house and grounds. Take images with your comp-vid, Assistant Director, and send those and your notes to me when we get back."

"For the Second Advisor's files?"

"Certainly for his files," I agreed absently, while keeping my eyes on Milli and Faram. Faram had just made the mistake of calling me a piece of ass with no other skills.

I will kill him if you ask it, Rigo informed me as he stalked away to follow Parak.

~

P'loxett

Gillen Wilker

"I will not risk you again until I find a suitable partner," the Prophet hissed at Je'Dik. Anyone else who had the temerity to question the Prophet's actions would be dead already. I had no idea why he'd allowed Je'Dik to survive—especially after the failed assassination attempt on Hraede, which resulted in Kault's death. Somehow, Je'Dik was far more important than I'd suspected.

Je'Dik was angry, but I couldn't see his eyes through the goggles he wore to tell how angry he was. I wondered if the Prophet could read his body language as easily as I could.

"I want another like Kault," Je'Dik demanded. "We worked very well together."

"You will take what I give you," the Prophet allowed his temper to show, now. "We have many scheduled for death. You will do this for me."

Nobody would have mistaken the force of that command; it vibrated throughout the room and settled in my bones. Anyone else would have fallen to the Prophet's feet and kissed them, if he'd allow it.

Je'Dik merely huffed and turned to leave. P'loxett, who also appeared unworried, stood nearby, relaxed in his stance. I, on the other hand, shivered from the command the Prophet had given another.

"P'loxett, have you enough of the formula to continue your work?" The Prophet turned to my companion.

"Yes, my commander," P'loxett dipped his head to the Prophet. "I have enough for four worlds before I am forced to create more. I am ready to go wherever you send me."

"Good. Go to Galk first, then to Corez, Kwark and Murazal."

"It will be done as you command. Come, Gillen. We have work to do."

~

Royal Palace, Galk
   Reah

While Ocenosek and Cudworth were both troubled by the disappearances of Tory and Denevik, Cudworth displayed the most concern. I considered that the brothers had gotten close to Denevik since coming to Galk and left it at that.

Meanwhile, Lexsi, Kory and Wardevik had come to visit. Mostly, Lexsi wanted to ask questions about her father's disappearance and Warde desired to know whether I wanted Tory as a husband again.

I doubted it would trouble him greatly—he'd gotten used to my other mates. My worry was whether I'd actually get Tory back from wherever he was, or even if he were still alive.

Would Randl know, because of the coin on Tory's chest? Perhaps I should send mindspeech to find out.

"We can pinpoint where and when they disappeared, but that's all we can do," Bel Erland mumbled. He was more troubled by the disappearance of his father, but all the disappearances concerned him, as they did Wyatt and me.

Bel Erland and Wyatt had even folded space to Karathia and Campiaa to determine what they could when their fathers disappeared, which wasn't much. Dee had seen Teeg's disappearance, but there was nothing extraordinary about it. At first, Dee imagined Teeg had folded space for some emergency. It was nothing of the kind.

At least Tybus was still there and standing in for Teeg while everyone available searched for the missing. As for Ry, Erland, his father, had seen him disappear and knew immediately that something was wrong.

Pieces of my heart were missing, as were three of Lissa's sons and her eldest daughter. All of us had taken terrible blows, and our hearts and our patience were now pushed to the limit as we continued our missions.

When the knock sounded on my study door, Wyatt went to answer it. Rezo Nilus stood outside.

"Come in, please," I invited. "You ought to know about the disappearances, as you're one of us, now."

"It's the King, isn't it?"

"His stand-in, just as I'm the stand-in for the Queen," I agreed as Nilus settled himself on a chair next to Wardevik's. "He is my husband, in reality, as you may have guessed."

"It has not escaped me that the two of you are far closer than your royal counterparts."

"Agreed. I hoped it would pass unremarked," I said.

"Most fail to notice anything the King does," Nilus replied. "I notice, because it is my habit to do so. That means that you need another to act as your King. Your advisor's absence can be easily explained away. An excuse won't hold for the King."

"I suppose you're right," I conceded. "Wardevik, are you prepared to step in for Tory?"

"If that is your wish."

Always the diplomat, I sent. *Is it what you truly want?*

I see the expediency of it, and it makes sense. I will do this, my love.

"Bel Erland, can you make Uncle Warde look like the King of Galk?"

"I can." He rose and went to Wardevik before casting the spell to disguise him.

"That's very good," Rezo Nilus complimented Bel Erland's work.

"He's my son and a Fifth-level Karathian warlock," I sighed. "Like his father, the missing King."

⁓

Corez

Vik

We only realized we'd been walking through a haze of carbon monoxide after we walked out of it. Someone with power had formed a dome of it over the capital city of Varalon and kept it there long after it had served its purpose.

Not only had it killed all the inhabitants, it also killed any normal creature thoughtless enough to walk into it. As High Demons, we weren't affected by the poisonous air, but it was easier to breath once we left it behind.

I thought it strange that we'd not found any humanoid bodies or skeletons on our journey out of Varalon. Perhaps they'd been removed by crews wearing protective gear.

"This suburban area is also deserted," Denevik pointed out as he began walking again. "You know we'll need food and water if we're stuck here."

Meerius, is there anything like that for us to find? I sent.

The closest drinkable water is fifty miles away.

"I think we'll have to fly if we want water anytime soon," I told Denevik. "Meerius says it's fifty miles from here."

"Can he direct us?"

"Yes."

"We'll lose our clothing."

"Yeah. Well, it's water or clothes, take your pick."

I will keep your clothing for you.

Meerius' words baffled me.

Miniaturization, he said, as if I should have understood that all along.

"Take your clothes off before you change," I told Denevik. "Meerius says he can keep them safe while we fly."

Falchan

Drake

We'd been biding our time, listening for the first signs of the attack. Drew and I had gone into our meditation poses while Gavin, whose hearing was far better than anyone else's in the Falchani army, stood watch outside our tent.

The three of us were waiting for dawn and the enemy to arrive.

I hear them, Gavin sent. *Gather your blades and come. I will transport you both to the front if you wish it.*

He could do just that, I realized. Our combined weight would be nothing to his vampire strength, and his speed would ensure that nobody saw us clearly as we passed.

Drew and I stood smoothly from our seat on the tent floor—as we'd been taught.

"Take us, then," I told Gavin while sheathing my blades.

Gavin wasted no time; he wrapped an arm about each of us and flew through the camp as if the god of haste had infused his body.

Ravers, Drew sent as we came to an abrupt stop before the vanguard of the enemy.

Ravers indeed, I replied and pulled both my blades simultaneously.

~

Murazal

Nissa

The last time I'd been in danger, I was twelve. Here, on the future Murazal, danger invaded our very pores. We'd found a blast crater on the outskirts of the city, where I placed a concealing spell against sight, sound and smell.

Afterward, Toff built a small fire using a spark of power, and Trik managed to find a scrawny rabbit for our dinner.

Most of the people we'd seen were hungry and angry. If we hadn't hidden ourselves behind spells, they'd have probably attempted to steal our clothing and shoes.

"What are we going to do?" I asked my husbands. "We can't stay here, but I have no idea where we should go."

"If I recall the maps of Murazal correctly," Trik began, "there was farmland to the west of the capital city. I say we head that way tomorrow. I have no idea whether another animal will show up within my spell range to feed us breakfast. There's certainly nothing growing in this area to feed us; everything has been scavenged by the people we saw earlier."

"I agree with Trik," Toff said.

"Then tomorrow, we'll go west. Let's hope we don't starve before we find a better place to be, and then try to figure out what the hells is going on."

"It's like whatever your mother and the others were trying to do failed completely," Trik told us. "Or that they'd never attempted it in the first place."

"It does have that feel to it, doesn't it?" I agreed with his assessment. "Something happened, that's for sure."

"I think we should do casting spells while we head west," Toff suggested. "In case we run across something that shouldn't be. If we find anything, we can report it if we ever get back to our own time."

"This," Trik waved a hand, "would certainly interest a lot of people, and Ildevar Wyyld, especially."

"Mom, too, unless she's caught up in this mess somehow, just like we are," I said. "If Zaria finds out, she'll certainly be on top of it."

"I wonder if anyone else was pulled away from our time," I mused.

"That could be," Trik acknowledged. "If they were, then I assume there's a reason for it."

"You mean a reason other than making us suffer and die?" Toff crossed arms over his chest and stared at the lip of the blast crater above our heads.

"We're not dead yet," Trik pointed out. "We have abilities at our disposal that the suffering inhabitants of Murazal do not. If there's a way we can help them, then now's the time to start thinking about that."

"He's right," I told Toff. "If the enemy placed us here, then we will do everything in our power to reverse his intentions. We'll need to fashion water flasks out of something," I said, suddenly seeing a path open before us. "And maybe something to carry food, too. We have no idea whether we'll find food whenever it's time to stop for the night, so we have to conserve when we do find something."

"Agreed," Trik said.

"Agreed," Toff sighed.

Galk

Rajeon

"This reminds me of something I read," Morrett took stock of our surroundings. Everything was either dead or dying, and we'd walked quite far from the city. Even in the distance, I could see little growing, and we'd seen no evidence of living creatures, either.

"What's that?" I asked absently, considering which animal to change to in order to find water. It was our most pressing issue, in my mind.

"It was in books from the Larentii Archives, about the Life Giver."

"Life Giver?"

"Queen Reah," Morrett shrugged. "She saved many worlds that had been sucked dry of their essence by a rogue warlock. They all appeared barren and dead after a while. Somehow, she was able to replace the power within them and bring them back to life."

"Then I suppose it's too bad she isn't here right now," I complained. "Look, do you think you can hold onto the feathers of a giant eagle? We need to find water, or we won't last more than a day or two. An eagle is the best way to see something far off, in my estimation."

"Then we have to try. I hope you can catch me if I happen to fall off."

"I'll do whatever it takes," I promised.

"Let's go."

More and more, I was coming to admire this Sirenali. He had a full measure of courage and determination, and it shored up my own. I went through the change, ruffling my feathers as I settled on the ground for Morrett to climb up.

Soon enough, he was settled right behind the base of my neck and gripping feathers as if his life depended upon it.

As it did.

Taking off would be difficult for him. With hope that his grip was firm, I launched myself into the sky and beat my wings forcefully to gain height and speed.

I find this intriguing, if a bit terrifying, Morrett sent to me.

Same here, I replied. *Hold on. I see sunlight glinting off something in the distance. We'll investigate.*

And so we did.

~

Kwark

Rylend Morphis

"You know what bothers me?" Teeg asked as we walked toward the outskirts of the city.

"What's that?"

"No bodies. No skeletons—nothing. All of that is gone. I can't scent anything decomposing that isn't plant life."

"Now that you mention it, that is odd."

"What do you know about Prophet's disease?" he asked.

"Not much, really—just that it's a thing. Bel Erland knows more than I do."

"I wouldn't know either, except they blasted that stuff all over the crowds in Campiaa City and infected several metric tons of residents. On top of that, the Prophet took the bones of people infected with it, crushed them with the concrete they died in, then sold it to be reused in several new constructions. People inside those new buildings went nuts afterward."

"What's your point?"

"That he may have infected this world with Prophet's disease, then took the bones, crushed them and set them loose in some way on other worlds."

"That's scarier than anything I've heard in a long time. Is there any way to tell if that's what happened here?"

"Think about it—civil wars, famine, shortages and deadly diseases? Some of the diseases were never identified, according to what I read."

"Then it could be Prophet's disease, plus other, unpleasant things, I suppose. I've heard he isn't the most merciful of despotic criminals."

"And he has a few rogue gods at his beck and call. It would be easy for them to conjure up a few incurable maladies to go along with the Prophet's disease. Kills the people faster and frees up their bones for other uses."

"Because you can only kill so many in a day, physically speaking?"

"Why not? He's all about making people suffer, too, so there's that."

"Where is the ASD, CSD and everybody else in all this?"

"No idea. Maybe the planet was quarantined or something?"

"Then something would have been in the records, stating that," he argued.

"Yeah. You're right. Did you see anything on there about the space station closing? This is a hub world—what about all the worlds it serviced? What happened to them?"

"Hold on," Teeg pulled the comp-vid out to look in the files again. "Uh-oh. This says the space station was closed more than a year earlier from where and when we are right now—everybody thought the disease was being carried in from other worlds. As for the other worlds, I'll have to *Look*—there are no records, or they were dumped."

His eyes lost focus for a few moments. While he *Looked*, I did the same. "Civil wars," we said in unison as we refocused on one another.

"If the same thing happened on other hub worlds, then the entire Alliance—or Alliances—could be at war, thanks to the Prophet and his likely minion, D'slay."

"What about Mom and the others who are trying to protect the hub worlds, then?"

"No idea. I've tried mindspeech—it either doesn't work off-planet, or they're not listening or plain not there."

"If they're not there, where could they be?"

"If I knew, I'd have told you already. I feel like this planet and the others around us have been shoved out of their places and abandoned."

"How could that happen? It makes no sense."

"Nothing about this makes sense, or have you not noticed?"

Falchan

Drake Tatsuya

How long did you say this battle lasted? Gavin had given up any pretense of using blades and had been fighting with his claws for the past two hours.

Until sundown, I replied. *That's another hour away, if I'm right about the sun's position this time of year.*

You never have to tell a vampire when sundown is, Gavin reminded me as he relieved two more enemies of their heads.

Where did they get all these people? Drew demanded. I wasn't sure about Gavin, but Drew and I were as thirsty as we could possibly be. Somewhere behind us, the water wagon servicing our battalion had been damaged or destroyed. I wished for the ability to fold space; I'd head for the nearest river for water.

Have you tried Pulling *water to you?* Gavin asked. Apparently, he understood our plight, although we hadn't told him about it.

No. I assumed since we couldn't fold space, I began.

Here. A full waterskin slapped me in the face while a second one hit Drew in the chest.

Damn and tarnation, Drew cursed before jerking the cork from the container and drinking. Gavin stood beside him, dealing with all who tried to reach him while he drank his fill.

My waterskin lay at my feet while I fought on.

Your turn, Gavin informed me as Drew got back to the business of fighting.

Pulling the waterskin into my hand, I did as Drew had, removing the cork and drinking the thing dry. I didn't drop it again until there was no liquid remaining inside it.

My turn, now, Gavin said. *Cover me.*

I took the front, Drew covered Gavin's back as the vampire emptied his waterskin in record time. Once that was accomplished, the claws he'd sheathed appeared again and no enemy stood before him for long.

One more hour, I reminded myself.

Only one.

CHAPTER 15

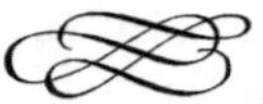

Kabbuc Mountain, Mardir
Toad

"Now that Kault is dead and Je'Dik has been called back to P'loxett until another partner can be found, it is up to us to assassinate the next target," D'slay snarled at me. He wanted no physical part in this, especially after Kault was killed so easily.

It was obvious to me that the one in Larvalis' place held power of some sort; I could think of no other reason why anyone would survive an attack from a misting vampire and another whose parentage I could only half guess.

"This is your target," he shoved his comp-vid at me.

He knew this one was very similar to the last—who'd killed Kault. "We can't hand him over to someone else to kill after we take him, so you're going to have to step up."

He knew what killing did to me—I would be disabled for weeks. He had no concept of the pain I suffered during that time; he'd curse me and my failings instead. Somehow, his obsession couldn't get past the illness that overwhelmed me whenever I ended a life on his command.

"Perhaps you should have bought some other wizard's child," I said, surprised by my own temerity.

"There weren't any others suitable," he snapped before slapping my face. "Get yourself together. I will accompany you to ensure that this termination is done properly."

"Of course." I bowed my head to the one who'd mastered me.

This would be nothing like Prime Minister Fallah's death, where the actual killing was done by another. All I had to do was move the body afterward, following D'slay's command to fix her internal organs to hide any trace of the acid employed in her death. I'd left the tiniest clue behind to indicate the manner of her death, but Security Forces on Corez turned out to be more incompetent than anticipated.

Now, D'slay wanted *me* to kill his next target.

Against my will.

⌇

State House, Corez

Lissa

"Is something wrong?" Winkler asked. He, Rigo and I were waiting for breakfast in Rigo's study before diving into more of the information we'd gotten from Milli and Faram. If those who worked the same jobs on Le-Ath Veronis supplied notes as bad as theirs, they'd be relieved of their duties quickly.

"I wish Faram's notes were as easy to read as Trevor's," I set my comp-vid on the table with a sigh. "Something makes me feel halfway itchy, too, but I can't quite figure out what's causing it."

"Trevor's notes are clear, concise and you can trust his observations," Rigo, who stood nearby, turned toward Winkler and me. We'd taken our seats at the table, waiting for food to be delivered. Rigo, on the other hand, was restless for some reason.

A knock on the door was followed by two servants wheeling in a cart filled with covered dishes. Any other wizard would have known to hide or dampen the scent of his partner in crime.

This one hadn't.

Even with time to consider other options, I'd still have come to the same decision, since I had no way of knowing what would come of it.

Ignoring the wizard, I aimed straight for the disguised Sirenali who guided the cart, blasting him to bits with power I barely realized I'd gathered. Winkler and I latched onto the wizard with power, so he couldn't escape.

Something pulled back against our hold on him; we struggled against an unknown strength that wanted the wizard as badly as we did. For the smallest of moments we held him, until our vision blurred for barely a second and our power skipped a beat.

Winkler howled the moment the wizard disappeared with a frightened shriek; we were helpless to stop him.

That surprised both of us.

The next surprise was even more unexpected—an earthquake rumbled into existence beneath our feet. It shook the foundations of the State House and rippled outward through the city, knocking down buildings and splitting streets with the massive roar of an angry beast.

~

Royal Palace Grounds, Galk

Reah

The good news here is we got everybody out. The bad news is that much of the palace is unsafe, if not reduced to rubble, I reported to Lissa. *The earthquake here happened shortly after yours on Corez.*

Zaria and her Larentii held the palace together on Kwark, but much of the city around it is in ruins. I suppose it's some sort of victory that D'slay appears to be dead, but his wizard got away. I suspect that all the earthquakes were a direct result of D'slay's death.

If you're saying this is by the Prophet's hand, then you are likely correct, Zaria joined our conversation. *Alrenardo misted Tamp and the Queen out of the palace on Hraede, but many other occupants weren't so lucky. He says at least sixteen are dead from falling debris or walls collapsing on them.*

What about Zanfield and the others on Murazal? I asked.

They weren't in the State House when the quake happened, and Travis and Trent managed to put a shield over them while Zanfield spoke at a court official's retirement party.

Zaria, is there a way to track the wizard? Lissa asked.

I can ask Randl to come have a look where he disappeared.

He'll have to stand on air; the entire room collapsed.

I think I can manage that for him.

How quickly can he be here?

He's on the way now.

State House, Corez

Zaria

Valegar and I shielded everyone there while Randl, standing on an air support I'd supplied, touched marble fragments where D'slay and the wizard had stood.

Minutes passed as Randl considered this fragment or that, before dropping the one he held and lifting another.

Finally, he turned toward me. "I see D'slay and his death," Randl confirmed. "As for the wizard, there's no evidence that he was ever here."

"How is that possible?" Lissa demanded. I'd already seen the images of the wizard in her and Winkler—I knew it to be true.

"Perhaps whatever pulled him away erased all traces of him, too, although I'm very interested in how that could be accomplished," Randl replied. "My concern is whether the Prophet will be satisfied with this method of revenge, or if he has other things planned to make us pay."

"My bet is on the latter," Zaria sighed. "He won't stop until he's destroyed everything, but that was his intention all along. Killing D'slay may have convinced him to move his plans forward, but I think they were already in place."

"Then all we have to do is figure out what those plans are," Lissa rubbed her forehead.

"I can fix the headache," I offered.

"Please. I can't think anymore."

~

Emergency Shelter, Murazal
Zanfield Staggs

"Miz, Lev and Mae are now doing our work on Sirena," Dave informed me as he and Sabrina thumbed through images, "since they can't leave the planet without the Prophet picking up their location."

We needed engineers and architects to assess the damage throughout the capital city. I didn't trust anyone else to give me accurate information. "This bridge between business complexes needs to be closed," Sabrina handed a comp-vid to me. "The piers and pier caps could fail any moment."

The bridge in question connected two complexes the size of small cities that stood on massive piers of their own on a large lake. "I'll take care of it." Travis began tapping on his comp-vid.

"The passenger train to both complexes travels that bridge," I pointed out. We may have to transport trapped employees another way. What about the piers beneath those complexes? Are they holding up?"

"Checking that now," Sabrina replied.

"Update on current death toll," Trent announced.

"Let me see it." His comp-vid was set in front of me at my makeshift desk. "Nearly three thousand," I pinched the bridge of my nose. "Fucking Prophet," I growled.

"So far, the only positive in all this is that D'slay is dead," Travis responded.

"At this cost?" I tapped Trent's comp-vid. "Damn. Can this day get any worse?"

"Don't tempt fate," Dave cautioned. "We don't need worse."

"Kwark has the fewest casualties," Trent said when I handed his comp-vid back. "But they had several Larentii there to dampen the earthquake and minimize the damage."

"I was hoping we'd find you here," Kell and Opal folded in. "We just came from talking with Ildevar and Tybus. As you imagine, they're not pleased with these simultaneous events on five hub worlds, because that points to a single perpetrator. We may be forced to inform both Alliances of how dangerous the Prophet has become."

"Five hub worlds?"

"Hraede was hit, too, along with Corez, Galk, Kwark and Murazal."

"Hraede completely slipped my mind, I apologize," I said. "This makes it so much worse. You're right Dave, I shouldn't have tempted fate," I turned to nod at the dwarf. "How did the Prophet do this—attack five worlds at once?" I asked Kell.

"We don't know, yet. I wish we could have gotten our hands on that wizard—we may have learned a lot from him, but he's probably with the Prophet, now."

"Wherever that is," Travis grumbled.

"We've already *Looked*; if the Prophet used anything other than raw power to cause the damage to five hub worlds, we can't find it," Opal said. "That means he's either grown more powerful, or he's hidden the catalysts behind bone dust."

"I think I agree with Zaria on this—she said he likely had all this in place before; we merely activated his plans earlier than he intended by killing D'slay."

"I hope you're both right," Opal sighed. "Otherwise, it's terrifying."

"I agree with Zanfield," Travis said. "All this happened immediately after D'slay was killed. Did he even have time to pull that much power in before unleashing it in five directions? And why attack the other worlds on a whim when D'slay died on Corez?"

"Unless he already had something in place," Kell nodded thoughtfully. "That makes sense, I suppose."

"I think that—and the disappearances of several of our colleagues means he knows we're filling in for the actual leaders of those hub worlds," Trent voiced the worry that bothered me most. "I figure he realizes that we won't die so easy, but he can sure get to some of us, as well as the planets and their population."

"Are Ildevar and Tybus preparing a statement, in case it's necessary to warn the Alliances?" Perri asked softly.

"They are—that's what the meeting was about. They'll hold back until it's absolutely necessary, but the statement is being written now."

"Zan," she took my hand and squeezed my fingers, "I want to go to the State House, to see whether I can detect any power residue from the quake."

"Sweetheart, I'm not sure it's safe," I argued.

"Zan, that asshole took the King of Karathia. *My* King. I'm really angry about that. If there's something I can do about it, then I have to try. I'll keep a bubble shield around the rest of me; I only need to touch a few things with my hands to search for a power signature."

"My love, you could be risking your life," I responded.

She went still and blinked at me. I didn't understand for a moment.

You called her your love. I think she's a little stunned, Travis sent.

I'd been holding that back, not wanting to crowd her or push her in any way, considering her past and how she'd been abused by her uncle Alken. If I ever got my hands on that piece of filth, he wouldn't survive.

"If you really want to go, then I'm coming with you. If something happens, it will happen to both of us." I stood and pulled her into a hug.

Travis

Even Kell and Opal went with us to the State House, or what remained of it. Kell found the most stable portion near the epicenter of the damage, and Opal employed power to keep the broken stone and rubble where it was until Perri could touch what she wanted.

Zanfield refused to leave Perri's side and walked carefully over the wreckage with her until she found a likely spot. With one hand, she gripped Zanfield's arm. With the other, she leaned down to touch the stones.

Perri's audible, indrawn breath made all of us jump. "Murazal is in trouble," she squeaked.

"We already know," Dave began.

"No. Murazal, the planet's spirit. He's in trouble."

"Who has him?" Trent demanded.

"Nobody," Randl appeared as if called. "Nobody carries Murazal—he, Kwark, Galk, and Corez remained neutral in all this."

"Zaria carries Hraede," Opal said. "Is he or she in danger, too?"

"I'll ask," Randl said before going silent for a moment.

Zaria arrived moments later, three Larentii with her. "Hraede went silent after the quake," she said, sounding worried. "This isn't good."

～

Falchan—Past

Drake

Sundown had come, and the last line of invaders was beginning to waver, until the first few turned and ran.

Had fear for their lives finally kicked in, or had these not been affected by the raver drugs like the others before them? Regardless, the rest of their army had died on Falchani blades—and one vampire's claws.

The losses on our side were just as steep as the history books claimed they were. Bodies of friend and foe littered the field behind us; the ground was slippery with blood and everywhere were discarded weapons and war trophies.

Gavin, I shouted mentally, as he began to chase after more enemy deserters. I shouldn't have bothered; he was already on them as they raced toward a far stand of trees. Even weary beyond reckoning, a vampire will still outrun a humanoid.

"Let's go get him," Drew came up beside me, breathing hard.

"Damn. I guess we'll have to—he's chasing after the first deserters, now."

Without much motivation, we began our walk toward the trees, where Gavin was about to disappear.

"What was that?" Drew hissed as a light appeared quickly amid the trees, only to disappear just as quickly.

"I thought my eyes were playing tricks on me," I confessed.

"I don't think that's it, bro." Drew broke into a run. With legs screaming for rest, I forced myself to follow him.

~

Murazal

  Nissa

If we hadn't formed invisibility shields around ourselves, we'd have been seen by the troubling number of ragged, desperate souls we found on a trampled path, heading toward the capital city. Toff, Trik and I'd already had a heated argument about warning them that there was nothing but violence waiting there for them.

We finally concluded that if they tried to attack us, we could end up harming them, so remaining invisible appeared to be the best course of action. We chose to listen to their conversation, but there was very little other than talk of disease, hunger and the need of basic shelter.

When we reached the first pile of bodies, which were being loaded into what looked like a garbage shuttle, we stopped still and held our breath.

Still, the travelers passed them by as if they didn't see it.

They don't see the ones loading the bodies, Toff hissed in mindspeech.

They don't see the bodies, either, Trik added. *Or hear the hover-loaders.*

They don't look starved, either—the ones doing the loading, I pointed out. *Their clothes aren't rags like the others.*

Should we ask them, I began.

No! Toff and Trik said in unison. *Listen closer,* Toff went on, *some of them aren't speaking Alliance common.*

What language is that? I asked.

Something I know a lot about, and that's not a good thing. They're using a language very similar to that spoken by the Green Fae. That means they're fae of some sort, and there isn't any way they'd willingly stoop to heaving bodies into a garbage shuttle, unless someone more powerful ordered them to.

Is it evidence of the Prophet's hand in all this?

It could be. We just have to escape their notice and try to find out where they're going with that load of bodies.

I'd bet three Grey House jewels that those bodies are infected by Prophet's disease, Trik growled.

I wish we could send mindspeech to Mom, I said. *I'm afraid that if we approach them to place a spell-tag on the shuttle, the Prophet will know. We're not strong enough to stand against that.*

I'm not sure anybody is strong enough for that, Trik agreed. *It's obvious they're taking those bodies off-world; that shuttle will get them to the space station, where a ship is likely waiting.*

Do you think all these people are infected—they just haven't realized it yet?

If the Prophet is involved, I'd say it's very likely, Toff said. *He's killing all of them, albeit slowly.*

Supply and demand? Killing sufficient numbers to get the desired amount of bone dust to spread elsewhere and infect new victims?

That's terrifying, Trik shook his head. *How can anyone be this evil?*

I hear the one who created him set him on this path, I said. *That sounds like double or triple the amount of evil imaginable. It's so horrible, it's beyond my comprehension.*

Unless he was obsessed, he had a choice in the matter, Trik pointed out.

There's that, I conceded. Nobody got to choose their parents or relatives. It was up to them to decide how they lived their lives. Trik understood that; he found his father's sins and criminal activity repugnant in the extreme. If anyone could be the exact opposite of Zellar, then Trik was that person. He knew Toff and I loved him, no matter who he was related to.

I think you should put a spelled mental record together, Toff said. *In case we don't make it, maybe they'll find us and check our remains for that sort of thing.*

Of all the wizard clans, only Grey House wizards held that ability, and the record would last as long as there was a single cell of a single bone left to relay the message.

Good idea. I'm beginning now.

~

Corez

   Vik

We'd reached the lake and drank our fill before examining the hulk of a crashed shuttle near our landing location. "This isn't an Alliance shuttle," Denevik pointed out the markings on a twisted piece of metal.

"No, that's from Greval, according to the markings." I named a world that wasn't a member of either Alliance.

"I thought Greval was dying from some sort of rampant disease," Denevik said.

"That was seven years ago. Besides, who better to steal from? I doubt the Prophet gets choosy when he sees ships and shuttles for the taking, and if the planet is too sick to fight back, even better."

"Why do you suppose this one crashed?"

"No idea. It doesn't appear to have been shot down," I sorted through more of the wreckage. "Maybe Greval wasn't big on safety measures, should the engine fail."

"Looks like it's been here for at least a year or more," Denevik noted. "No sign of bodies inside, either."

Perhaps it was crashed on purpose, Meerius suggested. *If those inside were infected with Prophet's disease, what better way to spread it?*

"That's a terrifying thought," I said aloud.

"What's that?" Denevik asked.

"Meerius thinks it could have been crashed on purpose, with whatever or whomever was on board infected with Prophet's disease."

"Damnation to Jufaleh," Denevik cursed. "Is there no end to his wickedness?"

Help me, a voice called out. It was so weak, I barely heard it.

It's Corez, Meerius cried. *She's here, close.*

"Fucking hell," I snapped. "Meerius, tell me where to go."

~

Galk

    Rajeon

We found water—a lake filled with it—but it was stagnant and undrinkable. "This isn't good," Morrett looked about him. Only a few clumps of weeds, mostly dead, covered the shoreline. Farther out, dead stumps of trees emerged from the ground like grave markers—a testament to an entire planet and the lives lost upon it.

Command me, Sirenali, a small voice filled my mind. Morrett gasped; he'd heard it, too. *Pod'l-morph, a drop of your blood. Please*, the voice continued.

"Who are you?" I demanded aloud.

Galk, the voice wheezed.

"The planet spirit is dying—we have to find him," Morrett began to search the area, desperate to find the owner of the voice.

Dig deep, came the next words. *Pod'l-morph. Help me.*

With the idea in my head that this could be the worst kind of trap, I became a tree and began to sink my roots into the sandy soil beneath my feet.

～

Falchan

    Drake

The blast fired at us almost took Drew and me down, we were so weary. Ahead, Gavin was nearly knocked off his feet; only the digging into the ground with his claws kept him from flying backward with the force of the power leveled against us.

Drew was faster than I was at firing back; I hadn't considered it until he tossed a fireblast against the second one hurled in our direction. Both met halfway and detonated, knocking down trees and flattening anything else in their path.

I see them, I shouted as drifting smoke and falling debris cleared enough. Four attackers stood farther inside the stand of trees; Drew's fireblast surprised them and took them unaware. Three were rising to their feet as a fourth rocked on his heels while attempting to sight us again.

No! Gavin rushed forward so fast, I wondered how he still had enough energy to do so. Two died.

Two escaped.

One, in his haste to fold away, dropped a vial of shining liquid.

Poison, Drew informed me.

How do you know that? I demanded.

Falchan told me.

Jerking my head around, I stared at my brother, who was walking toward me. On the bare skin of his chest, just above his leather vest, lay a gold coin. I went still. Travis and Trent had gold coins on their chests.

Drew carried Falchan—the spirit of the planet.

"We have to find a way to get that vial to the Larentii," Drew said, bending down to carefully lift the clear container. "Falchan says there are three others buried here, and we need the Larentii to lift them from their burials and take them away."

"How do you propose we do that?" Gavin growled at us. "We can't fold space."

"Nefrigar?" Drew spoke aloud and sent mindspeech at the same moment.

If he answered, it would be Nefrigar from the past, most likely, but Larentii had a way of sorting things out where time was concerned.

"You called?" Nefrigar appeared nearby. "Ah, Falchan," he greeted the coin on Drew's chest.

"He says we need Larentii to pull up the other three of these that those two buried, with their two friends, who managed to get away," Drew said, pointing toward decapitated bodies.

"Of course. I imagine that is a poison designed to kill Falchan and others like him?" Nefrigar surmised.

"Yes."

"Who do we have here?" Nefrigar strode toward the bodies in

question. "Ah," he said, as if expecting it, "Stone Wicke. Nicely done, vampire," he told Gavin.

"Who's the other one?" I asked.

"A child of Yaredolak Cordrifith," Nefrigar surveyed the body carefully. "I imagine Zaria would know more by searching his features."

"Wait—are you from now, or the future?" I asked.

"The future," Nefrigar shrugged as if I should have known it. "Drew is now powerful enough to send mindspeech into your own time, should he desire it. Apparently, he did just that."

"*Now* it works," I rolled my eyes.

Nefrigar smiled. "Shall we search for the poison, before we forget it's here?" he asked.

"I suppose we should get on that," I agreed.

~

Kwark

Rylend Morphis

"This is the only fresh water I could find within walking distance," I said. I'd had to scry for it, too, although once we were close enough, Teeg could scent it for himself.

"Is it drinkable?" Teeg asked.

"I don't find anything wrong with it," I answered after performing another scrying spell.

"Then we'll hope for the best," he said, dipping hands into the small stream and lifting water to his lips. With a sigh, I did the same, trusting that there wasn't anything there that could fool my spell and kill us anyway.

"This water is still safe," a voice sighed beside us, making us jump in surprise. "It is all I can do, now. Nothing else lives here; I lost everything else last year."

I stared at the image of the man—that's all he was. A ghost of something that had once been powerful, if my warlock's gifts told me anything at all.

"I am Kwark," he introduced himself. "Although I feel myself fading with every sunset that passes across this stream."

"What happened?" I asked, while Teeg stared and attempted to get a scent off this wispy stranger.

"I hear he calls himself the Prophet," Kwark shrugged fading shoulders. "I have a favor to ask," he added.

"What favor would that be?"

"I need to restore what I have lost. I beg you to allow me stay with you until I am myself again."

"Your power, you mean?"

"Yes. Or I will die with my planet and will never be reborn."

"Vik carries a world spirit," Teeg pointed out, as if attempting to convince me.

"Vik?" Kwark asked, suddenly interested.

"Our brother," I explained. "He came by it because he works with Randl."

"Reviendus," Kwark breathed, as if the title was a holy one. "How I wish I had gone to him. Now, it is too late, and he will not come for me."

"I am here, now," I said. "How can I carry you? My brother holds his in a gold coin on his chest."

"I no longer have enough energy left to do that for myself. I can only send you the image of the coin I wish to be. You will have to do the rest."

"Are you sure about this, bro?" Teeg asked.

"I think I need to do this," I said. "Send the image," I turned back to Kwark, who was now so transparent I could barely see him. He was fading fast, likely from the energy it took to remain visible and speak to us.

The image formed in my mind—an ancient coin from Kwark itself. Gathering power, I formed the spell that would lock Kwark inside gold, then scryed for the closest source of that metal.

"Hurry, he's almost gone," Teeg warned. I felt Kwark slipping away as I *Pulled* a chunk of gold from farther upstream.

Had he known or hoped that someone would come to this particular stream, where gold still lay hidden?

I didn't have time to consider that idea—not if Kwark were to survive.

Almost there, I sent mindspeech to him, begging silently that he wouldn't die while I hastened the spell to form gold into a coin.

A rushing sound came the moment the coin was fully-formed and hanging in midair in front of me. Before I could do anything else, the coin slammed into my chest and I felt my power being drained—so rapidly that I dropped to my knees from intense pain and sudden weariness.

If Kwark survived, would I, also?

Murazal

Nissa

We stayed where we were until the last of the bodies were loaded onto the shuttle and it lifted from the ground, eventually flying out of sight.

"Where to now?" Trik asked.

"Water and food, Toff suggested. We won't last long here without water first."

"I can try *Looking*," I said. I saw water in my mind, but it was nearly two miles away and I couldn't tell whether it was safe to drink. I relayed my findings to Toff and Trik.

"We'll take a look," Toff said, sounding determined. "If it's not drinkable, we'll find the next closest source."

"We have to leave this road behind," I told him.

"I think we've seen enough sick people for today. Dead ones, too," Trik pointed out.

"You're right," I agreed. "Let's go."

Corez

> *Vik*

She's there—in the water, Meerius shouted. *Wait, she's sick.*

I'd reached for the gold coin shining in half a foot of water when Meerius warned me.

Please, I need blood to counteract the poison, Corez sounded as if she were weeping.

"What's wrong?" Denevik slid to a stop next to me, his boots splashing the water around us.

"Meerius says Corez is sick. Corez says she needs blood to counteract the poison."

"High Demon blood, then," Denevik frowned at the coin in the water. "What are we waiting for?"

"It could be extremely dangerous," I said. "Deadly, even."

Emotion crossed Denevik's face. "When I started this mission, I was looking for an honorable way to die," he said. "But I've seen that there may be something to live for, thanks to Zaria and you. Corez," he spoke directly to the coin, "I will do my best to live, if you will do the same."

Denevik turned to his smaller Thifilathi, and with a clawed hand, ripped open the skin at the center of his chest. "Come, then, my lady," he lifted the coin and slapped it onto bloody scales, "we will attempt to survive together."

Meerius and I shouted our dismay as Denevik dropped to his knees in the water and roared in pain.

<h1 style="text-align:center">CHAPTER 16</h1>

oad

"Where am I?" I demanded.

"In a cage, where you will do no more damage," the man informed me.

"Where is the cage, then?" I rephrased my question.

"That is not for you to know." He slid a plate of food beneath the lowest bar, then followed that with a cup of water. The bars of the cage didn't harm him like they did me when I attempted to touch them. I'd also been prevented from using any of the power normally available to me.

This man—so far, he was the only one I'd seen, although I knew there were others somewhere. I couldn't say how I knew that; my cage was in the middle of a field, or so it appeared.

The dark-haired, tall man who tended me would walk away until he vanished behind a shield or barrier of some sort, while the vision of the field continued uninterrupted. If this were the Prophet's way of punishing me for D'slay's death, he'd chosen well. I wanted to weep at my isolation, except at meal times.

Those, at least, were not neglected and the food was good. Often, I worried it would be poisoned, but hunger always won. If it killed me, perhaps I would be better off anyway.

I expected to be tortured and questioned, in that order. Nothing of the sort had occurred as yet, and that only ramped up the fear of what my final fate would be. Perhaps this was the form of torture they'd chosen; to keep me uninformed and frightened.

My stomach growled, reminding me that food was waiting. I sat cross-legged on the floor of my cage and pulled the plate into my lap. This time, there was fruit on the plate, in addition to cooked fish and vegetables.

Better fare than I'd ever gotten with D'slay, and I doubted the Prophet's people ate this well, too.

Where was I, and why had I been brought here?

~

Galk

Rajeon

As a tree, I'd hollowed myself and formed steps so Morrett could descend until he came to the coin which held Galk's spirit. Once there, I'd open a huge root so Morrett could grasp the coin. Then, I'd pull us both up until we reached the surface.

The method I'd employed wasn't lost on me; it could have been my death long ago, had I been chosen by the Avii Queen—to dig deep and allow her to deposit a collection sphere in a hidden land called Fyris, on a now-dead world called Siriaa. Travis and Trent explained it to me when I asked if they knew.

I hoped my fate wouldn't be that of the pod'l-morphs who'd been selected for that task on Siriaa; as far as I knew, they were all dead.

Likely, it had been the doom of my family, as I appeared to be the only survivor. "I'm here," Morrett spoke aloud, before reaching for the coin. I'd formed a bowl over it, so dirt wouldn't cave in on the coin before he could take it.

"I have the coin," he announced.

Command me, Sirenali, Galk whispered to both of us. *Pod'l-morph, a drop of your blood, please. I do not have much time remaining.*

Hold on, I told Morrett, and using my strength, I pulled in roots, became a diamond vine and shot toward the surface, spilling Morrett out before becoming myself—except for a diamond thorn on one finger.

Without a second thought, I cut myself.

Morrett held out the coin. I allowed several drops of blood to fall on it. "Live," he commanded the coin, obsession vibrating in his voice.

First came the blinding flash of light, and then Morrett's shriek as the coin tore from his fingers, burned a hole through his shirt and attached itself to his chest.

"Morrett," I shouted, reaching out to catch him as he fell, unconscious, to the ground.

~

Murazal

Nissa

"This was once a forest." Toff sighed at the number of stark, broken tree stumps surrounding the lake.

"The lake is drying up, too," Trik observed. He was right—parched, cracked mud lay before us, with the water lying many yards away.

"Just looking at it reminds me how thirsty I am," I sighed. "We should use a spell to purify every handful we drink, though."

"Agreed," Toff nodded.

"Shall we?" Trik began walking toward the edge of the water, which lapped against the moist-but-drying perimeter surrounding it.

I followed Trik; Toff followed me.

"What's this?" Trik reached the water first, then leaned down to lift something he'd found there.

I found it difficult to describe what happened next. The gold coin Trik found was sucked from his hand and adhered to his chest in a blinding flash of light. That strange and unbelievable act caused so much pain and confusion for Trik—he screamed and fell while Toff and I struggled as if our legs were engulfed in quicksand to reach his side.

~

P'loxett

V'dar

Thirty-four dark, sharp spikes dotted my shoulders, representing thirty-four rogue gods I'd absorbed to combine their power with mine. Only when I was alone did I allow my robe to fall away from them—to admire their symmetry.

I'd discovered that should I desire it, I could peel away this one or that, reshape them, and send them elsewhere to do my bidding. I'd done that a few times already, and sometimes, I did so because I missed the spheres I used to clack together in my fingers—as a soothing exercise.

Two of them currently slid smoothly through my fingers as P'loxett approached me, looking pleased. Pulling my heavy robe over my shoulders with power, I adjusted the hood to hide the studs, although P'loxett knew my secret already.

"I told you the formula and my plan would capture those powerful enough to serve you well," P'loxett informed me. He smiled as he spoke, which wasn't usual for him.

"You did very well. How long will it take before they come to me on their own?"

"The mixture was more potent than I imagined and has worked faster than I could ever comprehend. They succumbed so quickly; I felt them stumble and fall. In only a few days, they will begin to straggle in," he bared more teeth in a vicious grin. "Even those planets barely affected will eventually feel the pull and bring you mighty gifts. I have arranged for them to arrive in stages, so you may bend them to your will without interruption."

"Excellent. Well done," I told him. "We will await this first group before venturing out again. I consider the loss of Stone and Reddy necessary to bring me the one from Falchan."

"I believe you will be quite pleased with him," P'loxett agreed. "And with the others as well. The loss of Toad, however—that must be avenged. I know not where they took him, but I will find him if he still lives."

"He has gifts most wizards only dream of," P'loxett agreed. "Finding him is quite important, especially if we wish to traverse time once more."

"My thoughts precisely. In addition, my people are almost finished with the new escape world, should we be found," I said.

"You will not need it, once your newest slaves arrive. As for Stone Wicke, you will forget all about him when you see his replacement."

"Who might that be?"

"None other than the King of Karathia himself," P'loxett laughed. It was evil and jarring, that laugh.

I liked it very much.

~

SouthStar, Avendor

Ashe

"You've been watching the events on your planets all along," I told the gathering of world leaders. "Now, it is time for you to go home and take your places once more. As you've seen, all of you are fortunate to be alive, although some have lost your positions—temporarily, of course," I nodded to Doy Haris.

"Aren't we still in danger?" Queen Myriae of Galk demanded.

"Yes, but not as much as before," I told her. "D'slay is dead, and the Prophet has achieved his desires. We have troubles now you cannot imagine. Gather your things; you will be transported back to your planets to make plans for rebuilding."

"Make plans—perhaps," Doy Haris rose from his seat, his face indicating deep thoughts. "I cannot imagine this Prophet allowing anything to proceed normally from now on."

He was right—things could go downhill in a tremendous hurry if we couldn't find a way to avert greater disasters to come.

"You are now in charge of Corez," Haris turned to former Second Assistant Doril. "I assume you understand what must be done?"

"I hope to have your assistance," Doril dipped his head to Haris. "I will not be as good a leader as the one who took our places."

"Undoubtedly," Haris agreed. "I will do whatever is required of me, short of breaking any laws, to put Corez to rights again—should that be possible."

"Then keep your hope alive," I cautioned him. "We don't know whether this latest blow will become insurmountable as yet."

~

Corez

Lissa

We're bringing the hub world leaders back; it's time to set them in place again, Ashe sent. *We have other problems to solve, now.*

He was right—we had plenty of problems to solve, and some of those problems involved getting friends and family back.

"What is it, Tiessa?" Rigo asked.

"The ones we replaced are coming back, so we can work on more important things."

"Yes. There are many other, more important things for us to focus on," he agreed. "However, I dislike leaving them with a pile of rubble rather than a seat of power," he added.

"Honey, they have their lives, and that's more than they would have had if we hadn't come. The fact that they've been relieved of obsessions should never be taken lightly, either."

"True," he conceded. "That, and the gift of their lives, is the ultimate gift. When will they arrive?"

"How about now?" I pulled Rigo around as Trajan appeared with Haris, Doril and Second Assistant Blaren.

I figured we'd get dumped on pretty quick, so I grabbed Rigo's and Winkler's arms to fold the hell out of there.

"We owe you," Doy Haris stepped forward. "We understand that you are a former King of Hraede?" He offered his hand to Rigo.

"And who might you be?" he turned to Winkler.

"Her werewolf mate," he pointed toward me.

"And you?" He finally came around to me. The woman in the room. *How typical.*

Allowing my disguise to drop, I revealed myself. "The Queen of Le-Ath Veronis, at your service," I scowled at him. "And, if you can stop being a misogynist for a few seconds, I'd suggest firing that asshole masquerading as a Chief of Police. Frankly, he can't find his own butt cheeks with both hands."

"Tell him also this," Rigo gritted his teeth. "He will never be welcome on Le-Ath Veronis. I cannot account for his safety should he desire to visit."

Haris stood there for a moment, his mouth dropping open in surprise.

"Chief Farram insulted Queen Lissa," Winkler drawled. "Frankly, he probably should stay away from Karathia, Hraede, Kifirin and Campiaa, too."

"He has a tendency to belittle women," Doril waved his hand, as if that should explain everything.

"Then he has no business being in that position," I snapped, feeling even angrier now than I'd been moments earlier. "But you keep shoving that shit under the rug. See what that gets you."

"Tiessa, we have no need to stay here and be insulted further," Rigo reminded me.

"Yeah. Let's go." I folded space, bringing Rigo and Winkler away with me.

Galk

Reah

"Is there anything I should know before you leave us?" Queen Myriae asked me as I and my crew prepared to go.

"Stay alive," I told her. "It's important."

"I will certainly do my best," she said.

"If I were you," I added, "I'd make an effort to form a closer alliance with your husband, the King. You'll be stronger together than you are apart—even if it's only a political alliance."

"I—see," she said, considering my words.

"Are we ready?" I turned to Wardevik, Wyatt, Bel Erland, Cudworth and Ocenosek.

"We're ready," Wardevik replied.

"Good fortune to you," I told Myriae, before folding my group to Kifirin.

~

Murzal

Travis

"Zanfield Staggs—is it really you?" President Ylisis strode forward and held out his hand to Zanfield.

"It is," Zanfield grinned and took the offered hand. "I've watched your career with great interest," he added.

"I used to keep up with you in the society journals," Ylisis said. "I haven't seen anything come up on you in a while."

"He's been hiding out," Trent clapped a hand on Zanfield's shoulder. "With us."

"Where might that be?"

"If we told you, we'd have to erase the memory," Zanfield laughed.

"Is he joking?" Ylisis turned to me.

"Maybe," I shrugged.

"Well, if you ever need a favor," Ylisis told Zanfield, "you know where I am."

"I'll keep that in mind," Zanfield said. "Sorry about your State House."

"It's a building," Ylisis said. "That can be replaced. Lives, on the other hand, mine included, can't. I have plenty of work to do, now, consoling and rebuilding, but it could have been much worse."

Meet us in my library, Mom sent.

We said our good-byes to Ylisis, then folded space to Le-Ath Veronis.

~

Kwark

Zaria

Tears and gratitude. That's what I saw on Queen Ilise's face when she came forward to take my hand. "We'd all have died," she quavered. "Thank you."

"You'll have to find another chef and steward; we replaced those two with some of our own."

"I can't believe some of our own tried to kill us."

"That's over, now," I pulled her into a hug.

"Thank you," she gave me a watery smile when I let her go. "I won't forget this, I promise."

"Neither will we." Edden, who stood beside me, nodded to the Queen. "We must go; some of ours are now missing, and we must find them if we can."

"If I can help in any way," Ilise offered.

"Save your people and your planet," I told her. "That should be your focus."

"I will do my best."

I folded my bunch away; Lissa was waiting in her library to speak with us.

~

SouthStar, Avendor

Ashe

"I refuse to go back. I renounce my throne," Larvalis insisted.

"You can't stay here," I told him as evenly as I could. Of all the hub world leaders, he'd chosen not to watch what was happening on

Hraede. He had no idea what he was going back to, but he understood it wasn't pleasant.

"Fine. I have funds in secret accounts. Renellia and I can live anywhere we want and raise the baby however we want. Take me back and I will certainly renounce my position."

"You have no heir as yet," I pointed out, losing patience with this unworthy coward.

"The child will not be a legitimate heir, once I renounce the throne. I care not what happens to Hraede."

"Well, then, I suspect you need to speak with a certain group of people on Le-Ath Veronis, including Ildevar Wyyld. He may be very interested in those secret funds you say you have."

Larvalis cringed at Ildevar's name, telling me he'd siphoned those funds away from the state treasury for his own use.

"Let's go," I gripped his collar. "Renellia can stay here while we sort out your business with Ildevar."

~

Hraede

Tamp

"We're meeting in Mom's library at the palace," Trent explained. "I came to take you there."

"I see there's more to this story," I said, watching him carefully.

"There's a slight hitch where Hraede is concerned. That's why Queen Mephista should come with us."

Trent had wakened all of us in the middle of the night where we were. At least Mephista's temporary absence should go unremarked while we held a meeting with the others.

"We'll certainly come," Alrenardo sighed.

"Is Larvalis all right?" Mephista asked.

"As far as I can tell," Trent replied. "Let's go. We only have a few hours before someone will notice you're gone."

"We're ready," Al nodded.

Seconds later, we found ourselves in Queen Lissa's palace library, where many others were now gathered.

Including Larvalis.

Queen's Palace Library, Le-Ath Veronis

Lissa

We needed to focus on other, more important things, yet here was whiny Larvalis, claiming he wanted no part of being King of Hraede any longer, and vowing to abdicate the moment he got back, if we forced him to go.

If Gavin were here, he'd certainly have something to say about this.

"I believe we may be of some assistance in this matter," Graegar and Garegar appeared. Father and son Larentii—both were members of the Wise Ones, so I nodded to them to speak.

"Larvalis is not fit to rule Hraede," Graegar said immediately, which drew a protest from Larvalis.

"Do you want the Kingship back?" Garegar gave him a hard stare. "I suspect that information is finding its way to the surface, concerning tax monies that were diverted into personal, hidden accounts."

"This interests me greatly," Ildevar Wyyld stepped forward. "Is this true, Larvalis?"

"You will not lie," Rigo came forward to place compulsion.

"I-I did take some, ah, yes. I diverted tax money." Larvalis stuttered, he was so terrified.

"Great. What's the solution, then?" I asked.

"I would like to speak," Mephista said.

All of us turned toward the Queen of Hraede.

"Queen Mephista, you have the floor," Ildevar nodded to her.

"I don't want Larvalis back."

That's a no-brainer, I sent to Ildevar. I saw a slight smile tug at his mouth in reply.

"What do you want?" Ildevar asked in reply.

"I," she began, before hesitating. "I want Alrenardo to stay."

Another no-brainer? Ildevar sent.

"Alrenardo—you were once King of Hraede and carry that bloodline. What say you?" Ildevar turned to him.

"While I would love to stay and rule beside Mephista, I have no desire to carry the burden of someone else's crimes."

"I don't blame you," Ildevar agreed.

"I think I can offer a way out of this," Zanfield spoke.

All eyes turned to the wealthiest man in both Alliances.

"How is that?" Ildevar lifted an eyebrow.

"I have property everywhere. I can sign over a house to Larvalis and his ah, lady friend, and supply enough money for them to live comfortably for several years. Doled out according to need by one of my agents, of course. This offer depends on his willingness to repay what he has taken, and also upon the mercy of the powerful here, to set aside the evidence, as they know an innocent man will take the throne of Hraede."

"And a guilty one will go free," I pointed out.

Larvalis looked as if he wanted to whine again.

"I think if we watch him carefully from now on," Ildevar frowned at Larvalis.

"I swear I will never do it again," he held up a hand.

"I can make sure of that," Rigo offered.

"Do it," Ildevar agreed.

"You will never knowingly commit another crime," Rigo placed another compulsion. "And you will never be able to tell anyone you were once the King of Hraede."

"I think that's good enough," I said. "Graegar, will you and Garegar work out the details with Zanfield? We have other fish to fry, here."

"Of course." He smiled a beautiful, Larentii smile and disappeared with Garegar, Larvalis and Zanfield.

"Now, on to other things," I sighed. "That includes missing mates, children and friends. Where the hell are they?"

~

Zaria

While Graegar was speaking with Lissa and the others, Garegar sent mindspeech. *Nefrigar has need of your assistance, as do we, Vanaraszh.*

Does he need me now? I was ready to take Valegar with me and go straight to the Larentii homeworld.

It can wait until this meeting is concluded, he told me. *Then, I'd suggest bending time.*

How far back?

Yesterday, shortly after dawn on the homeworld.

I'll be there.

Thank you. We must go now, to sort out the difficulty Larvalis presents. While he never took an official name as King, I believe Alrenardo will be free to do so.

Good. Every time I hear Larvalis, I think of larvae, and that's not always a pretty picture.

For one with your native language, it certainly wouldn't be. I will see you soon.

He and Graegar disappeared, taking Zanfield and Larvalis with them. *I hope you're ready to serve your second term as King,* I sent to Alrenardo. *At least Mephista will make it more worthwhile.*

She will, indeed.

Valegar's arms folded about me. He'd heard Garegar's words, too. I hoped whatever Nefrigar needed wasn't something that would ultimately break our hearts.

~

Lissa

We'd played the images over and over of the disappearances; Connegar provided what he could, with life-sized images in each circumstance.

We watched Tory and Denevik disappear. Drake, Drew and Gavin. Morrett and Rajeon. Nissa, Toff and Trik.

We found nothing that we could point to as a reason or catalyst in each episode. The only one Connegar refused to reproduce was the disappearance of Zaria and Valegar's child. I figured it would be far too painful to make either relive that moment.

Were they together, wherever they were? If not, what was the point?

"We have much to consider," Rigo said. "Alrenardo and Mephista must return to Hraede before they are reported as missing. The rest of us must eat and rest before we take up this conundrum and our duties."

"You're welcome to stay here," I told the crowd.

"We'll stay and wait for Zanfield," Travis told me. "Besides, we're still working out where our dads could be—and Nissa and the others."

"I have to get back to Karathia," Bel Erland stepped forward to hug me. "Wyatt has to get back to Campiaa, just in case."

"Yeah." I understood all too well what *just in case* could really mean.

"We're going to the Larentii homeworld, for a brief respite," Valegar said as he and Zaria came forward. "If we determine anything that may be useful to you, we'll let you know."

"Thanks for everything," I pulled Zaria into a hug. "I'm so sorry things turned out like they did."

"I know," she mumbled against my shoulder.

I watched as she and Valegar disappeared.

~

Larentii Archives

Zaria

"Father, we are here," Valegar said. We'd arrived to find Nefrigar with his back turned toward us while piddling about with beakers on a sterile, steel table.

"Good. Very good. Come. See what we have to deal with, now."

Val and I approached the table; the liquid in the beakers was pale gold and shining. "This," Nefrigar held his hands above the vials, "has been named *gol-korethus* by the Wise Ones."

"Planet slayer?" I translated the Larentii into Alliance common.

"Yes."

"Well, I didn't know what to call it," I said, *Pulling* in twenty more vials and setting them alongside Nefrigar's collection. "These are from Hraede. When he came back to himself after the earthquake, Hraede told me about them."

CHAPTER 17

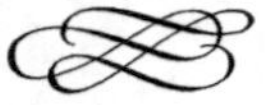

"Hraede is the only hub world who chose a companion," I said, as Nefrigar studied the coins on my left shoulder blade.

"You believe the other hub worlds were attacked this same way?"

"The moment the Prophet felt D'slay's death. I believe he pulled the trigger on this attack—perhaps sooner than he planned and sent earthquakes to distract us."

"Will it help to contact the spirits of those worlds—if that is possible?" Valegar asked me.

"Hraede has made the attempt. He gets no answer from any of them."

"Hmmmm," Nefrigar studied the vials I'd set beside his. "These are somewhat different," he said after a while.

"Do you suppose it's because the worlds are also different?" Valegar said.

"Could be, but with only these samples, it is difficult to say for certain."

"Ah, you are here," Graegar and Garegar arrived. Both began to study the vials on Nefrigar's table.

"Gol-korethus," Nefrigar sighed.

"Out of curiosity, where did your vials come from?" I asked him.

"Falchan—in the past."

"You know something I don't, then," I accused.

"He knows some things, as do we," Graegar soothed. "We need you to come with us now, so we may know more."

"Come where?" Val inquired.

"To visit our captive."

"You have a captive?"

"They called him Toad. We believe his name was not that in the beginning."

"You have the wizard?" I breathed.

"Come see for yourself," he invited, holding out his hand.

The wizard was enclosed in a cage built by the Wise Ones, sitting cross-legged at the center, his head bowed. I had no doubt that they'd provided clean clothing and washed his skin with power. Still malnourished, however, but the Larentii were attempting to correct that much of his former mistreatment.

"He's working to throw off the obsession D'slay placed on him," I said, as we stood outside his cage. At the sound of my voice, he lifted his eyes. Automatically, they filled with tears.

"How close is he to eliminating those foul commands?" Graegar asked. He'd disguised himself for this; he had dark hair and pale skin. I understood he'd worn this disguise whenever he'd interacted with this one.

"There are layers and layers of them," I sighed. "He has to work through each layer, because D'slay kept placing them."

"Can you tell who he is—or was?"

"Not until he rids himself of those first layers of obsessions, and my guess is that they were laid when he was young."

"How young?"

"I was six," Toad said. "When my mother sold me to D'slay and one other. I never knew his name—or if I did, I can't recall it."

"Honey, you were six," I told him. "Don't worry so much about it."

"He made me do things I didn't want to. D'slay did."

"We know. That's why you're still alive," I explained. "I doubt you'd have done any of that without those obsessions."

I studied him as he ducked his head again. Dark-haired and gray-eyed, he reminded me of many things.

Or many people, in this case. "Do you know how old you are now?" I asked him. "Where you were born?"

"I can't say for certain; D'slay always said to forget those things because they didn't matter."

"Of course he did."

"Do you recall going to Falchan—to help Stone Wicke and Reddy Cordrifith plant poison?" Graegar asked.

Gray eyes met mine. He remembered escaping from there, after a vampire relieved Stone and Reddy of their heads.

"Where is Gavin now?" I turned to Graegar.

"With Drake and Drew," he shrugged. "I beg you not to read it in me just yet."

Closing my eyes, I drew in a calming breath. "All right—I assume you have a good reason."

"You will know more soon."

"Thank you." I turned back to Toad. "I dislike calling you Toad—it doesn't suit you at all. Do you have a name you'd prefer?"

"Eli."

"Eli, are you comfortable enough? Do you need or want anything, other than your freedom?"

"I have more here than I ever had with D'slay."

"I'll make sure you have fresh water at your disposal all the time, and snacks and juice in-between meals." *Feed him vegetable proteins only, and all the fruit and vegetables he wants,* I told Graegar.

I'll see to it, he agreed.

I think the animal protein D'slay was feeding him made him ill.
You suspect something, don't you?

Yes, but we can't discuss it here.

"You think he's a descendant of the Grey House wizards?" Nefrigar lifted an eyebrow at my statement.

"He has the look of many of them, especially along the lines of Raffian Grey—and his father, Glendes."

"DNA will tell," Valegar suggested.

"I will return shortly." Graegar disappeared.

Queen's Palace, Le-Ath Veronis

Lissa

"Eli is a half-brother to Glendes Grey."

Zaria's words stunned me. "Glendes' father had an indiscretion?"

"It looks that way, and that means Eli was born long ago. More than thirty-thousand years, actually, because Glendes has been Eldest of Grey House for nearly that long."

"What else are you not telling me?" I studied Zaria's bright-blue eyes.

"I think Liron found him back then, and brought him forward, handing him to D'slay. Eli has many Larentii gifts, including bending time. This explains a lot of things, including D'slay's visit to Earth's past."

"They bought him when he was six—the right time to waken the wizard's gifts." I felt ill saying it aloud.

"Who knows—Liron could have manipulated his birth, too."

"Please say you don't think there are others."

"I can't say that with any certainty at all."

"Then we could have a virtual army of almost-Larentii, at the beck and call of the Prophet." My voice was high-pitched and close to hysteria.

"There may be other problems associated with this," Zaria

stepped forward and placed her hands on my shoulders. A calming relief washed through me—she expended healing power to achieve it.

"Let me sit down, first," I begged.

"I'll sit with you. Before I say anything else, we need to include Strength, Wisdom and Love in our discussion."

~

"They're thinking about things," I told Winkler when the conversation with the original Mighty was finished. "Zaria went back to the Larentii homeworld to get some rest. I don't know where the Three went—they wouldn't say."

"You can't tell me what it was about, can you?"

"No, honey. Just believe that it's a problem they're working on, now."

"Sounds serious."

"It may or may not be. How's that for an answer? Damn, I'm tired."

"I think we can clear your schedule for the rest of the day, and have dinner sent to your suite."

"All right, but I'd like to have a talk with all my mates before that happens."

"I'll send mindspeech."

"Thanks, Winkler."

He leaned down to give me a gentle kiss. "We'll find Gavin, Drake, Drew, and your children. I swear it."

"Thanks, hon."

~

Grey House
Breanne

Glendes Grey knew something was wrong; he merely waited for me to tell him what it was. He sat behind his enormous desk, his fingers steepled as he studied me, waiting for me to speak.

After so many years of being Eldest of Grey House, he'd finally learned patience.

He also owed me a favor.

Or three.

He probably wouldn't like what I was about to tell him. *At all.*

"You have a half-brother," I said. Glendes blinked in surprise.

"You can't be serious," he insisted after several seconds of mental shuffling passed. He was attempting to process information that refused to fit into any category in his mind.

"I am serious. The Larentii have confirmed it."

"Where?"

"Safe. From us and we from him. For now."

"He shouldn't be a danger—not in the powerful sense, if his ability was never awakened," Glendes said.

"Normally, that would be true," I agreed. "In this case, Eli's power was wakened, after he was bought from his mother at age six."

"Another wizard clan awakened it? They're the only ones who can," Glendes half-rose from his chair.

"We suspect that Liron woke his power," I said as calmly as I could. "We also suspect that Liron went looking specifically for—certain talents."

"What certain talents?" Glendes was now standing at his full height.

"Those that your many times great-grandmother Larentii passed to Grey House. While under D'slay's command, Eli exhibited the talents of bending time and nexus echo, among other things."

"Say it isn't true." Glendes leaned forward until his hands rested on the top of his well-kept desk.

"I can't say that, and you know it. The Larentii line still runs in your blood. Liron found the richest source and manipulated it for his own purposes. Then, he gave the boy to D'slay, so that fool could have a ride throughout time. Assassinate someone? No problem. Eli could bend time and remove him from the deed completely."

"You suspect that Eli was forced to assist in the assassinations, don't you?" Glendes sagged onto his chair again with a sigh.

"Ordered to, by obsession," I admitted. "D'slay is now dead, thanks to Lissa. It's also safe to say that the Prophet is pissed because of that, and probably even more pissed that the Larentii found Eli and took him away."

"Does the Prophet know the Larentii took him?"

"Not yet, and we hope he never finds out."

"I'd hate to be the one to declare war on the Larentii."

"As would I. There are other troubles associated with that concept, however, that I can't discuss with you now."

"What can I do to help?" Glendes said.

"I'm glad you asked," I smiled at him.

~

Corez

Vik

My greater Thifilathi lifted Denevik's smaller one and held him while his breaths came in short gasps.

"Corez is quite ill," a Larentii appeared, and, making himself as tall as I, looked upon Denevik, who struggled with the pain of Corez's sickness. "I doubt the ones who created this poison ever considered that High Demons might play a part in this."

With care, the Larentii placed his hand over the coin that held Corez's spirit. I closed my eyes when the healing light became so bright it threatened damage.

"Corez has been healed, with your blood and my power," the Larentii smiled at Denevik, who was now breathing more evenly. Setting him down, I reverted to my usual form while the Larentii decreased his size.

"Who are you?" I asked. "I can't recall seeing you before."

"I am Tenigar. You have seen me, but only from a distance," he replied.

"Can you take us back?" I whispered, while searching my mind for a reason a Larentii Wise One would become involved in Denevik's and my troubles.

"I will take you away from here, but you cannot return to the time and place you left. The reason for this will become clear eventually."

"Where, then?"

"A place where no damage can come from your presence."

Somehow, that sounded as if we were radioactive, or something.

Wait. Were we?

∼

Kwark

Teeg San Gerxon

"Can you move?" I asked Ry for the third time. I'd carried him to a shady spot beside a boulder, because he no longer had the energy to walk. The longer he held the gold coin on his chest, the weaker he became.

"Need. Help," Ry's eyes were dimming as I knelt beside him. What could I do? My brother was dying in front of me and I had no skill as a healer, or anything with me that would help him.

"Do not fear," a Larentii was beside me, making me jump and my heart to stutter.

"What can we do?" I begged, once my heart and breathing normalized. Larentii were the best of healers, if they chose to use those skills.

"He needs energy, food and rest." The Larentii lifted my brother as if he weighed nothing. "Come, I will take you away from this place."

I opened my mouth to ask him where we were going, but he transported us before I could utter the words.

∼

Galk

Rajeon

. . .

Morrett was suffering and there was nothing I could do to help. Healing was never a talent with the pod'l-morphs, because we were never ill. In all my life, I'd only seen one poison that could kill us, and it was the one planted on Siriaa in the past.

Even then, we had to come close enough to the source of it to die of its effects. When my people were instructed to dig deep, they'd reached that source to plant a collection sphere.

The subsequent gathering of the poisonous creatures overwhelmed the pod'l-morph involved, which caused their trees to wither and die. A terrible, prolonged death was their reward for helping to save the planet.

"If I die," Morrett began. I cradled his head in my lap, wishing I had something to lessen his pain.

"I refuse to allow it," I whispered.

"Tell Zaria how much I love her," he breathed, ignoring my words.

"You will tell her yourself." A Larentii appeared and knelt beside us. "I am Meligar, and I will relieve Morrett's pain before taking you away from here."

"I cannot thank you enough," I said, brushing away tears of relief.

~

Murazal

Nissa

Tears blurred my eyes as I sat on dried mud with Trik's head held against my chest. Toff was bringing handfuls of water, to attempt to bring down the sudden fever that assailed Trik.

I glared in anger at the gold coin, now adhered to his chest. We'd already tried to remove it, but it only made the pain worse.

I blinked—and blinked again to clear my sight, if only to make sure that the appearance of Garegar was real, rather than a dream.

"I am real," he assured me with a smile. "First, I will help Master Trik, and then I will take the three of you away from this place."

I couldn't hold back the sob of gratitude as Garegar began to heal

Trik. Toff knelt beside me and held me while Garegar performed his healing.

Cloudsong—Distant Past

  Breanne

"I barely recall the planet like this," Glendes and I walked a cobbled street of the capital city at dusk. In this time, Cloudsong had been ruled by a fair and just king. Many thousands of years in the future, it would be misruled and the planet would die, thanks to Zellar and his crimes. Eventually, Reah and Zaria would bring it back to life—to house people from a destroyed world.

"Your father is here; I tracked him to this point," I told Glendes quietly. I steered him toward a rowdy public house, where light spilled from windows and sounds of laughter could be heard.

"No doubt about it, Father did like his pints," Glendes sighed. "Please say we will not witness the indiscretion."

"We don't have to witness it; we only have to peg the woman and keep track of her," I replied.

Glendes scraped his boots on the board beside the outside steps; I cleared away dirt and mud from my shoes with power before following him into the pub.

Sure enough, Quendes Grey sat in a corner booth, a pint of dark beer in front of him and a woman sitting opposite. *I suppose it's time to see who Father dallied with,* Glendes sounded resigned.

You're disguised and the place is crowded; perhaps we should join them, I suggested.

Remind me to voice my objection later.

We'll only stay for a bit, then pretend to leave. I can shield us well enough that she won't know I'm tagging her.

How long must we watch?

Only until they go upstairs, and I receive ah, confirmation.

I feel ill. I suppose it's a blessing my mother never learned of this.

Probably.

"May we join you?" I asked Quendes with a smile. "There are no other seats."

"Please," he gestured with a hand. "Allow Koris to move to my side, and you can have her bench for yourselves."

Koris rose, aimed an angry glare at Glendes and me, then schooled her face and moved to sit beside Quendes.

Yep, she's the type to sell her kid, all right, I sent to Glendes.

Are you saying she accepts all methods of payment? His sending was dry.

That's what I'm saying, I agreed. *She's pretty enough; I suppose that's what caught his eye.*

Why don't we just render him sterile, so this entire episode will have no repercussions, Glendes suggested.

That could cause even more harm, in ways I can't begin to describe. Just bear with me in this, all right?

What will you do when the child is born?

I have a plan. Do you wish to be present?

It's my half-brother. I want to be there.

Good enough.

"Actually, I'm nearly finished with my pint," Quendes lifted his mug. "We'll leave the table to you." He drank the last of his beer, then nudged Koris. She stepped away from the booth; he followed. Glendes and I watched until they disappeared through a doorway, which led to the stairs and the upper portion of the pub.

How long will this take? Glendes asked as a barmaid arrived to take our order.

You can drink at least half a pint, I think.

"I'll have a pint," Glendes told our server. "And bring one for my companion as well."

You know I'm gonna change mine to wine the second it's set on the table, don't you?

What kind of wine?

Riesling, probably.

Make mine Riesling, too.

Unknown Medical Facility

Vik

Do you know these Larentii? Denevik, while sitting up in a hospital bed, now felt well enough to sip a protein drink and look about him. The door was open to Denevik's room, and we watched as several Larentii passed back and forth, focused on duties we couldn't decipher.

"Ours introduced himself as Tenigar," I shrugged. "I don't know where we are, but at least you're not dying. I'm just grateful the Larentii came for us."

"What happened? My mind is blank after this," he tapped the coin on his chest.

"Let's just say it wasn't pretty," I told him. "Tenigar says you did better than most would have because you're High Demon."

"Tory?" Drake wandered into the room.

"Uncle Drake," I breathed before rushing forward and pulling him into a hug. He thumped my back a few times and grinned when I let him go. "Damn, I'm glad to see you're all right," I said. "Are Drew and Gavin with you?"

"They are, although Drew is wearing Falchan, now," he tapped his chest and nodded toward Denevik. "I hear you have Corez," Drake told him.

"Oddly enough," Denevik lifted his drink to Drake.

"The Larentii brought in the others, too, but one from each world is sicker than Denevik, so they'll take more time and more healing before they'll be ready to get up and around."

"Who are the others?" I asked, feeling confused. "What worlds?"

"Sit down," Drake pointed to guest chairs in the room. "It's a long story."

Cloudsong, Distant Past

Zaria

"You're sure she's tagged?" Glendes mumbled as we walked out of the pub and onto the street.

"She's tagged. Let's fast forward a few months." I took his arm and bent time, to check on our pregnant quarry.

~

Unknown Medical Facility

Teeg San Gerxon

"Dad?" The comp-vid dropped from my lap as I stood quickly; I'd been seated beside Ry's bed, waiting for him to wake and playing a stupid game to waste time.

After all, I couldn't get the comp-vid to connect to anything anywhere, so I had to settle for a game embedded in its memory.

My father, Gavin Montegue, stood in the doorway to Ry's room, a strange expression on his face. "Son? How did they manage to take you, too?" he asked.

"The Larentii do what they want, I guess," I replied.

"I'm not talking about the Larentii. I'm talking about whatever it was that took us away from where we were."

"Oh. I have no idea," I confessed. "When we landed on Kwark, it was dead or dying. We found Kwark's spirit, but he was nearly gone, too. Things went south fast when Ry and Kwark, well," I didn't know how to explain their joining.

"I heard about that," Dad sighed. "Come here and give me a hug. I feel as if it's been forever since I saw you last."

"Do you know where we are?" I asked as I moved toward him.

"No idea, and the Larentii won't tell us. I figure it's for our safety, and perhaps theirs, too."

"Who could threaten the Larentii? Who *would* threaten the Larentii?" I asked as Dad pulled me against him.

"Strange things are happening, Gavril," Dad's voice was muffled against my shoulder as he spoke my given name. "In this case, your mother would say, *don't poke the bear.*"

Cloudsong, Distant Past

Breanne

Well, that explains a lot.

I'd taken Glendes four months into Cloudsong's future, to check on Koris. We found her, just as she was beginning to show. She had a visitor in her room above the pub, and one who wasn't interested in sex with her.

Who is that? Glendes asked about the male guest.

It's better if you don't know. Watch and listen, I warned.

"I will pay you handsomely to carry the child to term," the visitor smiled.

"How handsomely? I don't need to be stuck with a child to raise," Koris snapped.

"Oh, that will be the best part," he continued to smile. "Carry the child, and when he is born, I will take him."

"How much?"

"Ten thousand."

Koris lifted an eyebrow, considering whether she should take the offer before it was withdrawn, or whether she should hold out for more. In her day and time, ten thousand was equivalent to half a million credits.

A penny went a long way back then, Glendes observed.

"Make it twenty, and I'll do it. I'll have to have another place to live, you know."

"I shall pay fifteen and not more."

"Done. How do I contact you—to come and get the child?"

"Do not worry; I will know when and where."

I watched as Liron—yes, *that* Liron, stalked toward the door to leave. I was never so grateful to see anyone's backside before as he shut the door firmly behind him.

What do we do now? Glendes sent.

We make a few adjustments and ensure that monster never knows about them. Lifting a hand, I placed Koris in stasis. She wouldn't recall my visit, or that anything had happened.

Glendes watched curiously as I placed my hands on Koris' belly. I intended to set undetectable limitations on what Liron had already measured and manipulated.

～

When I returned Glendes to his study, it was only seconds after we'd left it to begin with. He'd seen much while we were gone, however. The last thing, of course, was the birth of his brother. Eli had claimed that someone bought him when he was six years of age. That meant Liron would pass the boy to a wet nurse, who'd bring him up to the proper age and act as his mother until Liron appeared to waken his talent.

As promised, Liron arrived right after Eli's birth, and just as I suspected, he brought a woman with him. My shoulders sagged as I recognized her; Irina had served as a brood mare for D'slay and for Liron—too many times to count. Then, D'slay dumped her when she was weakened and no longer useful to him. Too bad D'slay was dead in the future. If he weren't, I'd hunt him down myself.

Irina carried another child with her—the first of more to come, and now she would act as a foster mother for Eli.

"For your efforts," Liron tossed a small bag of gold coins on the bed where Koris lay, still bloody from the birth. He didn't bother to hide his exit this time; once Eli was held against Irina's chest, he transported her and the children away.

Koris reached out to grasp the bag of gold; it convinced me not to help her, as she needed help after birthing Eli.

She'd be dead in six days, and I didn't intend to interfere with that.

"What now?" Glendes asked, breaking into my thoughts and scattering the memory of what we'd witnessed together. "Will I ever see my half-brother?"

"I can't tell you that at the moment. There is still work to do, but your part in it is finished."

"What about Nissa, Toff and Trik? Has this helped them in any way?"

"That was part of my intention. Keep your hope alive that all goes well from here on."

"What should I say to Shadow? That's his daughter, and he is devastated."

"Tell him what I told you—to keep his hope alive. Remember, not a word about Eli or any of the rest of this."

"I wouldn't know where to begin, even if I had the urge," he muttered and settled uneasily on the chair behind his desk.

CHAPTER 18

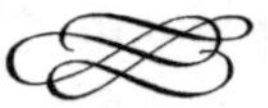

"Ah, there's our Sirenali, awake and hungry." Meligar leaned over Morrett's bed as he woke for the first time since we'd left Galk.

I'd sat patiently by Morrett's bedside for six hours or more; Meligar provided me with food and drink while I waited. I was grateful for Morrett's waking—I worried at times that he wouldn't.

"I feel better," Morrett admitted, in a voice dry and raspy. "Thank you for saving us."

"Oh, I haven't saved you completely, yet," Meligar replied. "That will come eventually, if our efforts are successful. I will return with proper food and clean water."

Meligar disappeared; Morrett turned his head to blink at me. "What did he mean?" he asked.

"I don't know, but I am so grateful you are alive, it gives me joy," I told him.

"I had strange dreams," Morrett sighed. "Of pain—of drying up and dying." He ran fingers over the coin on his chest. "I think those visions came from Galk."

"The pain also," I reminded him. "His suffering caused yours, I believe."

"He has yet to speak to me again," Morrett admitted. "I have no idea what to make of that."

"Perhaps he is regenerating and will speak later."

"I hope so. I dislike the idea that all this was in vain."

"Not in vain," Meligar was back and setting a tray of food on a table beside Morrett's bed. "You and the others are our best hope to combat the enemy."

"What others?" I asked before I could curb the question.

"You were not the only ones sucked away and left in precarious circumstances. Before long, we will bring all of you together, but that time is not yet upon us. Enjoy your food, and, if boredom threatens, we have puzzles, vids and other distractions for you while you recover."

Meligar disappeared again, leaving Morrett and me blinking in confusion at one another. "Here, let me pull the table around so you can eat." I finally recalled my manners and rose from my chair to help.

"Thank you. I am quite hungry, as you may imagine," Morrett admitted.

Nissa

Why did it go to Trik, instead of one of us? I asked Toff in mindspeech. Trik was still asleep on the hospital bed where he'd been placed by Garegar. We'd been told that Trik would sleep for a while and wake hungry.

Garegar promised to return when that happened and bring a meal for him.

Meanwhile, Toff and I'd been served food and drink shortly after our arrival. I still nursed a cup of tea, rewarming it with power when necessary.

I have no idea why it would attack him, Toff frowned and crossed arms over his chest. We sat on guest chairs inside the small hospital room, patiently waiting for Trik to wake as promised.

"Nissa?" Trik's voice was cracked and rough when he spoke. Toff and I were on our feet immediately and rushing to the bedside.

"I'm so glad you're all right." I hugged him as well as I could, while tears leaked onto the blanket covering him.

"Hey," he wrapped his arms around me and kissed my hair. "I'm still here, my love. Stop worrying about me."

Toff sniffled behind me, letting me know he was just as worried.

"Ah, time for food and drink," Garegar appeared in the room with a tray. "How do you feel, Master Trikleer?"

"Better," he sighed. "I have a question, though."

"What question is that?" Garegar lifted a blond eyebrow.

"When did our protection jewels disappear?"

It hit me, then. We hadn't had them the whole time we'd been on Murazal. Would they have prevented Trik from being joined with the planet's spirit coin?

"A good question. Perhaps we'll find an answer for you soon, eh? Until then, our Trikleer must eat and regain his strength. There are things waiting for us to do, and we cannot delay them for a moment."

There was something Garegar wasn't telling us, and I knew there was no use trying to pry information from a Larentii who wasn't inclined to say anything else. They tended to fold space, and there was no finding them after that.

He'd already refused to tell us where we were, because we'd asked him shortly after our arrival. "Does Mom know we're okay?" I asked instead of the other questions crowding my mind.

"She will know soon. Don't worry; there is a plan, and it must unfold according to its destiny." Garegar then busied himself with touching Trik to check on the progress of his recuperation. "Everything is fine," he told him. "Eat as much of your meal as you can, and I will return later."

What is he not telling us? Toff asked as he lifted the glass of juice and helped Trik hold it while he drank.

I wish I knew, I answered Toff. *Where did our protection jewels go? Did the one who kidnapped us manage to take them away? Until now, I'd have said that was impossible. No protection jewel has ever been taken from an unwilling bearer.*

The one removing it generally ends up dead, Toff agreed. *Garegar may know, or he may have a good guess; he's just not telling us.*

This whole thing is really strange, I began. *Who put us on Murazal, and why? Will he know we're not there anymore? How did Garegar find us? It's obvious nobody else could, or we'd have been rescued earlier.*

He said your mother still doesn't know, so Lissa won't know where we are, either. Have you tried to send mindspeech?

No.

I have. I tried to reach my father. There's something here blocking the sending.

What if it's the Larentii? Why would they do that?

I have no idea.

Sirena

Travis

"Do you think we'll find Vik and the others?" Trent asked. We sat at a small table in Randl and Dori's suite of rooms, having dinner with them. It was a small gathering; only Trent, Sabrina, Perri, Zanfield and I had been invited.

Until now, Randl had remained silent, listening to the rest of us talk—about the ones still missing, contacting Zaria and Lissa for news, and several other topics. Everything always came back to our missing crew, friends and family—and for Trent and me—our missing fathers.

Randl lifted his eyes to blink at Trent; to anyone else, he'd appear to be blind. With the uncanny ability he held, not only to see everything around him in his mind, but past those things, too, Randl saw so much more than the rest of us would ever know.

"I haven't lost hope yet." Randl's answer to Trent's question sounded very much like a diversion. As if he knew something that the rest of us weren't prepared for, as yet.

"Did the Prophet do this to us?" Trent demanded.

"I really can't say."

What the hell does that mean? Trent sent to me.

I have no idea. I've never known him to lie to us before, though.

Let's hope he's not lying now. I really don't want anyone to think they're sparing our feelings. I need a target. Something to go after and obliterate.

I understand that, bro. Maybe this is his way of holding us back from doing something stupid and getting ourselves killed.

D'slay's dead. The Prophet has to be behind this.

And we don't know where he is, do we? That eliminates pounding on him —even if we could. Right now, none of us, separately or together, may be strong enough to do it anyway.

You're giving up?

Hell, no. I'd just like to even the odds a little more before jumping on that bastard. Trent frowned at me for a moment.

"Randl?" Trent spoke aloud.

"Trent?" Randl's sightless eyes were now locked on Trent's face.

"Is the Prophet really a bastard?"

"In every sense of the word."

~

Royal Palace, Kifirin

Reah

"If Daddy could, you know he'd send a message," Lexsi placed a hand on my shoulder. "Great-grampa Denny, too."

"That's what worries me, baby girl," I sighed, covering her hand with one of my own. "Unless they're—incapacitated, they'd let us know where they are."

"I really thought they'd be back by now," Lexsi pulled her hand away. "Kory is having a hard time with this, too. That's why he went to his father's house, to help rebuild a wall that fell down."

"Moving heavy rocks is a good way to clear your mind," I agreed. "Does he need help?"

"He didn't ask for help, but I can send mindspeech."

"Send mindspeech to Nedevik," I named Kory's father, who was the eldest (and wisest) living High Demon. "He'll know whether we should show up or not."

"He says physical labor can sometimes help us think," Lexsi said after several moments of silence.

"Let's go, then. Warde can hold down the fort while we're gone."

"Has a wall ever been built by a Queen of Kifirin?" Lexsi asked as I rose from my seat.

"I built some fences back when I was raising gishi trees."

"But you weren't Queen, then."

"True enough. Let's go. Maybe we'll get an epiphany while we're working."

Royal Courtyard, Hraede
Alrenardo

"Randl sent mindspeech. I'll be leaving tonight," Tamp informed me.

"I was hoping you'd give advice on how to rebuild this pile of rubble," I waved a hand at what was left of the palace, which was mostly a mound of broken stones. Everything that could be salvaged from the debris had already been retrieved and stored.

"Start at the bottom and build up," Tamp slapped me on the back. "You and Mephista will do just fine. Ask her. I hear her uncle is an architect, and less bossy than her father."

"Don't get me started on her father," I growled. "He was willing to sell her to Larvalis, you know."

"Think of it this way," Tamp told me. "One of them had to have a level head. Just be grateful it was Mephista."

"I'm still trying to come up with a pet name, but what can you make out of Mephista? It defies explanation."

"Fessa," I said. "I hear that's what her mother called her when she was little."

"The mother who died when she was young, and not the stepmother?"

"That's the one."

"How did you get this information, and I didn't?"

"If you recall, I can take many shapes. Sometimes, all one has to do is listen—and have a mate who can bend time."

"You went back there? Saw her when she was little?"

"I did. You're welcome. I have to go put my things together. Someone will be here soon to take me to Randl."

"Because this isn't over."

"Not by a long way."

"If we don't meet again," I grasped his right arm with mine, in the way the Rith Naeri have always done when one of us leaves for a dangerous assignment.

"If we don't meet again," he reciprocated, before releasing me and walking away.

~

Queen's Palace, Le-Ath Veronis
Lissa

"Alrenardo just informed me that Tampirus has left for Sirena," Rigo said.

"That's where Travis and Trent are, too. I hope they're plotting ways to get our people back."

"Randl is quite cunning, Tiessa."

"If Connegar hadn't told me I needed to stay out of this, I'd be out there looking," I fumed. "Even if I have to visit every damn planet there is."

"There are times when we have to place our trust in others," Rigo pulled me close. "I feel this is one of those times."

"Well, I'll trust for three days. After that, it's game on."

~

P'loxett

  V'dar

"I anticipate a certain variety of enemy," P'loxett said, handing a long, slender case to me. "This is to destroy any pod'l-morph who stands against us."

Setting the case on my desk, I carefully opened it. Inside, resting on a bed of silk, lay a shining dagger.

"Ah. You've found a way," I breathed, lifting the dagger and hefting it in my hand. It was well-balanced and cleverly made.

"Yes. I detected the blood of one of them, you know. They are quite difficult to kill, as we discussed. Therefore, you now have a weapon to use against them."

"Is this the only one?" I asked, turning the blade this way and that to capture the light on its gleaming surface.

"There are eleven more," P'loxett grinned.

"You think of everything, don't you?" I set the blade in its case and snapped the lid shut. "I'll distribute them when the time is right."

"Of course. That is why I made them, after all. Now, as you know, wars will begin shortly on many worlds. We have laid our groundwork; all is in place and ready. Once those we've pulled to us arrive, we will set them up as generals for our armies, and chaos will overcome the Alliances."

"And once we have them in place, we will take everything we want."

"It will be as your visions have shown you," P'loxett gloated. "I have waited so long for this day. Revenge will be ours."

"Just as you were left to die long ago, so we will leave all other worlds," I vowed. "I am more than pleased that my efforts to save you have not gone unrewarded."

"I will serve you forever," P'loxett promised. "Until the end and beyond."

"Will you watch with me while the Alliances crumble? I will have vengeance against my enemies."

"Of course. It will give me great pleasure to watch those worlds die."

~

P'loxett

Alken Wilker

"They are waiting for P'loxett's other plantings to bear fruit," Gillen muttered as we walked between rows of fruit trees. Somehow, P'loxett had coaxed trees and plants to grow in soil so poisoned it should have been impossible. Soon enough, the trees would begin to bear fruit.

I would not be eating that fruit, as each tree had been planted with a body part surrounding its roots. Anyone consuming the fruit would be caught by the Prophet and forced to his will.

Just as Gillen, Qatti and I had been.

"On the hub worlds?" I responded to Gillen's words.

"Yes. He cast a net for specific kinds of fish, and now he is reeling them in."

"What will he do with them when they arrive?"

"Set them up to lead his armies. The Alliances will be his to destroy. It is my hope that once the wars begin, we can slip away."

"Do you think we can get away with that? Do you? He crooks his finger and we must go to him."

"I hope he sends me out with Je'Dik," Gillen gruffed. "Or with P'loxett again, although he is not the most pleasant of working partners. I feel less confined when I'm that far away."

"I wish I was back on Karathia," I grumbled. "Anything would be better than this."

"You chose to leave," Gillen snapped at me. "And you sold my pathetic, powerless son to do it. I wonder if Zanfield Staggs has killed the boy, yet."

"I'm sure Pauley is pickled in brine somewhere in one of Stagg's homes. Too bad we couldn't grab Staggs. We could live like kings."

"In an Alliance set for destruction? Hmmph. You're more stupid than I thought. Soon enough, brother, this planet will appear to be heaven to those living in the Alliances. The Prophet plans to destroy them all, and P'loxett is determined to help him do it."

"Surely there will be something set aside for him and his servants."

"Not the way I see it. Keep dreaming brother," he slapped me on the back. "The timer is set and soon enough, all will be destroyed."

Queen's Palace, Le-Ath Veronis

Lissa

"You asked for me?" Corent River had come to meet me in my arboretum, at the topmost level of the palace. Around us were many kinds of trees and plants, while fountains and a small waterfall provided a soothing background. Corent, a member of a race of Green Fae, studied the growing things about us with a satisfied smile.

"Sit here with me; we have to talk," I patted the cushioned bench beside me.

"Is there something wrong?" Corent's hair was turning from blue to purple, a sign he was worried.

"I know you're close to the plants and trees—they grow in your light," I told him as he settled on the bench at my side.

"It is who I am," he confirmed.

"I'm sure you're aware that the Prophet has infected some people with his disease by contaminating their food," I went on.

"Yes; Breanne has told me this."

"Not long ago, there were ships pirated between Murazal and other worlds. One shipment contained seedling trees—mostly fruit trees. Another contained large barrels of organic cow dung to be used as fertilizer. What wasn't known until Zaria investigated was that each of those barrels contained at least one body infected by Prophet's disease. The third was a shipment of sand for glassmaking, but there was also uranium within those crates."

Corent's brow furrowed as he processed this information. "We've determined that the pirates were sent by the Prophet," I went on. "Now, I've been racking my brain for two days on how all that could be connected. The solution I've reached needs confirmation—from someone who can nurture and manipulate trees and plants, convincing them to grow and bear fruit."

"I'm not sure what you're asking," he said after several moments of intense thought passed.

"What would you do—and how would you do it, if suddenly, Le-Ath Veronis were poisoned by nuclear waste? Let's say every other livable planet is exactly the same. A few people have the talent or genetic makeup to survive. How do you feed them, when the plants and animals normally wouldn't survive in those circumstances?"

Corent became so still it was eerie.

"Is it possible," I said as he remained frozen, "to manipulate the plants and trees to survive under those conditions?"

"How many people do you think are already infected with Prophet's disease?" Corent's voice was barely a whisper, his eyes wide and terrified as he stared at me.

"No idea," I said, finding it difficult to breathe. "He's found a way to grow fruit infected by his filth, hasn't he?"

"It would be a logical solution." Corent turned away from me then. "I must think on this." He rose and folded space.

"You and me both, honey," I spoke to empty air.

~

Larentii Homeworld

Zaria

"Are you ready?" Graegar asked. He'd sent mindspeech, telling me to meet him in the Archives.

"Where are we going?"

"To visit Eli, first, and then we will make our way to another location. I ask that you trust me."

"I trust you," I told him. "You've never given me reason not to."

"Perhaps that will remain true." He took my hand and folded space.

~

Eli

When I opened my eyes, I felt as if a great weight had been lifted off me. Morning sun shone upon me and it felt better than it ever had before. So good did it feel, in fact, that I wanted to lie naked in it.

"I've never felt like this before," I whispered to the sky.

"This is how you should always have felt." The one who tended me was back. Turning my head in his direction, I found *her* standing beside him. Tears sprang to my eyes; she looked lovelier now than she had when I first saw her.

"Love placed a time limit on many things in the past," the male spoke to the woman. "I am Graegar," he informed me, before becoming what he truly was—a tall Larentii with blue skin and blond hair.

"I am Zaria," she said. "How are you doing, Eli?"

"Zaria," Graegar nudged her. "Make the change—for Eli."

"What?" I lunged to my feet and gripped the bars of my cage as Zaria became—*a vision.*

She stood tall before me, with blue skin, pale hair and white wings. Gold sparkled on her skin and wings; I had no idea how that could be.

"We call her Corinnelar when she is like this," Graegar informed me. I didn't respond; all I could do was gape at her beauty.

"Eli, you are no longer bound by D'slay's obsessions—or anyone else's," Corinnelar said. "You have come into your own, now. I can see it in you."

"What else do you see in him?" Graegar said softly.

"Many, many things," she sighed before hunching her shoulders. "We have work to do. So much work," she lowered her eyes to the tall grass at her feet. Wind whispered through it; the sound and movement mesmerized me.

"It is up to you," Garegar said. "You must decide now, before we leave this place."

With her eyes downcast still, I watched as a tear, like a crystal drop catching sunlight, fell to the ground.

"Eli?" She raised her head to look at me, unshed tears making her eyes brighter.

"Corinnelar?" I dropped to my knees before her.

"If you could choose, would you go forward from here, or go back to your birth and start again?"

"Go back to my birth, with the same events in front of me? Please no," I begged.

"No hon. With parents who love you. Who can show you wondrous things and teach you about them. Would you choose that, or go on as you are, with the memories of what your life has been?"

"I could have parents and love? Say it isn't a lie. Please."

Tears now fell upon my own cheeks, just as they trailed down hers. "How can you do this? It is impossible." I now wondered if this were a special kind of torture—one designed to make me suffer the most for all my crimes.

Close your eyes, her voice whispered in my mind. I had no real choice in the matter—I would do anything for her. Light flashed against eyelids closed tight, and that was the last thing...

~

Queen's Palace, Le-Ath Veronis

Lissa

"I believe I know why those three Murazalian ships were pirated," I announced to the crowd in my library. Everyone who'd substituted on a hub world was here, except for those still missing.

Randl had also come, with a few others from Sirena.

"Tell us," Reah said. Both she and Lexsi had come with Wardevik. Zaria and her group stood next to Reah's, and I could see that Zaria already knew what I was about to say. I suspected she knew more than that, too, but I wasn't going to call her out on it.

I began my explanation to a crowd that became quieter by the moment, until they were barely breathing at the end. "That would explain a lot," Winkler stood and shook himself, much like his wolf would do when he wanted to rid himself of whatever clung to him.

"I discussed this with Corent before bringing it to all of you," I added. "He said it was the logical thing to do."

"We believe the Prophet has commanded the services of scattered groups of fae, so your theory holds up," Graegar appeared at the back of crowd.

"How did you discover that?" I asked him.

"Information from various sources has come to us," he replied.

"Should we begin a search for anyone who has recently planted groves of fruit trees on Alliance worlds?" Edden asked.

"There are no records kept of plantings like that," Zaria said. "But sales of fruit trees are tracked. Of course, if the trees in question are coming from the Prophet, and he is randomly planting them here and there amid established groves, we're still screwed."

"I believe this is why the Prophet always buried his infected victims near stands of trees and thick vegetation," Randl rose to speak. "At first, he used regular trees, to determine if it were possible. Then, he began to develop fruit trees, after his initial successes."

"So the fae have been helping him, after he obsessed them to obey," I nodded.

"The Green Fae were always the ones most adept at growing and acclimatizing plants and trees to thrive in adverse conditions," Corent spoke up. "Regular fae have little talent for such, unless they have been taught. Their basic skills would be sufficient, should they learn patience and the process."

Corent spoke the truth; I'd seen the evidence myself after his people had turned a hostile valley amid high mountains into an oasis.

Toff—who was still missing with Nissa and Trik, had grown up among the Green Fae, but he'd never learned their methods because he lacked their talents. He was comesuli and not fae, after all.

"Who could teach the fae, then?" I responded.

"I have a theory about that," Zaria answered my question. "But before I tell you, I have to ask a question."

"What question is that?"

"Who among us is willing, at the risk of their own lives, to go to war—to buy some time for the Alliances?"

"Time? What are you talking about?" Rigo asked her.

"Time to quell coming rebellions. Time to find a solution to avoid total destruction."

"How much time can we buy? How much time do we need?" I asked.

"At least fifty years," she replied, her voice flat.

I closed my eyes as fear washed over me. Zaria had been to the future. Fifty years into the future, according to her own words.

What. Had. She. Seen?

CHAPTER 19

"We will only select a few of you," Graegar announced. Probably because everyone gathered in my library had volunteered for this assignment. What we hadn't realized at the time was Zaria wasn't in charge of it. The Wise Ones were.

There was a rumble of confusion after Graegar spoke—everybody wanted in on this, and they didn't even know what it was, yet.

"The reason we can only accept a few is there is limited space to maneuver where we're going," Tenigar, eldest of the Wise Ones, stepped forward to explain. "We need not only the strongest among you, but also the swiftest. I hope you will understand and accept our choices. Lives hang in the balance, and we do not wish to risk more than is necessary."

"Having said that," Meligar told us, "we ask that the following people join us in this mission. Lissa," he said my name first. "Reah," he announced. "Zaria. Randl. Cudworth and Ocenosek."

"Huh?" I breathed. They wanted the guards that Zaria found for Reah? I didn't even realize that they'd come for this meeting.

Except for Zaria, nobody knew them. How did she know them?

Who were they?

Reah went to both and hugged each of them while speaking quietly. This involved her first High Demon mate and her grandfather. I suppose it was fitting that two strange High Demons might be the best fit to help us in this, since the Wise Ones didn't choose Wardevik or ask for any others from that race.

"If those chosen will meet us in the adjoining room, Valegar and Nefrigar will see the rest of you safely home," Tenigar said.

"Here we go," Zaria was suddenly at my side and putting an arm around me.

"What will we be doing? I know you know something," I frowned at her.

"Well, there are some rogue gods out there, giving strength and advice to the Prophet," she sighed.

No wonder the Wise Ones chose whom they did. "Why aren't any of the Three coming?" I thought to ask.

"They have to hold everything together if we fail."

"They weren't kidding when they said what they did about risking our lives?"

"They would never lie or waver on that issue." Dropping her arm, she walked toward the smaller meeting room in the Archives, where the Wise Ones waited to tell us about our mission.

Reah

"Some of you will act as guards and protectors," Tenigar explained. "Others will employ power to engage those who will oppose us."

"Guards and protectors for what?" Lissa asked.

"For whom is a better question," Tenigar smiled gently at her. "We will take you to the place where they are recuperating, and the rest will be explained to all of you at the same time."

Lissa and I exchanged glances; Zaria didn't appear surprised at all. I suppose as a Larentii, they may have told her something already.

Or, she might know in other ways, although I couldn't say for sure.

"Is everyone ready?" Hiragar asked.

Moments later, we found ourselves in a strange hospital corridor. Rooms led off that corridor, but one person poked his head out a door before rushing toward Lissa.

Gavin Montegue was here, waiting for our arrival. Lissa shrieked his name as they collided in a mutual embrace.

"Reah?" A familiar voice called out from behind. I whirled to find Tory bearing down on me. I leapt into his arms and kissed him.

Then kissed him again.

Zaria

All the ones taken were here.

Except for one.

Valegar's and my child.

I forced myself to understand, while watching happy reunions all around me.

"Lissa?" I knew that voice. A head poked out of a room nearby, before Gavin came galloping toward Lissa. She squealed with joy as they united in a tight embrace. In seconds, she was surrounded by other mates and her missing children, all of whom wanted to hug her at once.

"Reah?" Tory's voice came from behind.

Reah raced toward him as he stepped out of another room. She hit him like a hurricane, and, like the steady High Demon he was, he didn't even rock back on his feet as Reah clung to him like a barnacle.

"Zaria?" Morrett touched my arm as I watched Reah kiss Tory several times.

"Honey?" I realized there were tears in my eyes as I turned to him. He and Rajeon stood there, patiently waiting for me to notice their arrival.

I love you so, Morrett sent as we embraced.

And I love you, I told him. *So much.*

~

Lissa

Gavin's fingers were twined with mine on one side; Drake held my other hand and Drew had me perched on his lap as we listened to Tenigar explain things.

"Morrett, Denevik, Rylend, Trikleer and Drew carry world spirit coins. Each of those world spirits have been affected by a poison created by the Prophet and his servants. We," he indicated the other Wise Ones about him, "were forced to manipulate things somewhat, so that the Prophet's plans would stray slightly from their original course.

"As of now, he believes the ones carrying Falchan, Murazal, Corez, Galk and Kwark are still on track to go to him voluntarily. Where we are, the world spirits I named, and those who carry them, are blocked from receiving the Prophet's summons. Once they leave this facility, they will have no choice but to answer that call.

"The Prophet also believes that his newest slaves will arrive in stages, so that he may place them under his command. This is another thing we have manipulated, so that all may arrive at once."

"Can't you reverse all this?" Reah asked, turning toward Zaria.

"Zaria could, as could we, if given sufficient time. I ask you this, however. How often have you received an opportunity to attack the Prophet and his minions—at his invitation?"

"You mean we're going to tag along with those who carry the affected spirits?" Tory asked. "To attack the moment we arrive?"

"Some of you, yes. Others, no. I do not wish to endanger Gavril, Toff or Nissa. Therefore, those three will stay here until the mission is over. Should we not return," he lowered his eyes for a moment and drew a heavy breath, "then someone we've designated will arrive to collect them."

"Why not take me, then?" Gavril demanded.

"Because you are the Founder of the Reth Alliance. We will not risk that, even though Tybus could replace you. Wyatt is your true heir, and he is not prepared to take the reins as yet. He has other things to accomplish before you give him your seat of power, one day. It is not your capability we question in this. It is your responsibilities that we consider in our decision."

Gavril still fumed, but he didn't argue. Anyone who chose to disagree with the Wise Ones was already on a losing side, in my opinion.

"Now," Tenigar went on. "We have searched extensively into the images planted in each world spirit involved, to learn specifics. What we've found is the same image each time—they will be called to a laboratory of sorts. I assume this is where the Prophet intends to place his new recruits under his obsession and remove all free will they have. The name of the planet, city or anyplace otherwise is not given, to ensure that nothing is left to chance in this.

"Each world spirit is called to find his way to that specific room, or will be, once they leave the safety of this facility. The rest of us will go with them, either as guards or warriors in this battle. We know not whether the Prophet himself will be waiting with his rogue gods in attendance, but we have little doubt that they will arrive quickly once we are revealed."

"They'll protect the Prophet until the very last," Randl said.

"As we expect them to do. However, should the Prophet escape, it is our duty to destroy those rogue gods, is it not? The Prophet is your quarry, Reviendus. I believe he will be much easier to kill if we eliminate his father's protectors."

"I intend to attack him first," Randl's voice was quiet and filled with menace at the same time.

"As we desire for you to do. This will bring his protectors, if they are not already there. Leave them to the rest of us; do what you must —learn what you must."

"What about those of us who've never been in a battle before?" Trik asked.

"Very good question. Graegar, Reah and Rajeon will be with you," he smiled at Trik. "They are quite adept at overcoming incomprehensible adversaries. Now, Lissa, when we are ready, I wish you to place all of us inside your mist, and once we arrive, only reveal those whom the Prophet has called to him. When they are approached, either by the Prophet or his minions, it will be up to the rest of us to take them down."

"What about the pull the Prophet has on us?" Denevik asked.

"Ah, High Demon, he never expected any of your kind. Turn and destroy whatever you can, while protecting those you love."

"If he didn't want or expect High Demons, how was I chosen?" Denevik asked another question.

"I've told you that we manipulated a few things. That was one of them."

"When are we going? Do we need to wear more suitable clothing?"

"I will dress all of us," Zaria said, before standing and forming light about us.

"Cool," Drew breathed against my cheek. "I can't see anything except everybody's head."

We were now dressed in something sturdy and light, and what it covered became invisible. I should have known she'd keep the knowledge of that technology, in case it was needed again. She'd transformed it into clothing, rather than a device. This was much more useful.

"Your suits have hoods—pull them all the way up and over your face," Zaria said. "The visor at the front will allow you to see your companions, and there is space at the bottom to let you breathe."

I did as she asked, and everyone now became fully visible to me.

"Stand," Tenigar commanded.

We stood.

Prepare yourselves for what is to come, he added in mindspeech. *From now on, this is the only form of communication you should use until this is over.*

Even though we were hidden by suits rendering us transparent, I employed my mist to cover all of us as the Wise Ones moved us from the protection of the facility. Once we were away from it, the pull on Drew and the others became obvious.

Hold onto those with spirit coins, Graegar shouted mentally before we were all dragged into a wormhole.

P'loxett

V'dar

"They're coming," P'loxett appeared next to me with a shriek.

"Which ones?" I was prepared to relocate to my lab and place heavy obsessions.

"All of them," P'loxett's voice remained shrill. "All of them!"

I yanked the spikes representing five of my strongest rogues off my shoulder. *I need your help,* I snapped at them. *Materialize and protect me!* Then, snatching P'loxett by the collar, I folded space to my lab. It could take all of us to corral several powerful beings without harming them—until they were properly obsessed and under my control.

Lissa

As instructed, I only released the five who bore spirit coins first. Somehow, Zaria controlled their suits and made them visible to those appearing in the lab to take them—five rogue gods and two others, one of whom was the Prophet.

Who was the other one?

Attack! Tenigar shouted.

Randl Gage

V'dar was my target. I leveled a blast at him that should have shaken him to the core. Instead, the blast split and curved around a shield he'd built around himself, before hitting the wall behind him.

The blast I'd fired continued through wall after wall of a massive compound, so large I couldn't see past the first few walls into thick darkness.

We were underground, somewhere.

"Show yourself, Randl Gage," V'dar shouted a challenge. Nearby, others had begun fighting the rogue gods, most of whom, no doubt, had assisted with the shield V'dar hid behind.

More walls collapsed, around us, raining debris into the room like flakes of dark snow. I imagined that someone in our party was now holding the space together with power, to keep who knew what from caving in on us. Shards of glass hit shields with tinkling sounds as the compound groaned beneath us.

Multi-leveled. We were standing in an underground compound; who knew how many levels it contained.

Perhaps it was built to withstand bombs. It wasn't meant to contain a battle between gods and the powerful.

I hadn't fired a second blast at V'dar, who'd now chosen to use the rogue gods as additional shielding.

Coward, I hissed at him in mindspeech.

He flung himself from between two rogues and fired a blast at me that blew out the entire section of his compound with a deafening rumble. His attack left us standing on an invisible, power-built floor while levels above and below us became visible when the dust and debris cleared.

Anyone with vertigo was probably feeling ill right now, as V'dar prepared to level another blast. I beat him to it, firing one of my own. It threw him back against his rogues, shield and all.

I thought the noise and fury of the battle around me couldn't get worse. I found I was wrong.

Reah

The moment the surrounding walls were blasted away, we were attacked from every side by the Prophet's soldiers. All of them bore some type of weapon, including ranos rifles. With a roar, Tory's Thifilathi tore a rifle away from a man and crushed it in his hands while the man attacked his legs with a knife and burst into flames.

Burn them, I shouted at Ocenosek and Cudworth. Both had landed in High Demon form; I was grateful they were hidden from our attackers by the suits Zaria provided. It didn't stop the waves of the Prophet's army from firing blindly, however.

Denevik followed Tory, knocking dozens of attackers away with wide sweeps of his Thifilathi's arms. Screaming and burning, they flew past the boundaries of the invisible floor and fell into an inky abyss. *Keep them safe*, I whispered to whomever might be listening and waded into the fray, cleaning up whatever got around the others.

Somewhere, far on the other side of this massive laboratory-turned-cavern, Randl engaged the Prophet.

In-between, Lissa and the others fought rogue gods and whatever else was sent against them, while protecting those who carried spirit coins.

Where were Zaria and the Larentii? I hadn't seen them since our arrival; I'd only heard Tenigar's mindspeech at the beginning, and then nothing more.

I'm hit, Denevik said. *Cudworth, too. Ranos blasts.*

I'm coming, I told them, and waded through a growing pile of bodies, which burned behind me as I forced my way forward.

Lissa

Liron had chosen well; these rogues were powerful themselves, and together, even more powerful. Either he'd taught them to work together as one, or they'd learned it from the Prophet.

Gavin, Drake, Drew and I continued to fire blasts at them, chipping away at a shield so thick it could take days to break through.

Ry was also contributing as much as he could to our efforts, although I could tell the weight of the spirit coin was draining him rapidly. Trik stood beside him, in much the same shape but lending his wizard's power to Ry to form more powerful blasts. Morrett had turned to his scaled and fanged alter-ego to slash at the armed attackers flooding into the space, much like cockroaches would after the lights went out.

For now, the shields I'd flung around them were working; bullets and ranos blasts threaded horizontally through the cavern like hurricane-driven rain. I'd long since dimmed the cacophony of sounds; there were loud booms whenever a power blast was detonated, amid the softer whines of bullets or ranos fire and the screams of the Prophet's troops as they died.

Where was Rajeon?

For that matter, where were Zaria and the Wise Ones? I hadn't seen any of them since before we landed here.

Also, who was the seventh man who'd come inside this space with the Prophet and his rogues, who still cowered behind them? The Prophet's army was expendable; why wasn't he?

～

Alken Wilker

Take what you were instructed to transport and go to the new location, the Prophet shouted into Gillen's, Qatti's and my mind. *Je'Dik and the daggers first!*

We had no choice but to obey.

"Come on, we have to get you out of here," I snapped at Je'Dik, who growled back at me.

"Do you want to live or not?" Qatti's hiss made Je'Dik recoil. From our secure shelter on the opposite end of the compound, we could hear the boom of fired blasts, and experienced the occasional shaking ground that accompanied it.

"Look at him; he wants to fight," Gillen laughed at Je'Dik. "You're not quite ready yet, youngling. There's so much more for the Prophet to teach you, before you become the terror that he desires. Take him and the daggers," Gillen told me. "Qatti and I will be right behind you with the weapons and selected troops."

Without another word, I hauled Je'Dik and the crate of daggers to the new compound on G'margis. As hard as P'loxett had been to find, G'margis would be far more difficult for an enemy to locate.

"Your new home," I swept an arm out to encompass the concrete-and-metal room about us. "Get used to the cold."

Rylend Morphis

At first, the pull was so subtle, neither Kwark nor I noticed.

Until it became painful.

Come, the voice instructed. *You are mine, now,* it added.

P'loxett! Kwark begged. *Do not do this—I beg you!*

He's trying to take us, Morrett's mindspeech was filled with agony.

I cannot fight him much longer, Trik wailed.

Stay strong, Drew sent, although I recognized the pain in his words, too.

P'loxett. A dead planet.

Not so dead, Kwark wailed. *If he takes us, we will never be ourselves again.*

I'm fading, Morrett's sending was filled with terror. *He's taking us! He's taking us!*

Lissa

Without warning, we became visible, as if our suits had suddenly stopped working. Weapons were fired with more accuracy as we struggled to destroy the massing army about us, all while battling five rogue gods who now threatened to gain the upper hand.

Turning my head, I watched a slow smile spread across the Prophet's face.

I blinked, and the blink took forever.

Noooo! I said as the Prophet slowly disappeared. The man behind him began to disappear with him, until—*wait.*

Diamond thorns closed around the unidentified man, somehow preventing him from going with the Prophet.

Would the Prophet return for him, or was he leaving without turning back?

Randl's shout of rage rang through my mind; his quarry had escaped.

The explosion bloomed around us—small at first, as if time had slowed even further. The rogue gods were still lofting blasts against us; I watched as they bloomed and exploded against my shields without sound.

Rajeon's thorns tightened ever so slowly about the man he'd captured, until the prisoner opened his mouth in a silent shriek of pain.

Tenigar and the other Wise Ones, with Zaria beside them, appeared behind the rogue gods who fought on, buying time for the Prophet to make his exit. I imagined they had plans to escape, too, as the explosions around us grew.

The Prophet was destroying his compound, and likely the planet that held it, too.

With eyes widening as slowly as possible, I watched another Larentii appear. One I didn't recognize.

Everything stopped. None of us moved—I found we couldn't. Something held us in place, and no exertion of power could prevent it.

Then, as if we'd been sliced out of the events that had stopped around us, we were removed from the scene of battle. Only my mind kept moving; my limbs were frozen in place.

Even Rajeon's diamond thorns had stopped tightening around his captive, although I saw blood on the victim's neck. If time ever resumed, the man's head would be shaved clean from his neck and shoulders.

With breath stopped and nothing moving around me, I saw the Wise Ones, Zaria, and the unknown Larentii break away from their paralysis.

Tenigar moved behind the rogues, before looking back and nodding at Zaria.

Did Zaria have tears in her eyes? My vision from that distance wasn't sharp enough to tell for sure.

Tenigar grew larger, and larger still, until his arms could encompass five rogue gods.

And then—no.

No. *Gods, no.*

CHAPTER 20

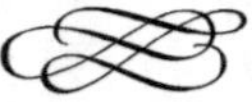

Zaria

Hurry; you must do this, Meligar commanded. I wept openly as I butted two timelines together, just as one of my mothers could do.

In this, I was following her template, although when she employed this trick, she hadn't had the help of any Larentii.

Now! Meligar insisted.

With a sob, I sent Tenigar, who was even now turning himself and the physical bodies of five rogue gods to sparks, into the time before any of them existed.

Flecks of gold swirled through, magnified by my tears.

I had to wait until the last spark of gold left this timeline before I ended the connection, and when it winked into the darkness, I shut the connection down and dropped to my knees. Shuddering sobs shook my body as I mourned the loss of the eldest Larentii Wise One.

Behind us, a shriek cut off; the movement of time had been restored and Rajeon had completed his task—that of removing P'loxett's head from his shoulders.

"Do not weep, I beg you." I'd never heard his voice before—but recognized it all the same. Then, he was kneeling beside me, gathering me in his arms.

"I can't help it," I whimpered.

"It was the only way, Mother," he soothed. "Tenigar planned it all along."

"Zaria?" Lissa lowered herself beside me. "We have wounded that are still in stasis."

"I will help," Graegar offered.

"I'll come, too, Father," Garegar said.

"Here," Lissa offered me a handkerchief.

Zarigar accepted it and began to wipe my tears. "Father will be upset if he finds you've been crying," he told me gently.

"Can somebody please explain what just happened?" Lissa asked. "Why are you calling her mother? Why are we where we are, and where is that, exactly?"

"We are situated in a slice of time that has been removed from all else," Meligar leaned down to lift Lissa and me to our feet. "Thanks to my grandson, here."

"That's not possible," Lissa frowned at Meligar.

"It wasn't before. It's possible now," Zarigar informed her. "It requires the ability to compress time, and then remove that pocket of time from its own timeline. I've been forced to do this several times, now, to save lives and rush the Prophet's plans, creating mistakes and hardships for him. Had we not destroyed P'loxett, then he would have continued to kill planets and gather recruits for the Prophet's cause."

"He intended to use Rylend and the others as generals for his conquering armies," I finally spoke, although my voice wobbled. "P'loxett promised him this."

"You mean a world spirit went rogue, too?"

"Yes," Zarigar replied.

"I suppose your talent for compressing time explains your shortened gestation period?" Lissa asked him.

"It was necessary. I regret the suffering it caused my mother and father."

"We all worried about you," Lissa grumped at him.

"I know. I hope this makes up for it."

"How do we get back, now? Does the Prophet believe he won this round?" Randl walked up, brushing debris off his clothing.

"He may believe that for a while," Zarigar answered. "I arranged for there to be signs of no survival after the planet was destroyed. That includes his rogues. It is my hope that this will make him easier to find next time, Reviendus."

"He'll be looking for revenge," I said, reaching out to touch Randl's arm. "While he may have hidden himself well, when he learns you survived, he'll come looking for you."

"Then I have plenty of plans to make," Randl sighed.

"Prepare the Formidables, too," Zarigar warned. "Wars will begin across both Alliances soon; that much of the Prophet's plan remains in place. The RAA and CAA will have their hands full on multiple fronts."

"Randl, you won't engage in those wars," I said, dropping my hand. "There is other nastiness planned, and you and your people will have to deal with that, instead."

"When?"

"In the future, roughly fifty years or so," Zarigar explained. "When you need a ride to that timeline, I will make myself available to you."

"How can you do that?" Lissa asked.

"My mother became pregnant in the future," Zarigar allowed a smile to appear. "This is the past for me."

"Zarigar is my grandson, and Tenigar's chosen replacement among the Wise Ones," Meligar informed Lissa and Randl.

"I thought he was Nefrigar's grandson," Lissa said.

"He is that, too," Meligar conceded. "Wisdom and I will have a conversation soon—about stolen children."

~

Queen's Palace, Le-Ath Veronis

Lissa

Two weeks have passed since we left Zarigar's slice of time behind.

Nissa and Toff were waiting here at the palace as I and my bunch arrived, bringing Trik with us. He still bore the spirit coin of Murazal, who'd been healed by Zaria and the Wise Ones.

Drew carried Falchan, which caused even his father, grandfather and uncles to dip their heads in respect.

Ry and Kwark were now having teasing battles upon occasion—after being healed, the planet's spirit showed a fine sense of humor.

Morrett and Galk were a good pairing; Morrett was often in the kitchen, cooking, and Galk made suggestions of what spices or flavors to add to certain dishes.

As for Denevik, who carried Corez, I heard from Tory that Corez was very pleased to be combined with a High Demon. Those two, along with Cudworth and Ocenosek, would be joining Randl soon on Sirena, to begin the search for the Prophet. The Formidables would eventually take on new roles, but for now, only Zaria, Randl and the Wise Ones knew what that would be.

"Lunch in the arboretum?" Gavin's brown eyes warmed as he entered my study.

"Oh, honey, I didn't even realize how hungry I was until you said lunch," I told him.

"Then come," he held out a hand. "We will talk of good things," he added. "And not the recent troubles, or those to come."

He was right; already there was unrest brewing on even more worlds, and I wondered how long the Prophet would play with us until he commanded his hidden recruits to openly rebel.

"Agreed." I took his hand, and he folded us to the garden at the top of my palace.

Travis

"Bro, there's something we have to do," Trent said.

"What's that?"

"We have to find Tedri Clurk."

"Oh. I forgot about that. His daughter's on Sirena."

"Vik and Zanfield are bringing her to Murazal."

"Sounds good," I agreed.

"I've done some research. This won't be a happy ending," he shook his head.

"Then we'd better get going," I sighed.

~

Temporary State House, Murazal

Vik

"Zanfield, so good to see you again," President Ylisis greeted him first. "Who have you brought with you?" He turned to Sharal Sawin, who stood between Travis and Trent.

"Tedri Clurk's daughter, Sharal," Zanfield said. "Tedri works in your Water Purity Department. Will you call him in, please?"

Ylisis was on his communicator immediately, asking for Clurk's presence in the President's office.

"Oh," Ylisis jumped when Opal and Kell appeared from nothing.

"This is Opal Tadewi; I am Kell Abenott, Vice Directors of the ASD," Kell introduced Opal and himself. "We're here to take custody of Tedri Clurk."

Sharal gasped; Ylisis was stunned momentarily.

"Tedri Clurk, sir," a receptionist opened the door to allow Tedri inside the office.

Tedri's eyes grew wide when he saw his daughter, who shouted "Papa," and ran to him.

We waited for the tearful reunion to settle, before Kell stepped forward and pulled Tedri away from Sharal.

"You are under arrest, Tedri Clurk, for providing the poison that killed Prime Minister Fallah of Corez," Kell placed power cuffs on Tedri, whose mouth hung open in shock.

"What? How?" Ylisis demanded.

"A year ago, do you recall that someone attempted to poison the water supply to the State House here on Murazal?" Opal's seldom-blinking eyes locked with Ylisis'.

"Yes, but that poison was destroyed."

"It wasn't," Opal disagreed. "Mr. Clurk, who has nurtured an anger against all Alliance leaders for his daughter's supposed death, made a deal with someone on Corez. That someone wanted Fallah out of the way; Tedri, here, wanted you out of the way. The one he dealt with was supposed to arrange both murders. You're lucky to be alive—twice over, I think."

"Who?" Ylisis was now furious. "Who committed this heinous crime against Fallah?"

"Three women," Tedri's lip curled in a sneer.

"We need Zaria," Opal whispered. "Now."

∼

Zaria

I'd ghosted through the Archives for weeks, trying to come to grips with what had happened, and what had yet to happen.

Opal's mindspeech reached me there. *We need you on Murazal*, she begged.

Without an answer, I folded space.

"Well, that explains a lot," I said after studying Tedri Clurk for only a moment. He'd been directly involved in Fallah's murder.

"Who?" Opal asked.

"Three Sirenali women," I sighed. "The same ones I saw on a pirated Murazalian ship. One of them is still in Lissa's dungeon."

"Good luck on getting an answer out of her, then," Kell hissed.

"I figure they passed some of their poison to Ethan Looms," I continued. "That's how he got it, I think. Then, he attempted to kill Queen Ilise and her mates."

"This is all starting to make sense now," Opal said. "I'd still like to know who was with that vampire who tried to assassinate the King of Hraede."

"That may be a while in coming," I said. "Anyone who knew him is probably obsessed."

"Was it worth it?" I turned on Tedri Clurk. "The punishment for direct involvement in the assassination of any world leader is Evensun. You wanted revenge for your daughter, who, as you can see, is alive and thriving. Things are not always as they seem, you know."

"Sometimes they're worse," he snapped at me.

"Most certainly," I agreed. "And sometimes, we've brought those things on ourselves. Is there anything else you need?" I asked Opal.

"No."

"Let me know if that changes." I folded back to the Archives, which were so quiet I understood that even Nefrigar was away.

Are you finished blaming yourself, yet? I jumped as Tenigar's voice startled me.

"What? How?" I demanded.

Was I fooling myself? Dreaming, perhaps?

Neither of those things, he informed me. *We have been together for a while, you know.*

Can Larentii be ghosts? I asked, feeling foolish for asking. I'd never heard of a Larentii ghost before.

I'm not a ghost. Tell me, what is the last memory you have of me?

"Gold sparks, disappearing through a time tunnel," I said aloud.

Pull the image into your mind. Magnify it.

At first, I didn't want to; I'd been trying to block that memory for weeks, now. It was far too painful for me to dwell on it.

Do it for me, he cajoled.

I pulled up the memory and displayed it in a three-dimensional image before me. With tears filling my eyes, I enlarged the image of gold sparks until I sobbed.

Those weren't gold sparks.

Every spark was a miniature gold plate.

The Metal Library.

For so long, I'd carried Tenigar with me, as the Metal Library. I sobbed again, although now, the tears that fell were tears of joy.

There now, stop weeping, niece. Meligar and I are related, you know. From now on, you only have to consult your ancient Uncle Tenigar for advice. As for Zarigar, he and I have been conversing for a very long time. I knew exactly when Wisdom arrived to take your embryo from Meligar, and I consoled him with the news of what you would become, and what great things you'd accomplish as the Vhanaraszh. Zarigar as my chosen replacement did not go amiss, either. Meligar and I—we have been blessed beyond imagining.

"Dearest?" Valegar arrived, noticed I'd been crying and wrapped his arms around me. "What has made you sad?" he asked.

"It started out sad, and then became happy," I reached up to caress his face. "Did you know that Tenigar is my uncle?"

"Ah. Father suspected, but he could not say for sure," Valegar smiled and leaned down to kiss me.

Nefrigar may be the wisest one of all, Tenigar said, then went silent as Val lifted me in his arms and folded us to mountain sunlight above a beautiful valley. There, Meligar and Zarigar waited for us. Meligar held Eliagar in his arms.

Val set me down; the child reached for me the moment my feet touched the ground.

"How's my little Eli?" I took him from my Larentii father and smiled when he laughed.

The End

Randl Gage and the Prophet's story will continue in *MindMaster, BlackWing Pirates, Book Four,* coming spring, 2019.

Rajeon Dare and the Formidables' continuing saga begins with *Buffer Zone, Future Wars, Book One,* now available.